A MOST EXCELLENT MIDLIFE CRISIS

GOOD TO THE LAST DEATH BOOK THREE

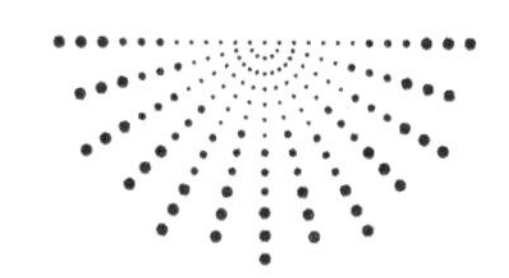

ROBYN PETERMAN

Copyright © 2020 by Robyn Peterman

All rights reserved.

No part of this book may be reproduced in any form or by any electronic or mechanical means, including information storage and retrieval systems, without written permission from the author, except for the use of brief quotations in a book review.

This book is a work of fiction. Names, characters, places, and incidents either are the product of the author's imagination or are used fictitiously. Any resemblance to actual persons, living or dead, businesses, companies, events, or locales is coincidental.

This book contains content that may not be suitable for young readers 17 and under.

Cover design by *JJ's Design & Creations*

Edited by *Kelli Collins*

CONTENTS

Acknowledgments vii

MORE IN THE GOOD TO THE LAST DEATH SERIES 1

Book Description 5

Chapter 1 7

Chapter 2 21

Chapter 3 35

Chapter 4 47

Chapter 5 59

Chapter 6 71

Chapter 7 79

Chapter 8 87

Chapter 9 103

Chapter 10 113

Chapter 11 129

Chapter 12 141

Chapter 13 157

Chapter 14 169

Chapter 15 177

Chapter 16 191

Chapter 17 203

Chapter 18 213

Chapter 19 231

Chapter 20 241

Chapter 21 257

Chapter 22 269

Chapter 23 285

Chapter 24 295

Chapter 25 307

MORE IN THE GOOD TO THE LAST DEATH SERIES 315

Robyn's Book List 319
Note From The Author 323
About Robyn Peterman 325

PRAISE FOR ROBYN PETERMAN

"Daisy's life has been turned upside down, and we get to watch the aftermath. Prepare to root for a new heroine. You'll fall in love with this hilarious hoyden and all of the hot water she dives into. Head first! Masterful and heartwarming, don't let this one get away!"

—NY Times Bestselling Author Darynda Jones

"Brilliant and so relatable! I laughed, I cried, I swooned, and I sighed. Heavily. Robyn Peterman has her finger on the pulse of midlife madness, and I can't get enough."

— USA Today Bestselling Author, Renee George

"I'd read the phone book if Robyn Peterman wrote it! It's A Wonderful Midlife Crisis is a home run of hilarious, heartwarming paranormal fun. Midlife's a journey. Enjoy the ride. Crisis included... Read it!"

— Mandy M. Roth, NY Times & USA TODAY Bestselling Author

"Hilarious, heartbreaking, magical and addictive! No one can turn a midlife crisis upside down quite like Robyn Peterman. A stay-up-all-night novel that will have you begging for more."

— Michelle M. Pillow, New York Times and USA Today Bestselling Author

ACKNOWLEDGMENTS

This series has been in my head for two years. It took a call and a nudge from Shannon Mayer to make me pull the file out and finish book one. Now you're getting book three! Each word was a joy to write and I owe Shannon for yanking me into the Paranormal Women's Fiction group. Playing in a sandbox with strong talented women who have each other's backs is a rare and special experience.

As always, while writing is a solitary experience getting a book into the world is a group project.

The PWF 13 Gals — Thank you for a wild ride. You rock.

Renee — Thank you for all your support, your friendship, your formatting expertise and for being the best Cookie ever. You saved my butt on this one. Forever in your debt.

Wanda — Thank you for knowing what I mean even when I don't. LOL You are the best and this writing business wouldn't be any fun without you. You make the journey more fun.

Kelli — Thank you for saving me from scary grammar mistakes. You rock. And thank you for letting me be late. LOL

Nancy, Susan and Wanda — Thank you for being kickass betas. You are all wonderful.

Jay — Thank you. Your cover captured what was in my mind perfectly.

Mom — Thank you for listening to me hash out the plot and for giving me brilliant ideas. You really need to write a book!

Mandy — You rock hard! So happy I can call you my friend.

Steve, Henry and Audrey — Thank you. The three of you are my world. Without you, none of this would make sense. I love you.

DEDICATION

This one is for everyone who knows the meaning of a hot flash. LOL

MORE IN THE GOOD TO THE LAST DEATH SERIES

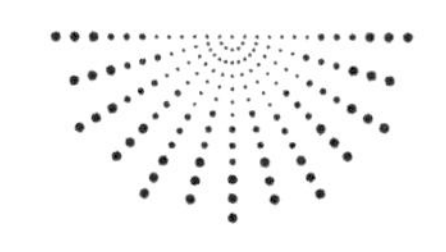

ORDER BOOK FOUR NOW

My midlife crisis. My rules. And if it doesn't put me six feet under, I plan to live it up in style—possibly for the rest of eternity...

After a Luke Skywalker/Darth Vader moment, I discovered I do indeed have a father. He comes with a hell of a lot of baggage, but I've decided to keep him. Not only do I have a father, I have a kickass new sister, a ghostly family, and super powers to boot. If you add to the mix that I'm dating the Grim Reaper, it's a freakin' party.

The only thing standing in the way of my happiness is the Angel of Mercy, though *Angel of Misery* is more appropriate. She's responsible for almost everyone I have loved, and who has loved me being taken away. With the help of family and friends, I will track her down and show her exactly what a perimenopausal hot flash looks like in action.

Job — Death Counselor — Supergluing ghosts back together and solving their issues is rewarding. For real.

Mission — Bring the seriously evil Angel of Mercy to justice without dying or getting anyone else killed in the process.

Team — A bunch of certifiable Immortals, including one who re-homes vibrators. Yes, you read that correctly.

How to do this? — Wing it. Wine, my Demon boyfriend, a houseful of deceased squatters, and good friends by my side will help.

Midlife's a journey. I will enjoy the ride. The crisis is happening whether I'm ready or not.

BOOK DESCRIPTION

A MOST EXCELLENT MIDLIFE CRISIS

Midlife's a bumpy journey. The ride is a freaking roller-coaster. The crisis is real.

With my life back to normal—*normal* being a very relative word—one would think I'd catch a break.

One would be very wrong.

With an Angel gunning for me and a Demon in my bed, life couldn't be more complicated. Not to mention, I'm going to have to make a rather *large* life choice.

Do I want to live forever?

Does anyone? Forever is a very long time.

Whatever. I'll think about it tomorrow… or next week… or next month. As long as I have my girlfriends, my dogs, a super-sized case of merlot and my deceased squatters, I'm good to go.

My midlife crisis. My rules. If it doesn't kill me dead first, I plan to have a most excellent midlife crisis.

CHAPTER ONE

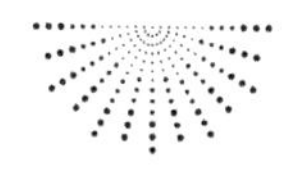

"Hell's bells," I muttered as I let my head fall forward. The swirling grain in the oak of my kitchen table was far more interesting than the shouting gibberish that was echoing throughout the house.

The furious disagreement between the two powerful men made me wish I'd told everyone to go home.

"Just be happy no one is throwing lightning," Candy Vargo whispered, picking her teeth with a toothpick.

I stared at her with my mouth open. I never knew if the woman was serious or just trying to screw with my head. "Is that an actual possibility?"

She winked. "Yep. You wearing rubber-soled shoes?"

"No," I hissed under my breath. "I'm wearing my funeral freaking best. Tennis shoes don't exactly go with dress clothes."

Candy shrugged and grinned. Lifting up her leg, she showed me her ratty tennis shoes. "I beg to differ."

It was truly horrifying that Candy Vargo, or rather *Karma,* was the Immortal in charge of fate. She was a hot mess of rude and some serious scary.

"I suppose you could duck," she suggested with a chuckle.

Rolling my eyes, I was tempted to flip her off. However, *tempting* fate wasn't a great plan. "Roger that," I said and turned my attention back to the action I hoped wouldn't take my house down.

The Grim Reaper and the highest-level Angel in existence fighting in a dead language wasn't what I'd envisioned when I'd called the meeting of the Immortals in my kitchen. It had been a heck of a long day, between Gram's funeral and over half the town in my home for the reception afterwards.

I was shocked as all get out that Bob Barker had shown up to pay his respects. He was Gram's *gameshow boyfriend.* She'd seen every episode of *The Price is Right* ever made—at least twenty times. I'd worried that she'd be upset he wasn't able to see her since she was dead, but Gram was just thrilled he came.

I wasn't thrilled when I'd learned that *Karma* had made it happen. Owing the deadly disaster of a woman wasn't my idea of a good time.

"You okay, Daisy?" Heather questioned quietly.

I smiled and shrugged. "Not sure I know the meaning of the word anymore."

She gave my hand a quick squeeze and watched as the undecipherable argument grew more heated. With a reassuring glance, she moved to the kitchen counter and observed the disagreement with an emotionless expression on her lovely face. Having Heather here was a blessing. Until recently, I hadn't known one of my best friends was the Immortal Arbitrator between Heaven and Hell. Now? I couldn't be happier about it.

My head felt like it might explode. Gideon, aka the Grim Reaper, and Clarence, aka Michael the Archangel—who I'd secretly nicknamed John Travolta because of the movie *Michael*—had been arguing back and forth in Sumerian for an hour. I couldn't understand a word. The ghosts had gotten bored and wandered away in search of a reality show to watch. Gram had stayed.

Gram had nodded off a few times and fell off of her chair, but in her defense, she'd had a big day. How often did one get to attend one's own funeral as a ghost? Gram's mid-service crash landing on top of her dead body in the casket she'd chosen to match her hair also wasn't an everyday occurrence. However, it did make for an excellent story. Holding back my laughter was one of the most difficult things I'd done. I didn't think having a Mary Tyler Moore slash Chuckles the Clown moment was a good idea, especially since there had been only a handful in attendance who could even see Gram's ghost.

"Eat this," Candy Vargo said, slapping down a plate in front of me at the kitchen table while the two men continued to debate. "Those nosey bitches who showed up left enough food to feed an army."

Glancing down, I couldn't quite understand what I was seeing. Candy was clearly as messy with her food as she was with her appearance. Potato salad was piled on top of the apple pie. Next to it sat a piece of fried chicken dangerously close to a large helping of banana pudding. The topper was the unidentifiable casserole with blueberries and ground beef in it.

It was all I could do not to gag.

"Umm... thanks," I said. "Not hungry right now."

"Try that," Candy insisted, pointing her ever-present toothpick at the blueberry beef surprise. "Looks disgusting. I want to know if it tastes as bad as it looks."

I pushed the plate over to her. "Then you try it."

Candy shrugged, removed the toothpick from her mouth and took a bite of the mysterious concoction. "Tastes like baked ass with blueberries," she muttered, swallowing with effort.

I was wildly pleased she didn't spit it back out onto the plate. Candy's manners were iffy at best.

"Can you understand them?" I whispered as I watched Gideon grow angrier and Clarence narrow his eyes in displeasure.

"Yep," she replied, putting her tennis-shoe-clad feet on my kitchen table.

"Nope." I knocked her feet back to the floor. "Tell me what they're saying."

"Can I put my feet back up?" Candy bargained.

"Only if you want to eat the entire blueberry ass casserole," I shot back.

"Spicy," Candy muttered with a laugh and scooted her chair closer to me. "They're arguing about if you can be trusted to tell the truth of what you see in Steve's mind. Clarence believes you're too close to be neutral. The Angel of Mercy stands to lose everything if she's deemed guilty. The Grim Reaper is on your side completely... of course, you're banging him."

"First of all, I'm *not* banging him," I snapped. "And if I was, it's not any of your business. While I do understand you're a badass who could probably incinerate me with a flick of your desperately in-need-of-a-manicure finger, I'd like to remind you that I punched a freaking tree and it fell over."

Candy eyed me until I grew uncomfortable. Unsure if she was going to tear my head off with her bare hands or laugh, I held my breath.

"You've got enormous nards," she stated, raising her brow.

"Lady balls," I corrected her.

"Whatever," Candy said. "It's impressive."

"Thank you," I replied, shaking my head. My Southern manners were ingrained. A rude compliment was still a compliment and required a polite response.

Candy stabbed the baked blueberry ass with her toothpick and pulled out a fresh one. "So, as I said, Clarence isn't on your side, Death Counselor."

"John Travolta is being a dick," I hissed under my breath. "And Clarissa *is* guilty."

"What you just said is proof of Clarence's issue," Candy pointed out. "You've already damned the Angel of Mercy without proof of guilt. While I hate the bitch, I have to side with Clarence on this."

Shit. She did have a point. I questioned how far I would go to ensure the safety of my dead former husband's afterlife. I would go very far… very, very far. Steve was my best friend.

"The problem is that Gideon has found in the text that it's impossible for another to join a Death Counselor in the mind of the dead," Charlie said quietly.

"Do you agree with John Travolta and Candy that I can't be trusted?" I asked.

Charlie was quiet for a long moment. He was round, polite and as kind as can be. It still blew my mind that Charlie was the Immortal Enforcer. He was married to the sweetest human in the Universe—my dear friend June. Of course, she had no clue, but I certainly did. As of about a month ago, I became very aware of the secret world that had been right under my nose my whole life.

"Trust is not the issue," Charlie explained. "Much more than you can comprehend is on the line. What I do believe is that your loyalty is with Steve. It muddies the waters."

"There's another way," Tim announced loudly.

Everyone stopped and stared at Tim. God, I hoped my new, socially awkward, vibrator-rehoming friend was going to make sense. As the Immortal Courier between the darkness and the light, he was full of shocking information.

"Speak," Gideon said tersely.

"Daisy is a hybrid Angel," Tim said, pointing to my eyes.

That woke Gram up fast. "What in tarnation are you talkin' about?" she demanded. "Her mamma was a human Death Counselor, just like me and just like Daisy."

"And her father?" Tim asked.

Gram sighed and shook her head. "I don't know."

"*If* this is true," I said, feeling strange and a little panicky. "What does it have to do with anything?"

"Interesting," Karma said, leaning in and studying my eyes. "I hadn't noticed. Very, very interesting."

"Again. Why?" I demanded. "How does the *possibility* of me being some kind of half-breed freak help get justice for Steve?"

Ignoring my question, Clarence leveled me with a hard look. "What is it that you want? To send your dead husband into the light or to destroy the Angel of Mercy?"

"The Angel of Mercy damned Steve to the darkness out of hatred of me. Her decision can't stand." I snapped. "So to answer your question... it's one and the same."

"Not necessarily," he replied.

"Bullshit," Heather said. "You would let the Angel of Mercy take a plea deal, so to speak? Get away with taking fate into her own hands unchecked? That is *not* how it works."

Clarence brought his fist down on the table in frustration. "Do you have any idea what stripping an Angel could do to the order of the Universe? Do you?" he shouted.

"I do," Gideon said coldly. His eyes turned red and his features sharpened. "I know exactly what happens when an Angel falls."

"With all due respect," Charlie said, nodding at Gideon. "We're not talking about a demotion. We're talking a removal of power, heritage and Immortality."

"Shit," Karma muttered with a laugh. "That would certainly suck."

"Enough," Clarence growled. "*If* the facts are indeed

proven against the Angel of Mercy, the punishment shall be doled out and the price will be paid. But..."

"But what?" I asked, feeling like my world was spiraling out of control. Was Clarissa going to get off scot-free?

"But I see no clear way to prove that your husband's death was indeed an accident," he finished, sounding tired.

The room was silent. Gideon's jaw worked a mile a minute and he looked like he wanted to kill Clarence. Heather was furious and pressing her temples. Gram was simply in shock. Candy seemed bored, and Tim...

Tim was grinning.

"I see a way," Tim said.

Tim had just moved to the top of my friend list.

"Out with it, Courier," Charlie demanded, focusing on Tim with interest.

"Blood-related Angels can see into each other's mind by touch," Tim reminded the others.

"This is true," Heather said, getting excited. "It can also be broadcast."

"Meaning?" Gram asked, as befuddled as I was.

"Meaning, an Angel could send—or rather, telecast—what he or she sees to those Immortals within close proximity," Gideon explained.

"Like a TV show?" Gram asked.

"Close enough," Candy confirmed, no longer bored.

"The point?" Clarence asked tersely.

"Daisy was sired by an Angel," Tim explained. "He can be used to show us what Daisy sees in the mind of her deceased husband. We would all relive the death and know the outcome. Daisy's neutrality or lack thereof would no longer be an issue."

My hope died as quickly as it had started. There was a huge hurdle. An impossible hurdle.

"I don't know who my father is," I said flatly. "The plan isn't possible."

"Nothing is impossible as long as you believe," Candy reminded me, twirling her toothpick in her fingers.

"While the idea is excellent, the reality is not. I have no idea who he is," I repeated.

"Clarence," Tim said, sounding ominous and cold. "Would you care to join the discussion?"

Everyone watched as Tim stood and walked to the back of the chair where Michael the Archangel was seated.

"I would not," Clarence ground out.

"Would you rather I deliver the news? I am the Courier after all."

Clarence Smith was not a happy man. It was very clear he knew who my father was. It was also clear that he didn't want to give up the information. Hatred for the man who had been so kind to me for years blossomed in my chest and made it difficult to breathe. Was he so taken with Clarissa that he would let her get away with unforgivable crimes?

I'd take a Demon over an Angel any day of the week.

"The conversation is over," Clarence said. "The meeting is done."

"The conversation has just started," Charlie said in a tone that made me want to hide. Charlie's eyes blazed silver and his hands sparked menacingly. "You will reveal the name of

Daisy's father, Archangel… or there will be hell to pay. Am I clear?"

The house shook, and I wondered for a brief moment if I would have to find a new place to live. I glanced over at Gideon, but his blood-red gaze was trained on Clarence.

No one knew who my father was other than John Travolta and Tim. That was abundantly clear by the reactions of the rest of them.

"The answer will be displeasing," Clarence said, devoid of emotion.

"I don't care," I said. "I want nothing to do with the man other than using him to save Steve. I'll use him like he used my mother. He is nothing to me other than a sperm donor, a deadbeat asshole, and a means to an end. Period."

"I'm quite sure he'll be relieved to hear that," Tim said with an undecipherable expression on his face. "Clarence, will you make sure to tell him what his daughter said?"

Clarence sat silently, and then genuflected.

"Making the sign of the cross won't save you," Tim said. "Speak now, or I shall."

I was ready to puke. I didn't understand what the heck the holdup was.

"Give me his name," I said. "Tell me where he is. I won't let him know how I found out. Your secret is safe with me."

"Oh, the irony," Tim said with a chuckle as the Archangel's body tensed in fury.

"Shut up!" Clarence roared at Tim then turned his angry gaze on me. "I'm your father."

The next few moments defined the term deafening silence.

The looks exchanged between the Immortals were ones of shock and confusion. Gideon was ready to strangle the Angel.

"Are you fucking kidding me?" I shouted, standing up and not caring that Gram heard me drop an F-bomb. "Are we in a *Star Wars* movie? Is this some kind of sick joke?"

Clarence closed his eyes and shook his head. "It's not a joke. I am your father."

I heard a thud and turned to see that Gram had passed out. I had no clue until now that a ghost could do that.

"Help her," I directed Candy, who hopped to her feet then sat down on the floor next to Gram. "I'm processing a whole lot of shit right now. The words disgusted and horrified come to mind, as well as hatred and revulsion. You have known me my entire life. My entire fucking life."

"I have," he said, staring at me. "It was for your own good."

"My own good?" I snarled. "That's certainly big of you, John Travolta. Thanks for that, you no-good son of a bitch."

"There is much you don't know," he said.

"Enlighten me," I replied.

The man who claimed to be my father said nothing.

"I'm talking to you," I snapped.

"And I hear you," he replied.

"Then answer me."

Again, he was silent.

I wanted to hit him. I wanted to destroy him. Why hadn't he wanted me? What was so wrong with me that he'd been around me my whole life and never acknowledged me?

My mother had preferred death to me, and my father hadn't wanted me. It was entirely too much to take in.

So, I didn't. I shut that part down. I'd turned out fine without a mother or a father. I'd had Gram, who had loved me enough for a hundred mothers and fathers. I didn't need a father. I didn't want one.

"Your explanation doesn't matter," I said flatly. He wasn't even worthy of my hatred. "You mean nothing to me. All I want from you is to touch me when I go into Steve's mind and share his death memories with the others."

"He is bound by honor and blood to obey your request," Charlie said, still shocked by the revelation.

"Correct," Heather said, coming to my side and placing her hand on my shoulder. "As the Arbitrator, I consent to the request of the daughter of the Archangel Michael. He is bound by the principles of virtue and goodness to aid in the case against the Angel of Mercy."

"His noncompliance shall result in punishment." Gideon stared daggers at Clarence. "By me."

"And me," Karma added, sounding delighted by the prospect.

"Your reply?" Charlie demanded of Clarence.

"As you wish," Clarence said with his gaze pinned on me.

I nodded jerkily at him and held on to my composure only by a thread.

"When shall we begin?" Tim asked, joining Heather at my side.

"Now," Gideon said. "I don't trust him to keep his word."

"My word is good," Clarence growled.

"Then what's the problem?" Gideon shot back.

"There is no problem," he said, sounding old and tired.

"Where is Steve?" Charlie asked.

"Upstairs," I whispered, light-headed and terrified.

Without another word, everyone stood and made their way to the stairs. My heart felt like it was going to explode out of my chest. This is what I had been fighting for and now that it was here, I was almost paralyzed.

Gideon and I were the last to leave the kitchen.

"Remember two things, Daisy," Gideon said as his eyes still blazed red. "One, I love you."

"And two?" I asked.

"The barrier between worlds may be thin, but not all that lies behind it is savage. We will win. Are you ready?" Gideon whispered.

"Yes," I said without hesitation. "I am."

Taking his hand in mine, I slowly led him out of the kitchen and into the violent storm that awaited us.

CHAPTER TWO

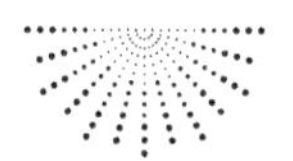

My mind raced. My thoughts were chaotic. Finding out that the man who I had secretly pretended was my father actually *was* my father was mind-blowing—and not in a good way. The sorry truth that he didn't want me was devastating. My childhood dreams had been smashed with a few words.

I now knew how Luke Skywalker felt—gypped and pissed. Only problem was, Luke was fictional.

I was not.

With each step up the stairs, my brain continued to roar with a hurricane of messy and disorganized thoughts—feelings of rage, sadness and inadequacy. But there was no time to focus on myself and my newfound crappy family member. Clarence Smith and I were not headed for a father-daughter happily ever after.

I had a mission and a goal that far outweighed my *daddy*

issues. However, my mind had its own agenda, with no plans of putting on the brakes anytime soon.

I'd lived without the knowledge of my father for forty years. I'd turned out relatively fine depending on with whom you spoke. I'd simply pretend *John Travolta*—my Immortal Angel sperm donor—didn't exist.

Good luck to me.

"Slow the heck down," I muttered.

Gideon glanced at me in confusion. "I'm sorry, what?"

"Whoops, not talking to you," I told him with a weak smile.

"Who are you talking to?" he asked, looking around for ghosts.

"The voices inside my head," I explained to a blank-faced Gideon. "I mean, not really," I added quickly, so he didn't think I was nuttier than I truly was. "My brain. It's on nonstop mode right now."

"Got it," he said with a nod. "That was a lot to take in."

"Understatement," I replied.

I was torn between wanting to hate John Travolta and wanting to make him love me. Both reactions were irrational and irrelevant. What mattered was that the time had come to right the wrong that had been done to Steve.

Clarissa, the Angel of Mercy—an oxymoron if I'd ever heard one—would not get away with trying to destroy me by hurting those I loved. I didn't care if my sperm donor was more concerned with Clarissa's fate than justice. John Travolta the Archangel was my father, but not in any of the ways that counted.

Still, I had *so many* questions.

"How in the hell does someone with little swimmers that are older than dirt even make a baby with a human?"

Gideon's chuckle stopped my forward motion.

Sighing, I closed my eyes. "Shit. I said that out loud, didn't I?"

"You did," he replied with a grin. "And to answer your question... the old-fashioned way."

"So, Clarence *banged* my mom?"

"Apparently."

For a second, I felt like a teenager and wanted to scream "gross". I sucked it back and winced instead. "I thought it was rare that an Immortal and a human could produce a child."

"Rare doesn't mean impossible," Gideon pointed out.

"Can an Immortal make a baby with another Immortal?" I asked.

"Again, rare. Again, not impossible," he replied, eyeing me with curiosity.

"Not asking for me," I quickly said. "That train has passed and I'm not exactly Immortal."

Gideon glanced down and bit back a laugh. "So, you were asking for a friend?"

"Something like that," I muttered.

Open mouth, insert foot should be my nickname. I owned it and had worn it embarrassingly well as of late.

I mulled over the new information and pushed every other question I had to the back of my brain. My focus had to be laser-sharp.

My priority was Steve and making sure he went into the light. Living through his death was going to suck, but if it freed him from the state he was in now, I would do it a million times.

I'd deal with the fact I was a hybrid Angel later—or possibly never. I had thought being a middle-aged human widow was complicated. What a joke. If the Angels were all like Clarence and Clarissa, I wanted nothing to do with that part of my heritage.

"Daisy, let everything go except the path directly in front of you," Gideon instructed.

"Impossible," I replied without thinking.

"Nothing is impossible if you believe," he shot back, repeating something I'd heard far too often lately.

"From your mouth to God's..." I began, and then zipped my lip when I mentally reminded myself that I was talking to someone who lived in Hell. However, the one from Hell was far more trustworthy than those I'd met from Heaven.

I gripped Gideon's hand like a vise. "What if Steve...?"

"No what-ifs," Gideon said, his gaze steady and his voice calm. "I don't believe it was a suicide. Period."

"Right," I said. "No what-ifs."

Part of me was terrified Steve's accident hadn't been an accident. He couldn't remember it. If it turned out that the crash had been by choice, my best friend was destined for the darkness and I was about to expedite the trip.

The possible outcome made my stomach churn. I'd been to the darkness, and I wasn't planning a visit anytime soon. I was sure I'd only scratched the surface. The bizarre fact that my hand was clasped in the warm embrace of the Grim Reaper further convoluted my thinking.

I was learning quickly that the good were not so good

and the bad were not all evil. The world was full of murky shades of gray. Gray was not my color.

The ruckus in the upstairs hallway pulled me out of my introspective thoughts.

"What's going on up there?" Gideon growled as he picked up his pace.

What the hell *was* going on up there? Had Clarence decided not to help and all hell had broken loose? The man said his word was good...

Racing to the top of the stairs, I stopped dead in my tracks—pun intended. I gasped and wasn't sure if I wanted to laugh or scream.

Quickly ducking and pulling Gideon down with me, we narrowly missed getting nailed by a detached flying ghost head. Of course, yanking Gideon to safety was unnecessary as the head would have gone right through him. But me? I could have gotten a lovely black eye or broken nose. Being the Death Counselor meant the ghosts were corporeal to me... and only me.

"What in the ever-lovin' hell?" I shouted over the howling wind, shielding my eyes from the strong gusts and the thirty or so ghosts going nuts.

"Insane," Candy Vargo yelled with a grin and a thumbs up.

Karma was correct. I grinned back at Candy and shook my head.

It was par for the course. My life had been spinning out of control for a while now. Why anything shocked me anymore was almost comical in a very unfunny way. I was a widowed forty-year-old who had a large posse of deceased roommates. I glued body parts back on with superglue and I could mind dive into the dead and figure out what problem they needed solved to move on. On top of that bit of bizarre news, my departed husband had shown back up to apologize for being gay and I was becoming the Hulk with superpowers.

However, what I was seeing right now took the cake.

The upstairs hallway was reminiscent of a big-budget horror film with seriously bad B actors. If I had to name the film, I'd have to go with *Drunk Circus of the Dead*. My dogs, Donna the Destroyer and Karen the Chair Eater, sat in front of the closed bedroom door and growled menacingly at the Immortals, who had pressed themselves against the wall in alarm. The dogs were enough to give anyone pause, especially since Donna was a Hell Hound.

But the ghosts had lost their damn minds.

My squatters were completely out of control, and I'd never been so proud in my life. The transparent brigade—led by Birdie, Gram and her new dead beau, Jimmy Joe Johnson—were gunning for Clarence.

I was fully aware they couldn't harm him, but they could cause a good amount of trouble—not to mention nightmares. Most of my expired guests were not in great shape. The longer they'd been dead, the greater the decomposition of their bodies. The flying appendages were a nice and macabre touch. Several heads rolled down the hallway and tumbled down the stairs, hitting every step with a thud. Arms and legs littered the floor. Putting my ghosts back together would be a shitshow, but the expression of horror on Clarence's face made the fact that I'd have to order more superglue worth it.

"Holy crap," I muttered, swallowing back an extremely inappropriate laugh as the headless Birdie shoved her detached cranium into the face of an appalled Clarence.

I figured Birdie had retrieved her head from the refrigerator during the reception after Gram's funeral. The crazy ghost loved to hide her body parts all over the house to freak me out. When I'd found her head in the fridge, I left it there. Her idea of a joke was gag-inducing. Of course, I planned to glue it back on after she'd learned her lesson, but I was thrilled she'd pilfered it. Clarence looked positively green.

"Call them off," my *father* hissed.

"They can't hurt you," I yelled with a wide smile. I ducked as a few unattached legs flew past my head.

I wasn't going to stop them because John Travolta had demanded I do so. I was going to stop them because I wasn't sure I had enough superglue to glue them all back together. The longer the flying dead freak show went on, the more body parts fell off of my squatters.

"Enough," I shouted over the melee. "While I appreciate the sentiment, the reality is not so hot—although, you guys get ten points for disgusting creativity."

Not one of them listened to me. Not even Gram. The action in the hallway was akin to *Beetlejuice* on crack. As amusing as it was, it did have to stop. Heather was surrounded by unattached feet and Tim looked as pale as the ghosts themselves. Charlie seemed somewhat entertained while my *father* was seriously put out. Candy was the only one really enjoying the show.

And Gideon? He simply grinned. The gorgeous man had my back for better or worse.

And this moment in time landed in the *worse* column.

"Listen up, dead people. There will be no reality TV for anyone if you don't stop right now," I yelled.

"Game shows too, Daisy girl?" Gram asked, pausing midair to clarify my threat.

"Game shows too," I confirmed, slapping my hands on my hips and eyeing the dead who had finally slowed down to listen. "I'm serious. If you don't cut this shit out and pick up your body parts, I'll put on the news channel twenty-four-seven."

The shrieks were terrifying to those who weren't used to the deceased. Even Gideon appeared taken aback. However, the ghosts despised the news. I didn't blame them.

"And I'd also like to say thank you. That was fairly magnificent in a revolting way," I told them as they preened with delight at my praise. "Your unappetizing defense of myself and Steve humbles me. However, I've got this. If I need you guys, I'll let you know."

Quickly and somewhat efficiently, my squatters floated around and tried to find their lost limbs. It was going to take entirely too long. Picking up a leg and an arm, I handed them to Gram, who luckily was still in one piece.

"Take these," I instructed.

"They're not mine," Gram pointed out.

"Yep, I know," I told her. "Right now, it doesn't matter. I

need all the ghosts to go back downstairs. We can figure out what belongs to who later."

"Roger that, sweetie pie," Gram said, herding the specters with a shrill whistle that could have burst an eardrum. "All righty, dead folks. You heard my Daisy girl. All the people missing a noggin, feel your way toward my voice. I saw about fifteen heads roll down the stairs so I'm guessin' some of y'all can't see shit from Shinola at the moment. If you need a buddy, raise your hand. If you don't have one of those, then raise a leg."

"I can't believe this is my life," I said as I watched the ghosts make their way back to the first floor.

Well, all the ghosts except for Birdie.

"Hoooooooookaaah," she sang.

The crazy old woman tossed her head in the air, did a backflip and caught it as she righted herself. The move was impressive. Candy Vargo applauded.

"Birdie, you and your head need to go downstairs with the rest," I told her as the Immortals in the hallway watched me with great interest. "If you do as I say, you'll be first in line to get your head reattached."

"Hoooooooookaaah," Birdie yelled, pointing at herself.

Glancing over at my audience, I held up my hand. "Give me a sec here."

"Take all the time you need," Candy insisted. "This is the best damn evening I've had in centuries."

"I do concur that it's fascinating," Tim added.

"Delighted to be of service," I said with an eye roll as Heather laughed.

Charlie shook his head and shrugged. "I've never seen anything like this in my life."

"It's not always this dramatic… or rather, traumatic," I assured him. "Birdie is special."

"That was very diplomatic of you," Heather said with a grin.

"Thank you," I replied. "It's my Southern genes talking."

"Hooooooooookaaah," Birdie repeated, smacking her bony chest with her head and wanting my attention back on her.

I squinted at her and mentally debated how to proceed. Pissing off Birdie could mean a foot under my pillow or even worse, an eyeball in my oatmeal. With Birdie, one never knew—not that her name was actually Birdie. I'd nicknamed her due to her excessive need to flip me off. She was in rough shape and had a bad temper. Although, she'd grown on me like a nonpoisonous fungus. She was a spicy-hot mess of rude and kept me on my toes. While I'd never admit it aloud, I'd miss her when it was her time to go.

"You were a hooker when you were alive?" I asked, hoping I'd read her clues correctly. Inappropriate laughter or committing myself to an institution right now were two reasonable choices. The choice was simple.

I laughed.

Not because it was funny, but because I was talking to a woman holding her own head and telling me she was a lady of the evening. The absurdity was overwhelming.

Birdie flipped me off.

All was normal in my abnormal world.

"Yausssss," Birdie hissed, zipping up and down the

hallway while holding her head and cackling like a loon. "Hoooooooookaaah."

"Mmkay. I suppose I shouldn't be all that surprised," I said. "Is there a reason I need to know this right now?"

"Yausssss, hoooooooookaaah dieeah foooor yooouah."

Her statement was alarming and confusing. I didn't know her when she was alive. "You died for me?"

"Naawwwooo," she bellowed with her overactive middle finger aimed at me.

Heaving out a sigh of relief, I waited for more. Another few minutes with Birdie kept me from having to relive Steve's death with an audience. "I'm not following what you mean," I told her.

"Dieeah foooor yooouah, hoooooooookaaah."

"I think she's telling you she'll die for you," Gideon whispered.

"I think you're right," I replied, wondering why in the heck she would offer such a magnanimous gesture when all she ever did was flip me off. "Birdie, that's very sweet of you. However, you're already dead. Plus, I would never ask you to die for me. I'm not that kind of girl. But I am asking you to go downstairs. We can continue this conversation later... or never."

"Hoooooooookaaah duuumb duuumb," she announced.

"Pretty sure she just called you stupid," Candy said, seating herself on the hallway bench and getting comfortable. "Whatcha gonna do about that smack talk, Daisy the Death Counselor?"

"Absolutely nothing," I replied, closing my eyes and realizing the day would come when I would have to dive into

Birdie's mind. It was going to be terrifying. Thankfully, today was not that day.

"Hooooooooookaaah duuumb duuumb asssssssssah," Birdie announced.

"She called you a dumb-ass," Tim pointed out unhelpfully.

"Yep. Heard that," I told him. I grabbed Birdie's foot as she whipped by and pulled her out of the air. "It's kind of hard to converse with a headless hooker," I chastised her. "You have a shitty mouth on you and you're rude."

She laughed.

Rolling my eyes, I pulled a tube of superglue from my pocket and dangled it in front of her. "This glue has your name on it if you haul your nasty butt downstairs immediately. You feel me? And if you don't, you're going to be headless for a long, long, long time."

"Looooogah?" Birdie asked.

"Long," I confirmed. "I'd also like to point out that it would be far easier to flip me off if you didn't have to carry your head."

"Yausssss, hooooooooookaaah," she replied, handing me her head.

"Umm, nope," I said, handing it back to her. "I have to help Steve right now. I promise I'll help you soon."

Birdie hung her head in shame. "Ssssoooorrry, Daaaau-usayy," she said. "Ssssoooorrry."

"Birdie, it's okay," I said, gently touching her shoulder. I would have normally touched her cheek, but since she was holding her head, that seemed a little odd. "I'm not mad. I think it's beautiful that all of you want to protect Steve and me. It's the same way I feel about you even though you don't make it easy."

"Daaaauusayy taaaaawlk hoooooooookaaah?" she asked.

I nodded and smiled. "Yes. We'll talk soon. You have my word."

"And her word is way better than John Travolta's," Tim pointed out as Clarence shot him an irate glare.

"We should get started," Heather said quietly.

Again, I nodded. "Birdie, go now."

"Saaaaafeh," she insisted as she floated away.

I smiled and waved. Being safe wasn't an option. Very little I did anymore could be considered safe.

Living on the edge was my new modus operandi, and I was about to test my limits.

"Are you ready?" Gideon asked, taking my hand in his.

"I am."

My statement was strong. It wasn't a lie. However, my insides were churning.

"Do you want a moment alone with Steve before we join you?" Heather asked.

I nodded gratefully. "I would. Thank you."

"Always, Daisy," Heather said. "Let us know when you want us to come in."

Again, I nodded.

What I wanted to do was cry, but that wasn't an option. Thankfully my lady balls had increased in size lately. I was going to need them.

CHAPTER THREE

"HEY, YOU," I SAID, CAREFULLY SITTING ON THE EDGE OF THE bed next to Steve and tucking the covers around what was left of him.

My old farmhouse was lovely. And the master bedroom was cozy and inviting just like the rest of the house. I'd done all the painting and some of the other manual labor, but Steve had been the one with the great decorating skills. All of the furniture was overstuffed and in soothing patterns and faded florals. The color motif of the bedroom was pale green and peach. It had always been my calm safe haven and was even more so now. Seeing Steve lying in the bed was tragically beautiful.

The day Steve went into the light would be the last gift I would give to my best friend. The thought of losing him again didn't undo me the way it had a year ago when he'd died. It would shred me to let him go, but it would also give me peace. Most importantly, it would give *him* peace and the afterlife he deserved. The injustice of what Clarissa had done by claiming his death was a suicide and trying to send him to the darkness would not stand when challenged. I believed it with every bone in my body. I had to. There was no alternative.

Steve had been a handsome man when he was alive—dark curly hair and the bluest eyes I'd ever seen. He was now a mere shell of his former self. It was difficult to find his beauty under the gray and papery skin, but it was still very clear to me.

"Dausseeeeee," Steve said with an attempt at a smile as I gently touched his face.

His communication skills had improved lately, but his appearance had not.

"We have a few minutes to talk," I told him, forcing a smile onto my lips that I hoped looked sincere. I was a crappy liar. He knew it and I knew it. My goal was to show him my confidence. I was terrified, but that was for me to know and no one to find out. "I'm going to go into your mind and prove to everyone that your death was an accident. It won't hurt."

I had no clue if what I promised was true, but I had a plan—possibly a very stupid plan, but a plan nonetheless.

"Dausseeeeee," Steve whispered in the lovingly stern tone I recognized so well.

"That's my name. Don't wear it out," I replied with a wink.

I didn't want to argue. I wanted him to be on the same page and I needed him to understand what was about to happen. However, a little gossip—at my painful expense—was also necessary.

"Remember when I told you about John Travolta?" I asked.

Steve made a sound and gazed up at me with an expression of confusion. "Chaawgeeeenge sssubjeectahs?"

"Yep," I said with a grin. "I'm changing subjects—kind of. It all relates in a bizarre way."

"Fiiiinah," he said with the tiniest shake of his head. "Joooonha Traaavoooooltah?"

"Michael the Archangel," I told him. "My boss, Clarence Smith? You remember him?"

"Yausssss,"

"He pulled a Darth Vader on me. He just admitted he's my sperm donor."

"Naawwwooo," Steve said, wrinkling what was left of his brow in shock.

"Yep. A total *Star Wars* farked-up moment. Gram passed out," I said, making light of what had just rocked my world off its axis.

"Luuuukah, ahhh amma yooouah faaawtheur?"

I couldn't help myself. I laughed, and then I started to cry—an ugly snot cry. I wasn't crying about John Travolta, but it was better to let Steve think I was. My best friend was in such horrendous shape, I was unsure if he would survive me entering his mind. Which I hoped was somewhat ridiculous since he was already dead.

"Ohhhhhhh, Dausseeeeee," Steve whispered, and then moaned softly. "Beeeeah oookaaay."

"I know," I said, wiping my eyes and inhaling deeply. "Everything will be okay."

"Dausseeeeee ffeeewl?" he asked.

"Honestly, I don't know," I told him truthfully. "Angry, sad, empty, cheated. However, I'm going to change the subject again. Cool?"

"Naawwwooo."

"Yes," I said with a half-assed attempt at a smile to lighten the mood. "Did you know that Birdie was a hooker in real life?"

Steve chuckled. It sounded more like a death rattle, but I knew the difference. "Naawwwooo."

"Yep, she informed me she was a hooker and that she would die for me."

"Reeeealllyah?"

"Really," I confirmed. "I told her thanks, but no thanks and pointed out that she was already dead."

"Meeeenah sooomthin eeelssse," Steve guessed.

"It could mean something else," I replied, thinking through the possibility that I'd misinterpreted Birdie's message. "I promised to talk with her later. I'll figure it out. So, anyhoo," I went on as if everything we had just discussed was normal. "Since John Travolta is my de facto pappy—in biology only—that makes me part Angel."

"Niiiiice," Steve said with a tilted grin.

"Nope," I corrected him. "Not nice. I'd rather be a Demon. Angels suck. That being said, turns out that *pappy* can touch me while I'm inside your mind and telegraph what I learn to the others."

"Whhhhyah?"

"Because John Travolta doesn't believe that I'm neutral where you're concerned," I told him, and then paused. "And even though I'll never admit it to the Immortals, I'm not. I'm not neutral where you're concerned at all. Apparently, taking Clarissa down is a huge deal, and I can't freaking wait."

"Dausseeeeee," Steve said, trying to reach for me.

I saved him the trouble and lay down next to him, careful not to knock off a body part. Steve was literally falling apart.

"What?" I asked, cautiously laying my head on his shoulder.

"S'oookaaay. Beeeeee nuuuuutraalah," he said.

"I won't have a choice," I pointed out. "The Immortals will see what happened at the same time I do."

"Assciideeent. Waassah assciideeent."

My head jerked up, and I stared at him. Holding my breath, I became light-headed and needed to clarify that I'd heard him correctly. "Are you sure? You remember? It was definitely an accident?"

"Reeemawbah soooomeah," he said. "Waassah assci-ideeent."

A massive boulder had just been lifted from my shoulders. Excitement coursed through my veins and the light at the end of the dark tunnel grew brighter.

"Okay," I said, rolling off the bed and pacing the room. Movement helped me think. "Don't tell me any more. Save your energy. When I go into your mind, we can speak normally. But remember, we'll have an audience."

"Whoooo-ah?"

"John Travolta, Charlie, Heather, Tim, Candy Vargo and Gideon," I told him, kicking off my heels and pulling my dress over my head. I quickly searched the laundry basket for some yoga pants and a sweatshirt.

Mind diving took a lot out of me. I didn't want to pass out in the dress I'd worn to Gram's funeral when I came out of Steve's memories. Hell, I should probably put on PJs. With what I had tentatively planned, I might sleep for a week when I finished.

Steve was quiet. His silence unnerved me a bit, but I was so damned relieved he was sure it was an accident, I wanted to cry.

"Are you ready?" I asked.

"Arrruh yooooouah?" he shot back.

"I am. My *lady balls* are huge and I'm wearing my favorite sweatshirt—only a few paint splatters on it," I said with a small smile tugging at my lips. "I've got this. You just have to trust me."

"Baaawlls."

"That's right, baby," I said as I gently kissed what was left of his forehead. "Everything will be okay. And remember, when we talk in your head, they can hear us."

"Roooouger thaaatah."

"NICE TO SEE YOU GOT DRESSED UP FOR THE OCCASION," Candy commented as she walked into my bedroom and glanced around.

"I'm taking a page out of your book," I shot back,

narrowing my eyes and daring any of them to gasp at the state Steve was in.

"Where would you like us?" Charlie asked, sucking in a barely audible breath of pity when his gaze landed on Steve.

He'd known Steve when he'd been alive. All of them had except for Gideon. I was well aware it was upsetting to look at him. His gray skin and partial head were all that were exposed, but it was heartbreaking to see.

"Why don't you all find a seat. I don't know how long it will take," I said.

Heather clapped her hands and an array of chairs appeared. The magic stuff still freaked me out. I had no clue why, considering I lived with ghosts and could knock over large trees with my bare hands. Everyone took a seat except for Clarence Smith, aka Darth Vader, aka John Travolta, aka Michael the Archangel... aka my father.

He stared at Steve in surprise and shock.

If he made even one rude comment, I would head-butt him and enjoy it. My Southern manners didn't exist where Steve's feelings were concerned.

Donna and Karen trotted into the room, hopped up on the bed and settled themselves at Steve's feet. It was clear that Donna wasn't pleased with the unfamiliar people who were in my bedroom. My Hell Hound had excellent instincts.

I wasn't thrilled either, but I was also thankful they were here. It was the only way to win.

And I had no plans to lose.

"And me?" John Travolta inquired, sounding tense. "Where should I be?"

God, if a punchline was ever waiting to happen, this was it. However, I needed him, and telling him where I'd like him to go wasn't in my favor.

Sighing and pulling on the ends of my wild dark hair, I stared at him and wondered briefly what my life would have been like if he'd been in it. I'd never know. The past was just that—the past. The future was mine and there was no room for him.

"I'm going to lie next to Steve on the bed and hug him. Grab a chair and put it next to the bed. You can touch my back," I instructed with very little emotion in my voice.

"As you wish," he replied formally.

Shaking my head, I bit back every snarly word that ached to leave my lips. He wasn't good enough for my anger. My focus was Steve.

"I want to be near you," Gideon said to me while smiling down at Steve. "Steve, is it okay with you if I lie on the bed as well?"

"Yausssss," Steve said, glancing up at Gideon with fondness.

Steve's reason for coming back was to make sure that I found real love with a man who could love me in a way he never could. Gideon was that man, and Steve was delighted.

"How about you?" Gideon inquired, looking at me in a way that made me feel truly seen. "Will that hinder you in any way?"

"Will it be weird for you?" I asked.

No one alive had ever been present when I went into the minds of the dead. I had no clue if I made horrible faces or noises. God forbid, the mortifying possibilities for embarrassing myself were endless.

Too bad. So sad. It didn't matter if I grunted the entire time I was out of my body. I was doing this for Steve, and I would humiliate myself a million times over if that was what it took. Besides, I was sure if I did anything out of the ordinary, Candy Vargo would be delighted to let me know.

"Define weird," Gideon said with a smile that made my heart skip a beat.

"Umm, fine point. Well made," I replied with a small laugh. Weird was my new normal. "I would like it very much if you were close."

Gideon nodded and lay down to the left of Steve. He gently put his hand on top of the blanket and whispered something in Steve's ear.

Steve smiled and sighed.

I was dying to know what he said, but it was none of my business. The illogicality of everything happening was strangely perfect. My dead gay husband and the man I was in love with were friends. Steve approved of Gideon. My best friend had succeeded in what he had come back to do and now it was time to let him go.

"John Travolta, you can touch my back now," I said, wrapping my arms carefully around Steve.

"Do you *really* have to call me John Travolta?" the Archangel inquired.

"Would you prefer deadbeat asshole?" I asked politely.

His pause was long. His chuckle was unexpected. "John Travolta will be fine."

"As you wish." I parroted the phrase he seemed so fond of and ignored the feeling of his hand on my back.

There was something so right and so wrong about my *father's* touch. It was something I'd longed for as a child. As an adult, I still longed for it. However, the man was touching me because he had to, not because he wanted to.

"Keep your hand on me until I come back," I told him flatly.

He had promised his word was good, but that didn't mean I trusted him. His alliance with Clarissa was too obvious to ignore. There was no way I wanted to dive into Steve's mind twice since it was unknown how it would affect him. I couldn't take the chance that John Travolta would remove his hand before I was clearly able to prove Steve's innocence.

"He will *not* remove his hand," Charlie said in a steely tone. "If he does, he shall be handless for the rest of eternity."

"Vicious. I like it," Candy said with approval.

Heather moved across the room and stood behind John Travolta. With a snap of her fingers, the Archangel's hand was bound to my back. The Angel hissed his disbelief at the disrespect and distrust that was being shown to him.

"Please tell me you can undo what you just did," I said flatly. "I do not need a John Travolta barnacle for the rest of my life."

"I can," Heather said with a grin. "Not to worry. I wouldn't burden you with the weight of a coward."

Without looking, I felt my father's body tense in fury.

"I'm sitting right here, Arbitrator," he snapped.

"I am well aware of that," Heather replied coldly. "I don't want any more surprises tonight. You seem to be full of those, Michael."

"Enough," Tim said. "We are spectators here. There will be no bickering."

"When did you grow balls?" Candy asked him.

"Same time you did," Tim replied rudely.

"Touché," she said with a laugh, and then added. "Mine are bigger."

"Doubtful," Tim muttered.

"I'm ready," I said.

The room went silent. Steve's deteriorating body trembled in my arms. My father's hand was magically secured to my back. The two men I loved the most were with me. Gideon's eyes met mine and a small smile pulled at his beautiful lips.

"You've got this," he said softly. "The truth is on Steve's side."

Nodding, I took a deep breath and let myself fall.

The fall wasn't without pain. I just hoped the pain to come wouldn't end me.

CHAPTER FOUR

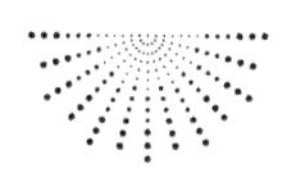

The cold. The cold went all the way to my bones and tore through my body like sharp, frozen daggers made of ice. Trying to catch my breath, I gasped for air but stayed calm.

My head pounded violently and every single cell in my body screamed for oxygen. I knew it was momentary, but it still sucked.

My mind went numb and my limbs felt like jelly.

Closing my eyes, I welcomed the icy chill that permeated my skin and seeped into my blood. It was proof that I was exactly where I wanted to be. I would never enjoy the sensation, but I'd become accustomed to it.

I'd become accustomed to a lot as of late.

I had no choice.

Or I was insane. It was a toss-up.

There was no rationalizing what I was doing. Gram had never taken a mind dive into the dead, nor had any other Death Counselor before her as far as anyone knew. While I did not subscribe to predestiny, I did believe that sometimes things happened for a reason. The simple fact that I could save Steve's afterlife with my gift was more than a good enough reason to be saddled with the strange talent.

"My Daisy," Steve said with such warmth in his voice. I felt tears prick behind my closed lids.

"That's my name. Don't wear it out," I said, counting to three and slowly opening my eyes.

My gasp was audible. My tears were unstoppable. Steve was no longer a shell of a person. He was whole and beautiful—inside and out.

We stood opposite each other in a cavernous room of emptiness. There was no floor. No walls to speak of—more of a vast landscape of nothing. Steve and I floated in a silvery mist. It wasn't frightening, but it would never be a place I would want to stay.

"Don't cry," he said, tilting his head to the side in concern.

"Happy tears," I promised. "You look so..."

Glancing down at himself, he chuckled. "Damn fine," Steve finished my sentence.

"Very damn fine," I agreed, grinning. "I wish we could just stay like this for a while."

"Why can't we?" he asked.

Shaking my head, I felt guilty for the words I was about to speak, but they were the truth. "The longer I stay in your mind, the harder it is for me to recover."

Steve pressed his lips together and ran his hands through his hair. "Let's do this then."

I nodded, feeling panic settle in my chest. "You're sure it was an accident?"

"I'm sure, Daisy. I can't remember exactly what happened, but

it was not by choice."

"Good," I replied, and then hesitated. "I..."

"You what?"

"I want to hold your hand," I said.

"Like the Beatles?" Steve asked with a raised brow and a twinkle in his eyes.

"Umm, yes, dorko. Just like the Beatles. I'll be Paul and you can be Ringo."

"That sounds kind of gay," he pointed out with a silly grin.

I shrugged. "If the ruby slipper fits..."

Steve's laugh went all through me, and I felt true joy. "We can really hold hands here?"

I nodded and reached for him. Steve placed his hand in mine and grasped it firmly. His hand lacked the warmth of a living person with blood running through their veins, but it was so familiar and felt so good.

"I know that you're dying to ask me something," Steve teased, tucking my wild hair behind my ear and giving me a lopsided grin.

"No, I'm not," I lied with a giggle.

"You want to know what Gideon whispered to me."

Rolling my eyes, I sighed dramatically. "Yesssss, I do," I admitted. "However, don't forget that we have an audience. If it's private, don't say it. I'll pry it out of him later."

"No need. Gideon told me that when other's look at you, they see your face, your smile, your kindness and your beauty."

"Mmkay," I said, not understanding why he needed to tell Steve that. "That's it?"

"Nope," Steve replied.

I eyed him and pursed my lips. "You're going to make me guess the rest?"

"If we had the time I would," he teased. "But since the clock is ticking, Gideon said that he sees your soul, and that he'll love you until the end of time."

I was flabbergasted, humbled and thrilled—so delighted that I forgot one very important thing...

"Gideon is getting so banged when I see him again," I announced to a grinning Steve.

"You haven't banged the Grim Reaper yet?" he asked, shocked. "His balls have to be purple by now."

"I'm sure his balls are— Oh shit," I said, slapping my forehead and wanting to turn back time about two minutes.

"What's wrong with his balls?" Steve asked, clearly not on the same page. "He looks very healthy to me."

"Umm, Steve—" I started, only to be cut off.

"Does he suffer from cryptorchidism?"

"What the hell does that even mean?" I asked, wildly confused.

"It's an undescended testicle," Steve told me. "Nowadays it can be corrected with surgery, but Gideon is older than time, so maybe it stayed up there. I don't think that it's a problem though. Have you seen his balls?"

"No," I shouted. "I have not seen his balls. But here's the problem. I know I haven't seen his balls, and I know you haven't seen his balls."

"Gideon also knows you haven't seen his balls," Steve added unhelpfully.

I wanted to scream. "Yes, while that is correct, now Heather, Charlie, Candy Vargo, Tim and Darth Vader also know I haven't seen his balls," I said, letting my chin fall to my chest in embarrassed defeat.

"Shit," Steve muttered, trying not to laugh.

He failed.

I joined him.

"How about we stop talking about Gideon's balls?" I suggested, still giggling.

"Sounds like a plan," Steve agreed, squeezing my hand. "Why don't you apologize to Gideon?"

"He's not here," I pointed out.

"True, but he can hear us, right?" Steve asked, grinning like a fool.

I nodded and punched him in the arm. "Sorry, Gideon," I called out into the nothingness.

I couldn't even begin to imagine the Grim Reaper's reaction to the last few minutes. Probably horrified and regretting his promise to Steve.

"I'm sorry too," Steve called out. "It's all my fault for suggesting that your balls hadn't dropped. Which, by the way, is not a big deal if they haven't. Just saying..."

"You should really stop now."

"Roger that," Steve agreed.

We stood in silence and stared at each other for a long moment. My mind was cluttered with fear laced with confidence. It had taken me a long time to get over Steve's death. I hoped like hell I wouldn't be thrown back to that dark place by reliving it.

It didn't matter. There was a price for everything, and I was willing to pay whatever it took to send my best friend into the light.

"I'll try to make this as painless as possible for you," I said.

"Do not do that," Steve said sternly. "I'm dead, Daisy. Any

pain I feel is phantom pain. Just watch it with me. Help me to remember what happened. Please. Am I clear?"

"I hear you," I told him.

He nodded and eyed me warily. "That was an answer with an omission."

"Possibly," I agreed. "Just relax and let me do what I need to do."

Steve inhaled deeply and exhaled slowly. He nodded and wrapped me in a tight embrace.

"Tell me what to do," he whispered with his face buried in my hair.

Honestly, I wasn't exactly sure. All of the others I'd visited in their mind had remembered what happened to them. Sam, John and Lindsay had known what they'd wanted to tell me. It took Lindsay some convincing to let me into the memories of her murder, but she'd trusted me completely.

Trust.

That was it... I hoped.

"Do you trust me, Steve?" I asked, pulling back and looking into his bright blue eyes.

"With everything I am, Daisy," he replied, taking both of my hands in his.

"Then close your eyes and open your mind to me. I'll be with you the entire time."

"I love you, Daisy. With all my heart, I love you."

"I love you too. I always have and I always will," I said, holding back my tears.

I was unsure how quickly he would leave once his innocence had been proven. The concept of sending him into the light was perfect. The reality was devastating.

No pain. No gain.

"Close your eyes, Steve," I instructed. "It's time. Try to get to the day you died and then just let it happen."

"I can do that. Will you be okay?" he asked.

"Yes."

I was unsure if I was lying or telling the truth. Okay was a relative word, so I agreed to a very broad definition.

Pictures raced across my vision so quickly I couldn't make them out. Again, it was like an old, static-filled black-and-white TV screen was inside my head. Catching glimpses of Steve's memories of me, I smiled sadly.

Hindsight was 20/20 and heartbreakingly obvious. My blindness astounded me, yet surprisingly, I regretted nothing. Again, I had to believe some things happened for a reason. The fact that Steve and I had been together made me the person I was now. I liked the woman I had become.

As I watched our life together flit past, I saw two people who adored each other as best friends—not as a man and a woman in a romantic relationship. It was very clear that we'd had an unbreakable platonic bond, not a sexual one. While I wouldn't change a thing, my heart still ached that neither of us had lived a full life together.

We'd lived a beautiful and loving lie.

I watched as Steve and I laughed at my first pathetic attempt at reupholstering a chair. I'd wanted to burn it, but Steve had proudly put it in his office and used it until the day he'd died.

"Oh my God. The chair," I said with a laugh.

"I loved that butt-ugly chair—wildly unattractive, but very comfortable," Steve said.

I still had the chair. It was one of my most valued possessions

—hideous, but filled with lovely memories.

Our wedding day and many other happy days rushed across my vision. It was invasive to know that it was being observed by others, but it was yet another price to be paid.

"I'm there," Steve whispered as I watched with sadness.

"And I'm here," I promised. "I'm not going anywhere."

"But I am," he said in a choked voice.

"Are you scared?" I asked, squeezing his hands.

"Not for me," he replied sadly.

"I'm wearing my lady balls and they're completely descended," I said in a light tone that belied the riotous emotions roaring inside me. "I'm good."

The day was rainy and gray. The sky was crying in anticipation of what was about to transpire.

The oldies station played on the radio and Bill Withers sang a prophetic song—"Ain't No Sunshine When She's Gone."

If the word she had been replaced by the word he, it would have been eerily perfect.

My breath caught in my throat and a chemical shift jerked through my body. I had as little control over it as I did in taking my next breath. My body no longer belonged to me.

My heart raced erratically and I glanced around wildly. Opening my eyes, I couldn't find Steve anywhere, much less myself. Shit. What had gone wrong?

The steering wheel in my hands felt real. The breath from my lips proved I was still alive. However, the breath was unfamiliar. Glancing down, I gasped as I realized why I couldn't see Steve in front of me.

I'd become Steve. I was driving the car.

My intention was to take the pain from him during the crash

—just like I'd done for Lindsay during her murder. Had I screwed myself with this plan?

Was I about to die for Steve?

Bill Withers continued to sing.

If the words to the song were my future, I was fucked.

"Bill Withers, you need to change those lyrics," I muttered, navigating the sharp curves on the country road. It wasn't exactly a switchback, but the drop-off on the side of the road was steep and deadly.

I knew I was getting close to the spot where Steve's car had gone off the road and wrapped itself around a tree. My anxiety grew as the tires began to hydroplane and the rain came down in torrents.

"Slow down," I shouted at myself and anyone who cared to listen. "You're going to die."

Someone was listening. God? Steve? Me? I didn't know and I didn't care. I was just happy the speed decreased.

"What the hell?" I cried out as something large appeared from out of nowhere in the middle of the slick road.

The winged creature glowed such a brilliant gold, I had to shield my eyes from the glare. The smile on the creature's lips was horrifying and the wingspan had to be at least eight feet on either side.

I knew her.

I despised her.

"Move," I screamed as I slammed my foot on the breaks and the car began to spin out of control. "Dammit, MOVE."

She didn't move. The Angel of Mercy stood in the road and was the reason I jerked my wheel to the right, causing the car to careen off the road and into a horrendous nightmare.

I didn't want to jerk the wheel, but it was exactly what Steve had done to avoid killing the beast that had come to kill him. The sound of Clarissa's maniacal laughter as the car tumbled off the road would live in my nightmares for the rest of time.

"I should have run you down, you bitch," I shouted as I lost control of the vehicle.

All I could hear was the scream of metal and Clarissa's unholy laugh.

Steve's death was not an accident. It was murder.

Somewhere in the far distance, I heard a male voice yelling at me. The words were undecipherable. Was it Steve? Was it Gideon? Strangely, it sounded a little bit like John Travolta.

The agony in the voice was unmistakable, but there was nothing I could do to comfort the man who seemed so upset.

"This is not real," I reminded myself. "This is not my life. Not my destiny."

The pain I felt was not my own. It belonged to Steve. This was a gift to him. He'd lived it once. I would not let him live it twice.

Shattering of glass, the shrill wails of the mangled metal as it twisted and deformed and the crunching of my bones as they broke in so many places beat against my ears. I lost the ability to think. I couldn't remember why this was a good plan.

"No," I screamed as the car rammed head-on into a tree.

Jerking forward into the steering wheel, searing-hot fire tore through my chest and I gasped for air. My heart pounded explosively. I could feel it all the way to my toes. The oxygen was snatched from my lungs as I cried out for help.

If I didn't die in the next few minutes, I would kill Clarissa with my bare hands in the very near future.

My mouth tasted of metal, but I couldn't recall what the taste was—pennies? Salty pennies? Blood?

Time refused to stop. Colors and images raced across my vision.

Strangely, riddles floated through my barely conscious mind. I tried to tell myself one to block out the agony. My voice sounded ragged to my own ears—as if I'd swallowed shards of glass. Maybe I had.

The line between Steve and me was invisible. I was him. He was me. I could see no way out even if I was willing to leave him.

"What can fly without wings?" I whispered, desperate to make the pain go away.

"Time," Steve choked out.

I was shocked to silence for a moment. Was Steve here? Was I dead too?

"I can bring tears to your eyes. I can resurrect the dead. I can make you smile. I can reverse time. I form in an instant and I can last a lifetime. What am I?" I asked, holding on to my life and sanity by a thread.

"You're a memory," Steve replied in a weak voice. "Leave me, Daisy. This is not your destiny. The truth has been revealed."

"I don't know how," I cried out, searching for him but seeing nothing but darkness.

"This is not real," Steve insisted. "It already happened. It happened a year ago. It was not a suicide. It was an accident. You found what you came for."

"It wasn't an accident," I said woodenly. "It was a murder."

Steve shuddered. The feeling was odd. The sensation was next to me, not inside me. I should have felt his shudder as if it was mine.

"I'm pushing you out," Steve insisted as I felt a violent jolt course through my body. "This is the last gift I can give you. Accept it, Daisy."

"Yes," I said as I grew weightless and woozy.

A hand reached for me, and I grasped it like a lifeline. It wasn't Steve's hand. It wasn't Gideon's hand.

The hand belonged to my father.

"Come with me now," the Archangel whispered. "It is not your time to go yet."

I couldn't see John Travolta clearly, but his voice was unmistakable.

"It was not an accident," I said, digging my nails into the flesh of his hand. "Steve did not commit suicide."

"Your husband did not commit suicide," he said.

"It was murder," I hissed, wanting to bite the hand that was trying to save me. "Clarissa murdered my husband."

My father was silent.

"Say it," I screamed. "Say the words. Prove you're not a coward for all to hear."

"It was a murder," he said in a sad whisper. "The Angel of Mercy is guilty."

My satisfaction was fleeting. An exhaustion I'd never known consumed me and a darkness pulled me forward. Closing my eyes, I let go.

There was nothing else I was capable of doing.

My mission was complete. Steve would go into the light.

I had no clue if tomorrow would come for me. The price had been higher than I'd ever imagined, but I would pay it again in a heartbeat.

CHAPTER FIVE

While I was fairly sure I wasn't dead, I was positive I'd landed in one of the rings of Hell. My body felt like it had been hit by a Mack truck and the argument I could hear defied logic.

"Quit gettin' your knickers in a knot," Gram chastised. "I'm tellin' you this for your own good. A toothpick hanging out of your mouth twenty-four-seven is uncouth. That habit is so ugly it would make a freight train take a dirt road in the middle of a flood."

"You're a pain in my ass," Candy griped.

"Tell me something I don't know, little missy," Gram shot back with a cackle of glee. "And while we're on the subject of rumps, you need a wardrobe overhaul. Those baggy clothes are a tragedy waitin' to happen—your dang rear end looks like a flat pancake. I'm tellin' you right now, you look like ten miles of bad road after you've been chewed up and spit out. If you want a male suitor or a female suitor, you're gonna have to do some laundry occasionally."

"You done with the compliments yet?" Candy inquired.

"Just gettin' started," Gram informed the Keeper of Fate.

Hell's bells, if there was ever a time to be stuck in limbo, this was not it. Gram was screwing with Karma. Of course, Gram was dead, but Candy Vargo didn't seem to be one who played by the rules. I had no idea if fate could mess with the dead.

"Give me your best, old woman," Candy said.

"Well now, ain't that the pot calling the kettle black?" Gram inquired. "How old are you?"

"Point to Gram," Candy said with a laugh. "And to answer your question, I'm older than dirt. Literally. So, give me your best, *young lady*."

"Much better, and I'm gonna do just that," Gram informed her. "You need some meat on you, Candy Vargo. You need to eat, girlie girl. You're so skinny if you stood sideways and stuck your tongue out, you'd look like a zipper."

Oh my freaking God. Laughing, screaming or duct-taping Gram's mouth shut were all fine ideas, but I was capable of none of those things. I tried with everything I had to pry my eyes or my mouth open, but to no avail. I wondered briefly if one of the ghosts had superglued them shut as a joke. Gram was skating on thin ice, and there was no way to stop her.

"Do you have a death wish?" Candy asked.

Gram laughed. "Too late for that. Already dead."

"Then why, may I ask, are you crawling up my ass?"

"Couple of reasons," Gram told her. "One, it passes the time until my Daisy girl wakes up. Two... I care."

"I call bullshit," Candy snapped angrily.

"Call whatever you want," Gram said. "You need some dang friends and I've decided that I'm one of them. You're a hot mess and I'm fixin' to set you up right before I have to go. You have nice eyes and a lovely smile when you decide to use it. Course, you need a haircut and a bath, but that's on the list."

"The list?" Candy asked, shocked.

"Yep," Gram confirmed. "It's about a mile long, but I figure if we knock off a couple things a day we'll be done in about a year."

"Shit," Candy muttered with a chuckle. "Your nards are huge."

"Lady balls," I whispered softly. "Gram has lady balls like me."

"Daisy's awake," Gram squealed.

I felt a rush of cool wind as the ghosts surrounded me and began to chatter unintelligibly. Slowly, my eyes opened —and I screamed.

Candy Vargo's face was approximately an inch from mine, and Gram's face was squished next to Candy's.

"Told you that you needed to work on your appearance," Gram told Candy as she fluttered around me. "Daisy girl, can you hear me, darlin'?"

"Yes," I whispered, sitting up in my bed gingerly. "Steve. Where's Steve?"

"Right here," he called out as he flew to my side.

Squinting my eyes, I wondered if I was dreaming or if

what I was seeing was accurate. Steve wasn't alive, but he was in the same state he was in when he'd first come back to me.

"How?" I asked. My throat was dry and my words felt rusty.

Steve raised his brow and gave me the same *look* he'd given me when I'd broken my foot years ago because I jumped off a ladder to grab a fresh paintbrush. In my defense, it was a small ladder, but the ground was hard. "Your little stunt in my mind reversed the damage the darkness caused."

"Are you mad at me?" I asked, trying to smile.

"Understatement," Steve said, shaking his head. "However, it doesn't change how much I love you."

"Good," I said, glancing around.

My relief that Steve hadn't moved into the light before I could say goodbye was overwhelming. Seeing him eased the pressure in my chest.

"Hoooooooookaaah," Birdie yelled with her foul middle digit raised.

I choked out a laugh. Never did I think that being flipped off by a cranium-challenged dead hooker would make my day.

But it did.

Birdie was holding her head and most of the squatters were missing appendages. Shitshow didn't even begin to describe the way my roomies looked. I was going to need a lot of superglue.

Wait.

"Clarissa," I growled. "Has she been punished?"

The room went silent. It didn't bode well.

"Not exactly," Candy hedged.

"Not at all," Gram added with disgust in her voice.

"Explain," I said as adrenaline fueled by anger helped me stand up. My legs were shaky, but they worked.

"She's gone missing," Heather said, entering the room and wrapping her arms around me in relief.

"I repeat. Explain," I said, hugging Heather back.

She pointed to the bed. "Sit."

"Nope," I told her, slowly beginning to pace the room. The ball of fury in my gut wouldn't let up. Moving was necessary if I was going to keep a lid on my temper.

"Fine," Heather conceded. "The Angel of Mercy's fate has been sealed. There is no doubt of her guilt. It's been reported and recorded. She will be stripped of her power, heritage and Immortality. However…"

"However, what?" I ground out.

"However, she has to be found first," Candy chimed in.

Pressing my lips together so I didn't drop an F-bomb in front of Gram, I attempted to gather my scattered thoughts. Had John Travolta given her a heads up and she'd gone into hiding?

With what he had done to save me, it didn't make sense. But sense wasn't necessarily going to be made out of anything that was happening.

"I have questions," I said in a tight voice.

"Shoot," Heather said, crossing her arms over her chest and waiting.

"Where is Gideon?"

"Gideon, Charlie and Clarence have gone in search of Clarissa," she said.

"What exactly does that mean?" I questioned.

"It means all Hell will break loose shortly," Candy muttered.

"Are you being *literal* or *figurative*?" I demanded.

At this point I assumed nothing. I'd had my fill of assumptions and they hadn't worked out so well.

"Figurative," Heather supplied quickly, understanding that literal explanations were imperative right now. "A state of mind can't break loose from anything."

"That's what Heaven and Hell are?" I asked. "Simply a state of mind?"

"It's the easiest way to explain it," Heather said calmly.

I was glad she was calm because I was anything but.

"So, Gideon, Charlie and John Travolta are searching the Universe for Clarissa?"

"Yes," Heather confirmed.

"Where's Tim?"

"Delivering the mail," Heather said.

I almost laughed except not much was funny right now.

"And is the search for Clarissa similar to finding a needle in a haystack?" I pressed.

Candy and Heather exchanged a cryptic glance.

"Yes and no," Candy said, taking the lead. "The soon-to-be-ex-Angel of Mercy can run, but hiding will pose a problem."

"Immortals have footprints for lack of a better word," Heather explained. "Wherever Clarissa goes, she'll leave evidence of her essence."

The news wasn't welcome. But it wasn't surprising either. Clarissa was well aware of what she had done and that she would be found out.

"Will they be able to find her?" I asked, testing out my fingers and arms.

"They will," Heather assured me.

"In a reasonable *human* time frame?" I asked. I knew we were dealing with Immortals. A hundred years was a mere blip in time for them. I'd be dead and gone in a hundred years and I wanted to see Clarissa brought to justice. Hell, I wanted to serve the justice up and shove it down her throat.

"Remains to be seen," Candy Vargo said, shrugging. "Just hope they find her before she finds you."

I cocked my head to the side and glared at Karma. "Do you know something I don't?" I inquired in a brook-no-bullshit tone.

"I know many things that you don't," she said. "But the end of this particular story? No. I don't know anything about that."

"Crap," I muttered as I continued to pace. With each step, I felt better and stronger. Part of me wanted to go for a run. I was sure that wouldn't go over real well with my company right now. They were all staring at me like I'd grown another head.

Maybe I had...

"How long was I out?" I asked, realizing I had to pee. Badly. "Hold that answer."

Sprinting to the bathroom, I did my business and brushed my teeth for a good five minutes. What I really wanted was to see Gideon, but I understood why he wasn't here. Heather tossed in a clean pair of yoga pants, undies, a sports bra and a t-shirt. She was a good friend. After a quick shower that felt heavenly, I got dressed and was ready to confront the world—or at least the people in my house.

My hair was a wild mess of long dark curls, but that was nothing new. Giving myself one last cursory glance in the mirror to confirm I wasn't sporting an extra head, I froze.

"What the heck?" I squinted to make sure I was seeing things correctly.

My eyes, normally a dark golden color, were now sparkling back at me in the mirror. I couldn't blame it on the sun shining through the window because it was overcast outside. My eyes were now more like John Travolta's—and I didn't like it one bit.

"Damn it," I said, narrowing my gaze at the image staring back at me. "Heather, can you come in here?"

"Yep?" she said, popping her head in the door.

"Shut the door behind you, please," I said and sat down at my vanity. "Can you look at my eyes and tell me if I've lost my shit?"

Heather stared at me for a long moment and sucked in a quick breath. "I think your shit is intact, and I think something is happening."

"Can you be more specific?" I questioned.

"No," she said. "I wish I could."

I nodded and considered punching something to release the anxiety building as my mind raced with frightening scenarios. However, I let that plan of action go fast. I'd recently knocked down a massive tree. I didn't need to punch a wall out of my house. Changing the subject would lessen the chance of a panic attack or property damage.

"How long was I out?"

"Two weeks," she replied, closing the lid of the toilet and sitting down.

"Are you kidding me?" I shouted. A panic attack was sounding more appealing with each new piece of information revealed.

"I kid you not."

"How was that explained?"

"Explained?"

"To June, Jennifer and Missy." They were human, and some of my dearest friends along with Heather. A two-week absence on my part wouldn't fly with my girls.

"I told them that Gideon kidnapped you with your full approval for a long getaway. With Gram dying, you needed a change of scenery. I also told them I was house and dog sitting for you."

"And they believed you?" I asked.

"June and Jennifer bought it hook, line and sinker," Heather said, and then paused. "But Missy seemed surprised and a bit hurt that you didn't tell her yourself."

Scrubbing my hands over my face, I wondered if I was going to have to weave a web of lies for my best friend since childhood. Missy was like a sister to me. I would be hurt, too, if she took off and neglected to tell me.

I sucked as a liar. The truth was so much easier to remember.

And I was certain Heather hadn't liked lying to Missy, either. They'd had a relationship in the past and were slowly trying again. A relationship full of lies was like a house of cards waiting for a gust of wind to blow it down.

"What do I do?" I asked. "Lie?"

"Lies aren't always kind," Heather said with a sigh. "But the truth in this case is not possible."

"Awesome. So, where did Gideon and I go?"

"How about a cabin in Maine with bad internet service?" Heather suggested. "It was cold and you didn't get out much, so you found other things to *occupy* your time."

I laughed then cringed. "Umm, how did Gideon react to… you know…"

"The undescended testicle discussion?" Heather asked with a grin.

"Yes," I replied with a wince.

"He laughed."

"He laughed?"

"He did indeed, and then offered to prove his nuts were outstanding if anyone was so inclined to look."

"Dear God," I gasped out. "Did he drop trou and reveal his balls?"

"Nope," Heather promised. "No one wanted to see his balls."

I heaved out a mortified sigh of relief and slapped on a little lip gloss. Maybe shiny lips would detract from my shiny eyes.

Or maybe not.

The burning question was on the tip of my tongue. I didn't want the answer, and I had no clue if Heather would *have* the answer. However, staying in the dark was unwise.

"Am I becoming Immortal?" I whispered.

She shook her head. "That's not how it works—at least not in my experience, and I've been around a very long time," she said. "One is *created* Immortal. It's impossible to *become* Immortal."

"Nothing is impossible," I said with a shudder. "If there's one thing I've learned recently, it's that."

"Point taken," Heather said, standing up. "Let's test a few things."

"There's a test to take to see if I'm Immortal?"

"No, but there are markers," she explained. "Put on your tennis shoes and a fleece and let's go outside."

"Is this a bad idea?" I asked, eyeing her warily.

"Probably," she admitted, grinning. "But it's a plan. You in?"

"Why not?" I answered with a groan. "But just so you know, I've never been good at tests."

"There's a first time for everything, Daisy."

Crapcrapcrap.

CHAPTER SIX

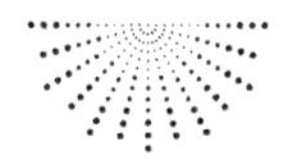

"WHY DO I HAVE TO GET RUN OVER WITH THE CAR? WHY can't you get run over?" Candy Vargo griped as Heather got behind the wheel of her sports car and started the engine.

"Because I'm wearing expensive leather pants and you're wearing shit," Heather yelled back.

"You gonna listen to me now?" Gram demanded as she flew circles around a pissed-off Candy Vargo. "If you'd take a little care with your appearance, you wouldn't have to be roadkill."

"Umm... what are we doing?" I asked, not liking the direction of anything that was transpiring.

While Candy might not be my favorite person, I liked her enough to not want her to die. Watching Karma get mowed down by a car seemed like a seriously bad idea. I had no clue how maiming Candy would prove I was Immortal.

"I'm going to run over Candy and you're going to try to save her," Heather explained as she revved the engine.

"Because?" I asked, buying time so I could talk Heather out of her insane plan.

"She wants to test your speed," Candy grumbled.

"We already know I'm fast," I said. "This is ridiculous. I really think—"

Before another word left my lips, Heather's lightning-fast sports car hurtled toward the Keeper of Fate.

Without a thought for my own safety, or any thought at all, I dove at Candy and threw her about thirty-feet in the air, narrowly missing getting clipped by the car myself.

Candy's squeal of delight almost made me laugh, but I swallowed it on a gasp and a bad word that made Gram throw her hands in the air in shock.

Heather's scream of terror made my stomach drop to my toes.

"Accelerator's stuck," Heather bellowed as her car careened toward my house. The ghosts sitting on the front porch watched the action with rabid attention. The car couldn't kill them since they were already dead, but it could harm one of my dearest friends and take out the front of the house.

Turning on a dime and channeling the Bionic Woman, I heard Candy hit the ground with a thud and a laugh as she fell back to earth. With speed that I didn't know I had, I sprinted toward the car, grabbed the driver's side door, ripped it off, shoved Heather over and slammed on the brakes so hard my foot went right through the bottom of the running board.

Thankfully, it also stopped the car's forward motion.

We were about two inches from the bushes that Steve and I had planted ten years ago. Not a leaf was disturbed. However, Heather's car was not as lucky.

Letting my head drop to the steering wheel with a bang, I closed my eyes and made a mental list of how to get Heather back. It was a long list.

"Pretty sure I hate you right now," I said, not looking at her.

"Pretty sure you're not just human," she said, stating the obvious.

"Did the accelerator really get stuck?"

"You want the truth?" she asked.

"Yep."

"No. The accelerator wasn't stuck."

"Would you have plowed into my house?" I questioned, still avoiding eye contact.

"Absolutely not," she said.

"So, the Candy thing was a warm-up? You wouldn't have mowed her down?"

"Kind of," Heather replied with a small chuckle. "I totally would have run her over. She's Immortal. She would have lived. Plus, I've wanted to mow her down for centuries. This gave me a legitimate excuse."

"There is so much wrong with that sentence, I don't know where to start," I said, trying not to laugh.

"Well, all I have to say is try living near Candy Vargo for a thousand years and tell me how you feel then," Heather said in her defense.

"Am I going to be around for a thousand years?" I asked, so quietly I wasn't sure she heard me.

Her lack of response made me repeat the question.

"Daisy, I don't know. You passed the markers, but you leave no footprint," Heather said. "It's as if you have the power without the life span."

"Is it because I'm a Death Counselor?" I asked, reaching for any kind of logical explanation—not that logic could be applied, but I was going to try. I knew now that I possessed a percentage of Angel DNA, but I'd had that my entire life and I'd been completely normal up until recently.

"No other Death Counselor has possessed this kind of strength, speed or power," Heather said, placing her hand on my back and rubbing gently.

"So, I'm just a powerful freak who can knock down trees, mind dive into the dead, juggle people, glue on body parts and pull car doors off their hinges?"

"Sounds pretty bad when you put it like that," Heather pointed out diplomatically.

"Not sure how else to put it," I said, glancing over at her with a small grin.

"Don't forget you're banging the Grim Reaper."

"Haven't banged him yet," I reminded her. "Haven't even seen his balls."

Heather laughed. I joined her. The reality that I called my life was so farked up, the only thing to do was laugh.

"Wait," I said, grabbing Heather as a thought occurred to me. "It's the mind diving."

"What's the mind diving?" she asked, confused.

"Every time I've done it, something in me has changed," I

told her as my excitement at having possibly figured something out ramped up. "After I dove into Sam's mind, my eyesight improved. After I dove into John's mind, I could run a marathon without breaking a sweat."

"And after you dove into Lindsay's mind, you took out a tree with your bare hands," Heather said, following my lead.

"Yep. And this time, after I went into Steve's mind, I ripped off a car door while the car was hurtling out of control and threw Karma almost as high as the roof of my house."

"I really enjoyed that," Candy Vargo said, sliding into the backseat with Gram on her tail.

"Great," I said with an eye roll. "Won't be happening again anytime soon."

"What if I let Heather try to mow me down again?" Candy suggested.

"You're out of luck," Heather said with a laugh. "My car is out of service for a while."

"Fine," Candy huffed. "You people are jackholes."

Ignoring Candy because I didn't have anything nice to say, I mulled over the discovery I'd just made.

"The key to not becoming a female version of the Hulk—or possibly Immortal—is to stop mind diving," I mused aloud.

"Gonna be hard for you," Gram pointed out. "You have a real soft spot for dead squatters."

I laughed. The words coming out of everyone's mouths were so absurd it was appalling. The worst part was that all of it was true.

"You're correct, Gram," I agreed, thinking of Birdie in

particular. Maybe the Ouija board would suffice. "But it's screwing with my DNA."

"I concur. The mind diving has to stop for the time being," Heather said. "We need to talk to Charlie."

"Why?" I asked. "What can he do?"

"His human day job is a lab tech over at the hospital," Heather reminded me. "I want him to take a sample of your blood and run some tests."

"What will he be able to learn by doing that?" I asked.

"Maybe nothing," Candy said, pulling a toothpick out of her pocket and picking her teeth. "Can't hurt though."

"What in tarnation did I tell you about that," Gram shouted at a shocked Candy, who quickly removed the toothpick and shoved it back in her pocket.

"Umm... something about a train and a flood," Candy mumbled, looking a bit terrified.

No one said a word. I bit down on my lip and sucked back a laugh with great effort. Gram meant business. I actually felt kind of sorry for Candy Vargo. When Gram got something in her head, there was no removing it.

For better or worse, Candy Vargo was Gram's new project.

Closing my eyes so I didn't accidentally see Candy's expression in the rearview mirror, I asked the next logical question. "So, what do we do now?"

"We wait," Heather said.

"For?" I pressed.

She shrugged. "Right now, your guess is as good as mine."

"Awesome," I muttered, glancing up at all my squatters

who were waiting patiently for me to do a little surgery. "I've got some dead people to repair."

"Sounds like a plan," Candy said, getting out of the car and hightailing it into the house.

I was sure she was going to hide from Gram.

"Gram," I said, turning around to talk to her. "You can't be too hard on Candy."

"Oh, sugar pie," Gram said with a dismissive wave of her hand. "She loves it. No one has given a rat's butt about that girl in a very long time. She might bitch and moan, but it makes her feel special."

I grinned. "It's special to have you riding her ass?"

"Darn tootin'," Gram said with a laugh as she flew right through the roof of the car and went to find her new *project.*

"Good luck to Gram with that one," Heather said as she clapped her hands and an enormous box appeared on the porch.

"What's that?" I asked.

"Superglue," she informed me. "You're gonna need it."

CHAPTER SEVEN

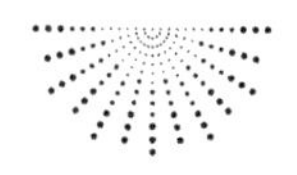

THE DAY DAWNED BRIGHT, SUNNY AND CHILLY. MY SQUATTERS were all repaired and a relative state of normalcy had settled back in. As of yesterday, Birdie's head was glued squarely back on her neck. She was thrilled to have her hands free to flip me off.

I'd slept like the dead after the *Mow Down Candy Vargo* fiasco and the subsequent *Let's Plow Heather's Car into Daisy's House* test—not to mention it took me five hours to glue all my dead guests back together. I was no closer to the answer as to whether I was becoming Immortal or not, but I was now sure I could defend myself and save anyone's life if the occasion arose… or at the very least glue them back together.

Here's to seriously hoping an occasion doesn't arise.

So, for lack of something better to do, I decided to do something stupid…

"Do you want me to vacuum the living room?" Heather called out.

"That would be awesome," I answered, putting the flower arrangement I'd had delivered on the kitchen table and sucking in a deep breath to calm my nerves.

I'd invited my friends over for lunch and was adding Tim and Candy to the mix. Socializing Tim had been my plan for a while. Candy was the wild card. Gram had insisted Candy was ready and desperately needed some friends. Gram was very aware that I was a sucker for the underdog—even if the underdog had hideous manners and could kill people with the flick of her finger. She'd sworn she made Candy incinerate all of her toothpicks. The inferno in the backyard firepit was the proof.

Living on the edge was my new way of life. There was a fine chance it would burn me like Candy had burned her bad habit in my yard.

"Everyone will be here in a half hour and June's bringing cookies," Heather said, wrapping the cord around the vacuum cleaner and putting it back in the hallway closet.

"This is a very bad idea except for the cookies," I said, pulling out plates, napkins and silverware. "I'm going to get busted for lying about my fictional getaway with Gideon. I'll have no friends left by tonight."

"I'll always be your friend, and you're not going to lie," Heather replied.

"No way, you crazy old freak!" Candy Vargo shouted as she sprinted through the house with Gram on her ass.

Donna and Karen thought it was a fabulous game and chased them while barking with joy.

"What's going on there?" Heather asked, raising her brow.

Putting the plates on the kitchen table, I sat on a chair and let my head drop to the wooden table with a thud. "Gram is making Candy wear a dress to the get together this afternoon. Told her if she didn't, she'd move herself into Candy's house and make her life a living Hell."

"Harsh yet creative," Heather said with a laugh. "I can't believe she convinced her to get a haircut. Candy's actually attractive minus the unruly mop. First time I've seen her eyes in a few centuries."

"Gram didn't convince her to get a haircut, she blackmailed her," I explained with a grin.

"Shut the front door. How does a ghost blackmail the Keeper of Fate?"

"No clue and never want to know," I replied, tracing the grain of the wood in the table with my finger. "Gideon called."

"And?"

"And they haven't found Clarissa yet. They think they've been close, but she's two steps ahead of them," I told her. "They're going to come back here and make a new plan of action. Besides, explaining Charlie's absence is getting complicated. June is worried sick."

Heather nodded and sat across the table from me. "I spoke with Michael."

"I prefer John Travolta or Darth Vader."

She chuckled. "Fine. I spoke with John Travolta. He basically said the same thing. However, if they keep coming up empty, the army will be deployed—that's a very last resort."

"The Angels have an army?" I suppose it shouldn't be shocking. They were certainly a violent group from what I'd seen so far.

"Nope."

"They're sending a *human* army out to hunt down an Immortal Angel?" I asked, getting more confused.

"Nope."

"The cryptic shit is going to give me gas," I said, narrowing my eyes.

Heather blew out a long slow breath and looked me in the eye. "The army is comprised of Demons. Using them is dangerous."

"Dangerous as in apocalyptic?" I questioned.

"No. Not at all," Heather assured me. "It can just be a bit problematic to have a few hundred Demons roaming Earth at the same time."

I was living in a bad movie with no ending.

"Should I ask who leads the Demon army?" I inquired as my stomach roiled.

"Probably not."

"Mmkay. I've become a rule breaker in my forties and I like to open and rewrap Christmas gifts early, then feign surprise Christmas morning. So unfortunately—for me, I'm sure—I'm going to ask. Who leads the Demon army?"

"Gideon," she replied flatly.

Finding out new and interesting facts about the man I was in love with wasn't always fun or good for my digestive system. The magazines had it all wrong. Researching your man was a shitshow—not info for a flirty conversation starter. Of course, I was dating the Grim Reaper and *Cosmo* didn't exactly cover that.

"Awesome." I pressed the bridge of my nose and promised myself not to ask questions I didn't want the answers to anymore.

Good luck to me.

Driving blind was the old Daisy. My eyes were sparkly and wide open now.

It sucked.

"Let's go back to a subject that isn't going to make me hurl," I suggested. "How am I not going to lie to the girls?"

Heather paled and began examining her cuticles with great interest. "Well... umm..."

"Out with it," I demanded, thinking I'd possibly picked the wrong subject.

"I *might* have subconsciously planted a few facts in everyone's minds." She winced and scrunched her eyes shut.

"Define that, please."

Heather suddenly found something very interesting on the ceiling. "Suffice it to say, you've already told them all about the Maine getaway, and you did tell Missy you were taking off before you left."

I was stunned to silence, but not for long.

"That's awful. I did no such thing," I shouted as I jumped to my feet and knocked the chair to the ground. "Is bending the truth with magic a common practice with all of you Immortals?"

Heather blanched and lowered her head. "No. I've only done it one other time and that was hundreds of years ago."

"Is it easy to do?" I questioned, wondering if it had been

done to me by any of the Immortals I'd been in contact with… especially Gideon.

"No. It's not easy and there aren't many who can do it," she admitted.

"Heather, this is bad. Lying is bad enough. Planting a revision of recent history in the minds of our best friends is freaking terrible," I snapped, yanking the chicken salad sandwiches and the mini quiches I'd made for the luncheon out of the fridge and slamming them down onto the table. "You have to undo it. If I get busted, that's on me."

She shook her head and looked like she wanted to cry. "God, caring about people can be a shitty thing," she muttered.

"Nope. Screwing with people's minds can be a shitty thing."

"That too," she agreed. "I did it for you. I didn't think it through—at all. There's so much at stake right now, I knee-jerked a plan without talking it over with anyone."

"My manners dictate that I say thank you, but I *really* want to head-butt you," I said, reining in my anger. "Can you undo it?"

"It might be worse if I did," she replied, running her hands through her hair in frustration. "It's complicated magic. I would happily accept a head-butt even though it would probably break every bone in my body."

I groaned and leveled one of my dearest friends with a stare that she met head-on. "As appealing as that sounds, it doesn't appeal at all. Violence isn't my thing even though you deserve it."

"I do deserve it."

"Well, at least we agree on something," I muttered with a strained laugh.

"I'm sorry, Daisy," Heather said.

"Promise me you won't do it again, and never to me," I insisted.

"I promise."

Shaking my head and wanting to head-butt myself for the direction of my thoughts, I went for it. "Is there a chance Gideon could have planted things in my mind?"

Heather was quiet for a long moment then shook her head. "No. Thoughts can only be planted in the minds of full humans."

"I'm a full human," I reminded her.

"No. You're not," she corrected me. "Michael the Archangel is your father. You have never been a full human since the day you were conceived."

"Heather," I warned with an eye roll of displeasure.

"My bad. John Travolta," she amended with a grin.

"Thank you," I replied primly, which made her grin grow wider. "I'm not fond of what you did at all. However, if I'm being honest—which is an oxymoron considering the conversation—I will admit that I'm relieved that I don't have to lie like a rug."

"So, I'm forgiven?" Heather asked sheepishly.

Sucking my bottom lip into my mouth, I eyed her then nodded. "Yes. You're forgiven, but I expect you to keep your promise that you won't do it again."

"Deal."

My knowledge of the strange and alarming kept growing. I wasn't sure how much more my brain could hold.

"Put these in your eyes," Heather said, handing me a small packet.

"What are they?" I asked.

"Contact lenses."

"I don't need contacts," I said, handing the packet back to her. "My vision is perfect."

"Not to see," Heather said, pushing them back across the table. "To hide the new color of your eyes. You could light up a room with those peepers."

"So, I *will* be lying," I said, opening the packet and popping them into my eyes.

"I call it living with a few omissions," Heather said with a small smile. "You'll get used to it."

I was getting used to a lot.

And only some of it was good.

CHAPTER EIGHT

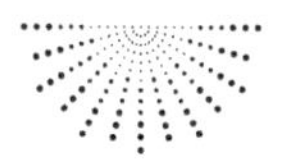

"WHAT HAS TWO BUTTS AND KILLS PEOPLE?" JENNIFER ASKED as she opened a bottle of wine and proceeded to pour a glass for everyone.

After the initial shock of realizing Tim and Candy had joined the lunch bunch, my friends accepted the new additions and included them with kindness. Jennifer, June, Heather and Missy were some of the best women I knew.

I was doing my damnedest to ignore the ghosts who were in attendance. Thankfully, it was just Steve, Gram and Birdie. Steve hadn't moved into the light yet even though it was possible now. I was secretly thrilled he was still here. Having no clue how long he would stay, I treasured every moment and was delighted to have him at the gathering. Gram wouldn't have missed it.

And Birdie? I had no clue why she'd joined the luncheon. She'd be difficult to ignore if she called me a hooker repeatedly and flipped me off for the next few hours. Thankfully, I noticed Gram having a few words with her, and she'd only given Gram the middle finger twice. That was excellent behavior for Birdie. I hoped she'd keep it up. The rest of my deceased squatters were happily watching a *Survivor* marathon in my bedroom.

"Come on, people," Jennifer said, handing Candy a glass. "Somebody needs to guess or I'm gonna be crowned the Queen of the World with a face like a baby's ass."

Jennifer's double dose of Botox was holding up frighteningly and exceedingly well. Not a single muscle moved on her face. She was completely Botoxicated and couldn't be happier about it.

"That's a pretty high and mighty title for someone touting info about a person with two asses," Missy pointed out with a grin.

"I have no issue with the title, I just want to know if two asses mean someone has two buttholes," Candy Vargo chimed in.

Missy let out a tiny squeak and bit down on her lip so hard, I thought she might draw blood. She was desperate to muffle her laugh. Missy's Southern manners were ingrained like mine. She'd rather die before making someone feel bad.

"That's an excellent question, Candy Vargo," Jennifer said, thoughtfully mulling over the logistics. "I'm gonna go with a yes on the anatomical query. Two asses would have to mean two poop holes. Drink up! I brought a whole case."

Candy covertly glanced over at Gram, who nodded her head that Candy should take a drink. I'd gone from being terrified of Candy Vargo to feeling sorry for her. However, I was sure Gram was correct about the Keeper of Fate secretly enjoying someone giving a *rat's butt* about her. Her need for Gram's approval was heartbreakingly sweet.

I just hoped Candy didn't try to talk to Gram while my human friends were present. I'd had a come to Jesus with both Candy and Tim before the gals had arrived. Whether it worked or not remained to be seen. Lunch had gone relatively well thus far. Even Candy's manners weren't too bad —nary a toothpick in sight.

"I can't think of anything that has two rear ends." June came out of the kitchen with a platter of her homemade peanut butter cookies piled high. "Not sure that cookies go with *wine* at two in the *afternoon*," she said with a giggle, rolling her eyes at Jennifer. "But I've never been able to attend a gathering empty-handed."

"And thank goodness for that," I said, pilfering a few cookies off the plate as June passed by. "I'd sell my soul for your cookies."

"That's a little dramatic," Tim said, staring at the glass of wine Jennifer had placed in front of him.

The sour expression on his face was proof that wine wasn't his thing. However, he sipped it politely and only gagged a little. He was doing his damnedest to fit in. It was adorable in a bizarre way.

"You'll understand when you taste June's cookies," Heather assured Tim.

"A toast to the chef," Missy said, holding her glass high. "I dream about that chicken salad. It was delicious as always. To Daisy."

"To Daisy," everyone said, following suit.

"Dudes," I said with a laugh. "It's as easy as sin, but thank you."

"It's my recipe," Gram reminded me.

Without even a glance her way, I repeated her. "It's Gram's recipe."

"To Gram," Jennifer said as her eyes welled up with tears. "I miss her something awful. Loved her like she was mine."

Gram zipped over to Jennifer and wrapped her in a ghostly embrace. Jennifer had no clue. Neither did June nor Missy, but the rest of us did.

Candy was under Gram's spell as well. She stood up, made her way across the room to Jennifer and awkwardly patted her on the head. Gram gave her a nod of approval and Candy blushed.

"Thank you, Candy Vargo," Jennifer said, sniffling. "Did you know Gram well?"

"Umm... I... ahh..." Candy was at a total loss. In her frantic search for how to answer, she went for a toothpick until Gram threatened her life and she immediately put it away.

Thankfully, June, Missy and Jennifer were oblivious to the fact the Gram had vowed to tear Candy an ass that would preclude her from sitting for a few centuries.

That would have been very difficult to explain.

Leave it to my vibrator-rehoming buddy Tim to save the day... or not.

Tim cleared his throat and let it rip. "I do believe Candy has learned more about Gram since her sad, tragic and untimely demise. Candy Vargo of the Piggly Wiggly wishes desperately that she had known Daisy's loving caregiver better, and awaits the day with bated breath until she meets the illustrious, wonderful and viciously threatening Gram in the afterlife. Candy Vargo is counting her toothpicks until the glorious time arrives, which almost came to fruition yesterday when she narrowly missed getting mowed down by a crazy woman—who shall remain nameless—driving a car. Not that I saw it. I just heard about it."

Tim's rather unconventional response caused about a minute and forty-seven seconds of confused discomfort among the guests. But we were Southern. Colorful and inappropriate behavior was in our DNA. A party wasn't a success unless someone stuck their foot in their mouth and pulled it out of their ass. It was usually Jennifer for the win, but Tim was the champion this afternoon. Bizarre conduct was expected and to a certain degree welcomed. It was also politely ignored.

"Well, then," said June, the adorable peacemaker of our group, nodding at Tim politely. "Would anyone like a cookie?"

The chorus of yesses let us gracefully move past Tim's outlandish defense of Candy. My new buddy was clearly not quite ready for group interaction, but being with my friends was a safe place for him to start.

"Back to the killer with two butts," Jennifer said. "Who has a guess?"

Candy gave it a shot. "Siamese twins with a vendetta against the diabolical shit-ass doctor who tried to separate them with a hacksaw?"

Karma wasn't quite ready for group interaction either.

"Nope," Jennifer said. "But that was a damn good guess and seriously gross. I like the way you think, Candy Vargo."

"I have a conjecture," Tim said, raising his hand.

"Is that contagious?" Jennifer teased with a laugh, grabbing a few cookies.

Tim, being a fairly literal guy, got perplexed. "No."

"She was joking," I cut in quickly.

Tim forced a polite laugh and slapped his leg so hard it was going to leave a bruise. His socialization was going *terribly* well…

"I shall rephrase," Tim announced, glancing over at me for approval.

I nodded and smiled.

"I have a guess," he said shakily.

I held my breath and waited to be horrified. Tim had already proven that he was capable of saying anything.

"Go for it," Jennifer said, slugging back her entire glass of wine then going for more.

"Did she drive?" I asked June quietly as she sat down next to me.

"Oh, heavens no," June said with a giggle. "I did. I'll get her home safely."

"A killer with two butts is an assassin," Tim revealed, to a delighted whoop from Jennifer.

"Yes! Get it everyone? Ass-ass-in… assassin! Two asses!" she shouted, impressed with Tim's useless knowledge. "Not to worry. I have more."

"Of course, you do," Heather said.

Heather and Missy sat on the couch together, bodies close. It made me happy to think they were getting back together. From what I'd surmised, it was Missy's hellfire and brimstone religious upbringing that had put a kink in their relationship last year. I didn't know what had changed, but I knew in my heart they were happier together than apart.

"Look at that," Steve whispered in my ear. "What the heck is Birdie doing?"

It was a good question. *What the heck was Birdie doing?*

Up till a few minutes ago, Birdie had been behaving herself beautifully which was shocking. She had perched on the couch next to Missy and watched the action with glee. She'd only flipped me off a few times and hadn't called me a hooker once. However, now she seemed obsessed with Missy. She'd wedged herself between Heather and my childhood BFF and was stroking her hair and peppering her face with ghostly kisses.

"Do you think Birdie was a lesbian hooker?" Steve asked.

Swallowing back my laugh was hard but doable. Since answering Steve was a no-no, I simply shrugged my shoulders and watched the show unfold. Birdie's behavior wasn't of a sexual nature. It was loving.

Was there a chance Birdie had known Missy in life? Was Birdie a relative of my friend? I didn't think so. I'd known Missy since we were small, but it was a possibility if Birdie's actions were anything to go by.

"How about we throw some facts out and whoever has the best or grossest info wins," Jennifer suggested.

"You've already won," June told Jennifer. "You're a font of unappetizing information, my dear."

Jennifer stood up and took a bow. "Thank you, June."

"It wasn't a compliment," Heather said, grinning. "It was a polite way of saying you only have one oar in the water."

"I meant it in a loving way," June said with a giggle. "Jennifer lights up my life and fills my head with nonsense. That's what friends are for."

"Damn straight," Jennifer announced as she popped open another bottle of wine. "Who wants to take me on?"

"I'm out," I said. "There's no way I can beat you."

"Count me out too," Missy said, unaware that she was being adored by a dead woman.

Heather, who was *not* unaware of Birdie's obsession with Missy, glanced over at me to check if I'd observed what was going on. I nodded covertly and shrugged. The Ouija board was definitely going to be put to use this evening. There was far more to Birdie than just an active middle finger and a foul mouth.

"I'll just listen," June said, pushing her wine away and sipping on lemonade instead. "I might learn something new that will make Charlie laugh."

"Is he back from his business trip yet?" Missy inquired.

"Tonight," June told her. "It's been two long weeks without my guy. I miss him."

"Tonight?" I asked, surprised. It was news to me. Gideon hadn't said when they would return, just that they would. Maybe Charlie was coming back first.

"Yes," June said with a giggle and a blush. "I'm going to go home and get gussied up in a bit."

June's blush made me grin. She was fifty-seven and blissfully married to a man who she had no clue was older than time. They were a fine example of marriage goals. June was the only one of us who had been successful in the relationship department. However, the rest of us were working on it. Jennifer, sixty-five and five times divorced, had a good thing going with Sherriff Dip Doody. She refused to marry him since she was wildly in love with the unfortunately named lawman. Heather and Missy were headed toward something, and I was head over heels for the Grim Reaper.

Strange, but somehow perfect.

"Alrighty then, since June needs to get ready to bang her hubby, let's get this game going. Who's gonna challenge me?" Jennifer asked.

"Pretty sure you already won the open-mouth-insert-foot title with that last comment," I said with an eye roll.

June simply laughed and shook her head.

"I will challenge you," Tim said.

Oh shit.

"Excellent," Jennifer shouted, causing everyone to wince.

I wasn't sure if everyone's reaction was because of the volume of her voice or the fear of what was about to go down.

"Let's get this over with," Heather said, knowing she'd live to regret her words. "On your marks. Get set. Go."

Rubbing her little hands together with delight, Jennifer teasingly narrowed her eyes at Tim. He was slowly getting the hang of being with others and grinned right back at Jennifer.

"Wombats poop cubes," Jennifer announced.

"Hells bells, do they have square buttholes?" Gram asked.

I glanced over at Gram and gave her a look. It simply wouldn't do for someone to answer her accidentally.

Tim nodded his appreciation of Jennifer's useless info and cleared his throat. "I challenge you with the fact that the ancient Romans used the crushed brains of mice as toothpaste."

"Yep," Candy Vargo confirmed. "Tasted like ass."

"I'm sorry. What?" Missy asked, wrinkling her nose. "You've done that?"

Candy looked like she was going to poop a brick... similar to a wombat. The Keeper of Fate had been alive during that time period and clearly had brushed her teeth with rodent cranium matter. However, she quickly recovered.

"Of course not," Candy said with a weak chuckle. "I meant that it must have tasted like ass."

"While that was impressive," Jennifer told Tim with a naughty grin, "I offer you that sixty-three planet Earths can fit inside Uranus."

"Not my anus," Heather muttered as Missy punched her in the arm.

"Outstanding statistic," Tim congratulated Jennifer. "I can beat that. If you consume fast food regularly, you eat about twelve pubic hairs a year."

"Okay. That completely ruined my life," I gagged out. "No more fast food for me."

"Or me," June added with a shudder.

Jennifer, never one to give up, continued. "Lorne Green had one of his nipples bitten off by an alligator when he was the TV host of that nature show."

"What the ever-loving hell?" Heather yelled. "No way."

"Yes way! Read it on the internet so it's true!" Jennifer shot back, massively proud of her nightmare-worthy trivia.

Heather squinted at Jennifer in disbelief. "You believe everything you read on the internet?"

"Hell no," Jennifer replied with a laugh. "But it's damn useful in certain situations—like right now."

"Very nice and hopefully inaccurate," Tim choked out with his hand over his shirt-covered nipple in solidarity with the possibly maimed Lorne Green. "But I am prepared to take you down. An early form of contraception included soaking dried beaver testicles in a strong alcohol solution and drinking it."

The entire group turned slightly green, including Tim. However, that didn't stop Jennifer.

"I'm gonna remember that one," she said, giving Tim a thumbs up. "It'll go over like a lead balloon at the next Gladiolas ladies club meeting. Thank you."

"Welcome," Tim said. "Do I win?"

"In your dreams," Jennifer shot back, eliciting moans of pain from Heather, Missy, June, Candy, me and even Gram. "There have been documented reports of vacuum toilets on planes and cruise ships sucking the rectums out of people."

"Good Lord, no more fast food, flying or cruising for me," June said with a wince.

"This party has gone to Hell," I said, shaking my head and regretting inviting Candy and Tim.

"In a handbasket," Missy agreed.

"I think my soul just withered up and took a vacation." June laughed, fanning herself with her napkin.

"Impossible," Tim replied, growing very serious. "Your

soul is propelled into your body when you're in the womb. At birth it becomes an invisible force that blesses you with life. At the end of your Earthly tenure, your soul is catapulted into a luminous dimension at the moment of your demise. So, don't worry about it taking a vacation. It's not in the bounds of reasonable actions for your soul."

The luncheon went from the bowels of Hell into the bizarre realms of Heaven. No one uttered a word. Although, Heather gave Tim the stink eye. It was insanely tricky to mix humans and Immortals… or maybe it was just Tim. He'd be getting a few more lessons on acceptable *human* etiquette before we tried this again.

Missy, in savior mode, quickly spoke up. "Speaking of souls. I come from a line of Soul Keepers. Old wives' tale in my family."

"You do?" Tim asked with such great interest it made the hair on my neck stand up.

"Yep," she said with a laugh. "As the story goes, I'm a descendent of Marie Laveau. Although, my parents railed against the voodoo magic in our family tree by becoming over-the-top Christian."

This was the point when Birdie lost her damned mind. She began circling Missy like a mini dead tornado.

"Snake handling?" Tim inquired. "Speaking in tongues?"

"Yep and yep," Missy said.

Birdie screeched unintelligibly at a volume I was sure would bring the rest of the squatters downstairs.

With a concealed snap of her fingers, Heather was able to mute Birdie's wails. But she couldn't stop the specter's frantic movement. Acting normal was growing increasingly difficult.

"I get these feelings sometimes," Missy said, tilting her head to the side in thought. "Like now. I feel an icy wind as if a ghost is walking over my grave."

"Now? Right now?" Candy asked, shocked.

"Yep," Missy replied with a laugh. "Crazy. Right?"

"Crazy," I agreed, forcing out a laugh that sounded strange even to me.

"End the luncheon," Steve whispered in my ear.

"And keep Missy here," Gram said.

Shit. I had no clue why Gram wanted Missy to stay, but questioning it was impossible with everyone here.

My acting talent wasn't great. It went hand in hand with being a poor liar, but necessity was the mother of invention… or in my case, a throwback to my high school drama class skills or lack thereof. I stood up, stretched my arms and yawned.

"Oh my! You're tired, sweetie," June said, jumping to her feet and giving me a motherly hug. "We should get going soon."

"Yep," Jennifer agreed, slapping Tim on the back. "You're a dang worthy competitor and right out of your ever-lovin' mind. Rumor has it that you x-ray and steal mail, but that doesn't bother me one bit. A little unlawful activity is healthy, but don't tell Dip I said that—don't want him to use the cuffs on me other than in the boudoir, if you get my drift."

"It would be *really* hard to miss your drift," Heather pointed out.

Jennifer simply laughed, gave Heather a thumbs up and continued her mostly socially unacceptable rambling. "Get this! When I had my Botox appointment, the receptionist went to the bathroom and I peeked at all the files. I have crap on everybody in town. Harry Johnson had a penis enlargement."

Candy Vargo barked out a laugh. "That is *not* his name."

"Oh, yes it is!" Jennifer told her with a wide grin. "Named his kid Richard—they call that poor boy Dick. But in their defense, Dick Johnson is a family name."

"Only in the South," Missy said, shaking her head. "So, there are a lot of *Dick Johnsons?*"

"Five that I know of and a daughter named Ima," Jennifer confirmed. "But here's the kicker. Anne Wilson Benang Walters had her knockers done... five times."

"I knew it," Gram yelled. "That woman looked like a hussy at my funeral. She tells everyone she was born with those rock-hard, pointy hooters. Anne Wilson Benang Walters is a liar-lair pants on fire. She'd pee down your back and tell you it's raining."

I almost told Gram to hush, but thankfully caught myself. "Umm... Jennifer, did that enlightening diatribe have a point?" I asked.

"Yep," she answered with a chuckle. "I'd like to invite Tim to dinner with Dip and me. I have a feeling it will be an illuminating meal."

"It would be my pleasure," Tim replied, surprised and pleased.

"Remind me not to go to that dinner," June whispered with a grin. "I've learned enough today to last me a lifetime."

"Ditto," I said, hugging her tight.

"Great lunch, Daisy," Jennifer said. "Great company. Great time. Do you want me to leave the rest of the wine?"

"No," I told her. "Take it home with you, but I wouldn't mind at all if June left a few cookies."

"They're all yours," June said. "I'll get my platter back later in the week. Charlie and I are watching our calories."

After a bunch of hugs and a promise that Heather would help me clean up, June and Jennifer made their exit. I didn't even have to ask Missy to stay. She and Heather were deep in conversation.

Turning my back to them, I whispered to Gram, "Why am I keeping Missy here?"

"Don't rightly know," she admitted. "Got a feeling in my gut."

"Me too," Steve added as he floated next to Gram and kept an eye on Heather and Missy.

"Hoooooooookaaah dieeah foooor yooouah," Birdie said, pointing to Missy.

My stomach dropped. There was no way Missy was going to die for me. Talking to Birdie was imperative. I just hoped I could find out what I needed to know with the Ouija board, since mind diving was on hold for the time being.

CHAPTER NINE

"You think I'm nuts, don't you," Missy said, drying off a platter and putting it back up in the slotted cabinet over the oven.

We were alone in the kitchen. Gram had let Birdie know under no uncertain terms that she needed to back off of Missy. Birdie called Gram a few unmentionable words with the F-bomb attached to all of them, then floated away in a huff. Candy, Tim and Heather had taken the dogs out to do their business.

"No. I don't think you're nuts," I told her, handing her another plate. "I think Tim is nuts and Candy Vargo is a close second."

"Speaking of... what made you invite them today?"

How to answer that question... Lying was out, but so was the entire truth.

Peeking out of the kitchen window to make sure they were out of earshot, I continued to wash the dirty dishes.

"They both need friends," I told Missy truthfully. "Tim and I have been chatting lately and I feel sorry for him. And Candy? I can't really explain it. I just feel like no one has ever paid much attention to her, and it makes me sad. She and Tim kind of remind me of the broken presents on the Island of Misfit Toys. I figured our group would be a safe place for them. So, if anyone is nuts, it's me."

Missy eyed me for a long moment then grinned. "Dude, I love you so much."

"Right back at you."

"So, the *Soul Keeper* thing didn't freak you out?" she asked, sitting down at the table and munching on a cookie.

"Nope. Didn't freak me out. Is it true?" I asked, drying off my hands and joining her.

She shrugged and laughed. "No. At least I don't think so, but it's a fun story."

"What does a *fictional* Soul Keeper do?" I asked casually as I filled up four plastic containers with cookies for Candy, Tim, Heather and Missy to take home. There was no way I was keeping dozens of June's peanut butter cookies. I would eat every one of them.

Missy plopped her elbows on the table and rested her chin in her hands. "As the legend goes, a Soul Keeper is a safe place for souls to reside before they leave this realm. They come to the Keeper when they're not safe elsewhere."

It was an odd statement. My breath caught strangely in my throat. I covered it with a cough. "Why would a soul not be safe?"

"The only stories I ever heard were from my great-granny on my mother's side when I was little. The family said she was insane and put her away in a home when I was around seven. I thought she was magical. I adored her," Missy said with a faraway gleam in her eyes. "She was beautiful—dark black skin and wild gray curls. Her eyes twinkled and she had a laugh that made me feel loved."

"What were the stories?" I was sure the answer was important. I couldn't put my finger on why, but I was going with my gut. Gram and Steve had insisted Missy stay. Maybe this *fictional* tale was precisely why.

"Oh, they were silly, but I used to hang on her every word," she said. "Apparently, a soul will come to a Keeper when an Angel wishes it ill."

"An Angel?" I asked, happy I was seated because my knees went weak.

"Yep. Read the Bible. Angels are not always the good guys."

No kidding. That was the understatement of the century.

"Does it happen a lot—that a soul needs to be hidden from an Angel?" I asked.

"Don't know." Missy squinted at me. "Do you believe in this kind of stuff? I thought you were agnostic."

"Up until recently, I thought I was atheist," I admitted. "After Steve died, I didn't believe in anything."

Missy was quiet for a long moment. "What made you change your mind?"

"You're going to think I've lost it," I told her.

"Umm, I just told you that I feel dead people walking on my grave and about the family lore of Soul Keepers. Don't think much is stranger than that."

She was so very wrong.

"Dreams," I said. It was the safest thing I could share. "Steve came to me in my dreams and I saw a golden light. I know he's going into it. It made me believe." It was a combination of a few different scenarios, but all were true.

As I spoke the words, Steve floated into the kitchen and seated himself beside Missy.

"Daisy," Missy said haltingly. "Can I ask you something? And you don't have to answer if you don't want to."

"Ask me." I knew what was coming.

"That day in my shop a couple of weeks ago... the day you slipped up and said you and Steve didn't have a sex life..."

"Tell her," Steve said, smiling sadly at me. "Tell her. It's okay. Let your best friend in on the truth as much as you can."

Looking down at my hands, I sighed. I didn't want Missy to be angry at Steve. There were always two sides to every story, and our story was complicated. I searched for a way to soften the blow and couldn't find one. I was a crappy liar and Missy knew me far too well.

Ripping the Band-Aid off quickly was the way to go.

"Steve was gay," I said.

Missy's sharp intake of breath was expected. Her tears were not. "Oh Daisy," she whispered, reaching for me. "I'm so sorry... for both of you."

There was a reason I adored this woman with every fiber in my body.

"Me too," I said, taking her outstretched hand. "We really had a great life together—a platonic, loving life. It kind of messed me up sexually, but I'm working on that. I didn't understand for a long time, and I don't think Steve understood, either. I'm not angry with him… or myself. I'll love him until the day I die… I just…"

"Wish that both of you could have been loved in the way you should have been loved," she finished for me.

I nodded. "But I wouldn't have found Gideon if I hadn't been with Steve."

I didn't add that Gideon was the Grim Reaper or that my dead husband heartily approved. That would be a little too much to take in.

"Life is some serious weird, dude," Missy said, squeezing my hand. "What's your opinion of Heather and me?"

I raised my brow and grinned. "What's *your* opinion?" I countered. "Your opinion far outweighs mine."

Missy laughed and closed her eyes. "Well, I'll never be able to bring her home to my parents, but since I never go home anymore…"

"Do you love her?"

"Love is a huge word," Missy replied. "Huge."

"Agreed," I said.

"What I experienced growing up kind of warped the definition for me," Missy went on. "Do I feel happier with Heather? Yes. Am I attracted to her? Absolutely. Does her well-being consume me? Yep. Can I live openly as a gay woman in a farked-up small Southern town?"

"Are you asking me to answer that last question?" I inquired.

"No," she said, shaking her head. "The real question is can I keep denying who I am so I'm socially acceptable, or will I continue to pretend and ruin my chance at real happiness… and dare I add love?"

"Look," I said, glancing over at Steve. "I didn't realize Steve was gay. If I had we would have figured something out. Being gay isn't a sin. Not living your truth or finding peace and happiness—that's the sin."

"Tell that to my mother," Missy muttered with a disgusted snort.

"Your mother isn't living your life for you, thank God. *You* are… if you choose to. Hiding is no way to live. That I can say with conviction. Look, I'm not exactly the person to go to for relationship advice, but since you asked… I say go for it. Life is short and love is hard to find. Screw people who don't get it. You don't like any of those asshats anyway."

Missy threw her head back and laughed. "You are correct. I don't. Daisy?"

"What?"

"Thank you," she said softly.

"Always, my BFF. Always."

Steve smiled and gently touched Missy's hand. Missy shuddered then giggled.

"So damn weird," she said, staring at her hand.

"What's weird?" I asked, glancing over at Steve, who backed away quickly. He stared at Missy in surprise.

"Another ghost must have walked over my grave," she said, shrugging. "I felt the chill on my hand. Beeeezarreo."

With a small nod at Steve, he took the hint and disappeared. "Speaking of beeeezarreo, tell me more about your family's side job as Soul Keepers."

"Seriously, dude?" she asked with a laugh.

"Seriously, dude. I find it fascinating."

"Mmkay," Missy said, wrinkling her nose in thought. "From what I remember of the stories, the soul doesn't take over the Keeper's personality like in a horror movie. Supposedly, it's peaceful. The Keeper might not even be aware that someone hitched a ride. The soul hides in a Keeper when it needs a safe haven."

"So, you're still you even if you're toting around a few extra people?" I asked with a giggle.

"According to my great-granny, yes," she answered, grinning. "No spinning heads or creepy-man voices. Honestly, I wish it was true. I think it would be incredibly cool."

I was so tempted to say beware of what you wish for, but kept my lip zipped.

"Oh, but there's more. When it's safe for the soul to move on, the Soul Keeper is supposed to find a Death Counselor."

I almost puked. Missy's great-granny knew a whole lot of things she shouldn't have known as a human.

"You okay?" Missy asked, touching my forehead. "You just went some serious pale, my friend."

"Fine. I'm fine," I said, plastering a smile on my mouth and hoping it didn't look like I was constipated. "So, umm... Soul Keepers are supposed to find a what?"

"A Death Counselor. Can you believe that shit? I should write a book and sell it in my shop. I'll call it *The Keeper and the Counselor Bustin' a Move on the Soul Train*. Maybe Great-Granny *was* insane—or maybe I am for sort of believing it." Missy shook her head and stood up.

"I would have liked to have known your great-granny."

"She would have loved you," Missy said. "I'm just so happy I knew Gram. I feel the same way Jennifer does—like Gram was mine, too."

"Tim, I really don't think it's necessary to share that," Heather grumbled as the trio came back in the house.

"They're her dogs," Tim insisted. "She'll want to know. I would want to know."

"Why doesn't that surprise me?" Heather asked with sarcasm dripping from each word.

"Congratulations. Donna pooped a damn mountain," Candy Vargo announced as she, Heather and Tim walked into the kitchen and sat down at the table.

"Karen's movement was quite impressive as well," Tim pointed out. "However, none of it was cubed."

"Remind me to stop spending time with you two," Heather said, smiling at Missy then narrowing her eyes at Tim and Candy. "You're both disgusting."

"Fecal matter is natural," Tim pointed out. "Nothing to be squeamish about."

"Awesome," I said, pushing his cookies toward him. "You can save that conversation for your dinner with Jennifer and Dip Doody. I'm sure it will be far more appreciated than it is right now."

"Of course," Tim said. "How did I do today?"

Missy giggled and gave him a thumbs up. "I'd say a B- with some extra credit points for beating Jennifer at her own game."

Tim clasped his hands together in delight and gave

Missy a jaunty nod of thanks. “I shall aspire to an A, but I happily accept your assessment of my progress.”

“I think I got a C,” Candy Vargo said, glancing around for Gram then pulling out a toothpick when she realized the coast was clear.

“You’re gonna drop to an F if you put that in your mouth,” I warned.

“Well, shit,” Candy griped, pocketing her toothpick. “All of you people suck.”

With that lovely parting shot, Candy grabbed a container of cookies and left.

“She needs some more work,” I muttered, handing Heather and Missy their cookies. “A lot of it.”

“I concur,” Tim said, standing up to take his leave. “Am I supposed to offer to help now?”

Biting down on my lip because I knew he was quite serious, I shook my head. “Nope. But the offer is always appreciated.”

“I shall put it in my notes,” Tim announced.

“You do that,” I replied.

“We’re out unless you need anything,” Heather said, holding Missy’s hand.

I smiled. “I’m good.”

“Me too,” Missy said, glancing over at me and winking. “Today was awesome.”

As they left, Heather silently mouthed that she would call me later. Tim was the last to leave.

“Missy is not normal,” he said as we watched them drive away.

"Define normal," I said, taking the contacts out of my aching eyes and putting them in a glass on the counter.

"She's not Immortal, but there is something unusual about her."

"Is she in danger?" I asked, remembering Birdie's warning.

"Isn't everyone?" Tim answered.

"Are you joking or being cryptic?" I demanded.

Tim stood silent for a long moment and considered his answer. "Sadly, neither."

Not the answer I wanted to hear.

However, forewarned was forearmed.

CHAPTER TEN

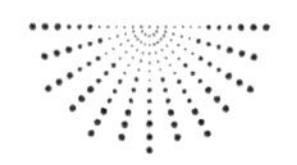

"This isn't going well," I said, twisting my hair in my fingers and groaning.

The Ouija board was not my friend this evening.

So far, I'd learned Birdie's real name was Ethel and that she'd been dead for over thirty years. Thirty years was an incredibly long time to have stayed around, but Ethel was an odd one. She wasn't fond of peas and she'd died of a heart attack shortly after performing fellatio on a famous politician who she refused to name. Not that I wanted to know who it was, but Gram was extremely put out that Ethel was keeping secrets.

"I'm gonna go Google it," Gram announced.

"Google what?" I asked.

"Who Birdie was blowin' the night she kicked the bucket," Gram replied.

Thank God I wasn't drinking anything because I would have snorted it out of my nose. "Umm… don't think you're going to find that on the internet. Plus, you can't exactly use the computer. You're dead," I pointed out.

"And that's where you're wrong, Daisy girl—not about the expired part, seein' I'm as dead as a doornail," Gram announced triumphantly as her deceased boyfriend, Jimmy Joe Johnson, floated next to her and puffed out his semi-transparent chest proudly.

Jimmy Joe Johnson—aka the Mayor of Squatter Town, as I'd named him—used to cry all the time. However, now that he and Gram were courting, he smiled constantly. As unsettling as it was that my dead grandmother was dating, if she was happy then I was happy.

"Enlighten me," I said, sure I would regret it.

"Well now, Jimmy Joe here discovered that if you yell the word *annexa* real loud at the black circle box thingie, it darn well answers you back. It's magic," Gram informed me, throwing her hands in the air with delight.

"Wait. What?" I asked, trying not to laugh. "*Annexa*?"

"Yep. Had to look the dang word up," she said. "Means an accessory or adjoining anatomical parts or appendages. Doesn't make much sense, but it works."

"I think you mean Alexa," I told her.

"Well, butter my butt and call it a biscuit," Gram yelled. "Are you sure? I mean, when I shout annexa, the dang black circle box thingie ignores me. But since my Jimmy Joe has somewhat of a passed-on speech impediment, he can make that piece of metal sing."

"I'm sure it's Alexa," I replied.

Ghosts using the Echo was yet one more unbelievable occurrence in my new normal. Of course, it shouldn't surprise me that the black circle box thingie could understand the dead when humans couldn't. It was a sly little contraption that I was pretty sure could read minds. All I had to do was *think* about something I wanted to buy and it was full of suggestions of where to purchase it.

"Good to know, sweetie pie," Gram said over her shoulder as she and her beau, Jimmy Joe, floated away. "I'll let you know what I find out."

"Great. Can't wait," I muttered, eyeing Ethel, who grinned and lifted her middle finger. "You're a pain in my ass."

"Hoooooooookaaah," she cackled.

"Listen to me, Ethel," I said, blowing out a frustrated sigh. "I can't dive into your mind right now, which is good and bad. Good because I'm terrified to take a trip into your head and bad because I probably need to. However, you're going to slap your hand down on the Ouija board again and try to answer my questions. You feel me?"

"Yausssss."

"Good."

Using the Ouija board wasn't like a dead man or woman mind dive. It was distinctly different. I'd learned that if a ghost and I touched the board at the same time, we could have a conversation of sorts. Ethel's voice was distant and slightly off. I could make out what she was saying for the most part, but was aware I was missing some of it. I would have been happy to have missed the circumstances around her pornographic death, but unfortunately that had come through loud and clear.

"Ethel," I said, trying again.

"No Ethel. Like Birdie," she said in a whispery voice, raising her middle finger.

I laughed. "Got it. Birdie, can you tell me if you knew Missy when you were alive?"

"No," she said.

"No, you didn't know her, or no, you won't tell me?" I pressed.

"Didn't know alive," Birdie said, her voice growing fainter.

"Shit," I mumbled. I needed to ask easier questions. I wasn't helping myself or Birdie. "You did not know Missy when you were alive. Nod your head if I'm correct."

She nodded her head vigorously. I was delighted it didn't fall off. I'd used two full tubes of superglue when I'd reattached it.

"When you said Missy was going to die for me, was that a literal statement?"

"No."

"Was it about Missy at all?"

"No."

My relief was visceral. It meant something else. What? That's what I needed to figure out.

"Okay," I said, wondering why in the heck she was all over Missy if she had no clue who she was.

Wait.

My stomach cramped and a headache developed over my left eye. Right now, I was my own worst enemy. If my mind kept creating farked-up scenarios, I'd be sporting a migraine soon. The direction of my thoughts sucked, but I had to take a stab at it. The chance of Birdie being able to communicate much longer was slim. I could barely hear her now

"Here goes nothing," I muttered, pressing the throbbing spot on my forehead.

My theory was a long shot and ridiculous, but no more ridiculous than the fact that I was using a game board to talk to a dead woman who referred to me as a hooker… or that I had repaired thirty ghosts yesterday with superglue… or that I'd ripped a car door off a moving vehicle.

Sucking in a deep breath and hoping like hell I was on the wrong track I asked a question I wasn't sure I wanted her to answer. "Did you know of Missy once you were dead?"

Birdie nodded.

My theory wasn't as much of a long shot anymore.

"Is there someone inside of Missy who you know? Is that why you were so obsessed with her?"

Birdie hissed and her eyes grew huge in the hollowed-out sockets.

Involuntarily, I stood and jumped back. My chair crashed to the floor. The Ouija board flew off the table as a cold wind blasted through the farmhouse. Birdie's scrawny body jettisoned to the ceiling and she wailed like a banshee, sending chills skittering up my spine.

"Yausssss," she screeched. "Yausssss, yooouah. Piiieeece yooouah."

Slapping my hands over my ears, I was sure I'd just lost fifty percent of my hearing. Birdie whipped around the kitchen like she'd eaten a vat of sugar and topped it off with ten gallons of coffee. The house literally shook on its foundation.

Her behavior was terrifying and her words baffling. I was definitely not inside Missy—nor was any piece of me. As far as I knew, I was physically in one piece. Mentally, I was a hot mess, but physically I was in one piece. Glancing down at myself, I counted my arms, legs and fingers just in case Birdie was correct and I was missing an appendage that had somehow hitched a ride inside my best friend.

I was not.

I almost laughed that I'd actually checked, but I wasn't above disbelieving anything at this point.

Of course, there was a fine chance Birdie was confused. I'd noticed it with some of the other dead who'd stuck around for a while. Birdie had been hanging around as a ghost for over thirty years. I wasn't sure how she'd stayed that long and I doubted she had her timing correct. The exact years didn't matter. Even if she'd been dead on this plane for ten years, her mind had to be muddled. However, her bewilderment was not going to leave me homeless.

"Stop," I shouted. "Stop right now."

Birdie froze midair and trembled violently. The cold wind disappeared as quickly as it had arrived and the house settled. Her small frame wafted back down to the floor and her face was a dark ashen gray. It was the worst I'd seen her look. Birdie's body had been semi-transparent since the first day I'd met her, but I could see through almost all of her now.

"Shit. What have I done?" I whispered with tears pooling in my eyes. "Birdie, are you okay?"

She nodded slowly and gave me a small smile. With a large part of her jaw missing it was macabre, but I'd never seen anything so beautiful. The ghost drove me nuts, but I secretly adored her.

It was time for the secret part to be revealed. Gram had taught me if you have something nice to say, you should darn well say it.

Reaching out and gently stroking her papery cheek, I leaned in and kissed her forehead. "I'm so sorry. I didn't know how much that would upset you. You're important to me, Birdie. As much as I've wanted to smack you upside your dead head, I also love you."

Birdie tilted her head and moved her mouth. Not a word came out. Never had I missed being called a hooker so much in my life. Her sunken eyes darkened with confusion when she realized she couldn't make a sound.

"It's fine," I said, plastering a smile on my lips that didn't reach my eyes. "I think you just lost your voice from screaming. You'll get it back in no time."

She nodded, but didn't look convinced. I wasn't convinced either.

"You'll be calling me foul names again tomorrow," I promised. "Wanna flip me off?"

Birdie shook her head no. My chest tightened.

"You want me to flip you off?" I suggested, desperately needing her to smile.

Again, she shook her head no.

"Umm… you want me to flip Gram off?"

That plan of action got a weak grin.

"Excellent," I said. "One middle finger salute to my grandmother coming right up."

Birdie had aged dramatically in a few short minutes. It was an odd observation to make since she was already dead, but it was as if the admission took what life was left right out of her.

No more Ouija board for Birdie. If I needed to speak to her again, I was going in. To hell with being careful. I lost the privilege the day I'd turned forty and started seeing dead people.

Besides, how much damage could one more freaking mind dive do?

~

"There's someone living inside Missy," I said.

Heather stared at me open-mouthed. "Missy's possessed?"

Heather had come back over when I texted her there might be a problem. She'd told Missy that one of her clients needed assistance. It was ten at night, but everyone knew Heather worked twenty-four-seven.

It wasn't a total lie...

I wasn't exactly a client since I technically worked for Heather as a paralegal, not that I'd been to work in a while. Jennifer and June worked for Heather, too. We'd all left our old firm, run by my newly discovered pappy, John Travolta, when Heather had decided to go out on her own.

Best move I'd ever made.

She'd raised our pay, included medical, insisted on a

bonus and had a profit-sharing plan. It was beyond generous, but then again, so was Heather.

"No, Missy's *not* possessed," I assured her, scanning the living room to make sure Birdie wasn't floating around. I couldn't afford to lose the rest of my auditory senses if she got upset again. "I think Missy's a Soul Keeper."

"That's real?" Heather asked, scratching her head. "I've honestly never heard of a Soul Keeper until this afternoon."

"Apparently, yes," I confirmed. "Birdie, whose real name is Ethel, but wants to be called Birdie, told me."

"Told you what?" Heather asked, walking over to the couch and gently pushing Karen and Donna over to make room for herself.

"Let me backtrack," I said, pacing the living room. "First off, Ethel was a hooker and died shortly after giving a politician a blow job."

"He killed her over a blow job?" Heather choked out, appalled.

"Umm... no," I said, unable to swallow back my wildly inappropriate laugh. "She had a heart attack after blowing the politician. My guess is that the blow job wasn't lethal."

"Got it. And that has something to do with Missy?" she asked, confused.

"No. I'm doing a terrible job with this story."

Heather gave me a lopsided grin. "I'm going to have to agree."

"Thank you," I said with an eye roll.

"Welcome," she replied.

I kept moving around the room. If I sat down, I might

implode. My brain was carrying too much information, yet not enough... It was a frustrating spot to be in.

"When Missy and I were doing the dishes, she told me the story of the Soul Keepers."

"And?" Heather pressed.

"And even though she thinks it's a wives' tale, I don't believe it is," I said, picking up my pace and jogging in circles.

"You're making me dizzy," Heather said.

"Can't be helped," I replied. "Gotta move."

"Fine. Keep talking."

"Roger that," I said, using the ottoman as a hurdle jump. "So, a soul goes into a Soul Keeper when an Angel wishes it ill."

"What the hell?" Heather muttered.

"Exactly what I thought," I said, breaking into jumping jacks. "And Missy's great-granny told her that when a soul is ready to move on, the Soul Keeper has to find a Death Counselor to help."

Heather gasped. "Get out of town."

"I'd love to," I replied with a laugh. "No can do since I just took a fictional two-week vacation with the Grim Reaper. So anyhoo, Birdie didn't know Missy when she was alive. She became aware of Missy after she died."

"Was that why she was so attached to her this afternoon?"

"Yes, and also because Birdie believes that Missy is carrying the soul of a person she knows," I said, dropping to the floor and doing pushups to change it up.

"She told you that?" Heather asked, now pacing the room.

"Kind of," I said. "I was using the Ouija board so it wasn't exactly clear. I also think she was confused. She told me she'd been dead for over thirty years and implied that it was a piece of *me* inside Missy."

Heather froze and examined me from head to toe.

I laughed. I'd had the same reaction.

"I'm all here," I promised.

"You sure?" she asked, worried.

"Yep. I'm positive. However, something is really wonky."

Heather was pensive as she moved to the window and stared out at the darkness. "I agree," she said softly.

"After the luncheon, Birdie pointed to Missy and said she would die for me," I explained, rolling over to my back and launching into a punishing round of crunches. The pain felt good.

"I'm sorry. What?" Heather demanded, whipping around from the window.

"Don't worry—even though I still am," I admitted. "When I questioned Birdie, she said that Missy wasn't going to die for me."

"Then what did she mean?"

I sighed and finally let my body relax. "I don't know. I'd have to mind dive to really talk to her."

"That's out of the question right now," Heather said firmly.

"Do you know something more than we already discussed?"

Heather paused far too long for my liking.

"Out with it," I said.

"I could be wrong," she said hesitantly.

"Or you could be right," I pointed out.

She nodded and rolled her neck. Clearly, she was feeling the tension. "It's a remote possibility that each time you dive into the dead, you're losing your mortality."

"You told me a person had to be created Immortal," I reminded her as I jumped to my feet and began to run in place like I was gunning for first place in a marathon. "I don't have a footprint."

"You don't," Heather agreed. "However, I can think of no other explanation. It's time to have Charlie test your blood."

"And that could solve the mystery?" I demanded, feeling like Alice falling through the Looking Glass.

"It might. It might not," Heather replied, running her hands through her attractive short pixie cut and making it stand on end. "I just don't know, Daisy."

"Charlie can take a sample tomorrow," Gideon said, standing in the foyer of my house.

I screamed.

"Not exactly the reaction I was looking for," he said with a grin as he crossed the room, pulled me to my feet and hugged me like he would never let go. "You scared the hell out of me when you almost didn't come out of Steve's mind, Daisy."

"That would be awful, considering Hell is where you reside," I said with a laugh as I breathed him in.

He smelled like sexy, soapy man. He smelled like happiness and home.

"Very funny," he whispered in my ear and took a little nip that sent happy chills through my body.

Heather cleared her throat. "I don't want to interrupt."

"Then don't," Gideon said.

"Be nice," I chastised Gideon as I disengaged myself from his embrace.

I felt the loss of his heat acutely, but since both he and Heather were here, we needed to talk.

"Are all three of you back?" Heather asked, getting right to the point.

Gideon nodded. "We are."

"Did you find Clarissa?" I asked. Her name on my lips made a fire burn in my chest. I despised her.

"No," Gideon replied, staring at me strangely.

"Do I have cookie crumbs on my face?" I asked, brushing my mouth with my hand in embarrassment.

"Your eyes," he said, squinting in shock.

"Angel eyes," Heather said, tossing me another small box of contact lenses to wear when I was around my human friends.

"That happened when you came out of Steve's mind?" Gideon asked, still staring.

"I guess it did," I replied, feeling wildly self-conscious. "Do you hate them?"

"I could never hate anything about you, Daisy," he said as relief washed over me. "I'm just surprised. That's all."

"You see why I want Charlie to test her blood?" Heather asked.

"I do," Gideon replied. "Not sure it will tell us much. Does Daisy leave a footprint?"

"No," I said, wanting to be part of the conversation since I was the subject. "However, I did throw Candy Vargo as high as the house and ripped the door off of Heather's car while it was moving."

"Don't forget you put your foot through the floorboard when you slammed on the brakes," Heather reminded me with a chuckle. "Totaled my car."

"Yep. Well, that's what you get when you try to mow down Karma and then crash into my house," I replied tartly.

"Should I ask as to why this occurred?" Gideon asked, biting down on his lip to suck back a grin.

"Nope," I replied. "Suffice it to say, each time I mind dive into the dead, I gain new super powers."

"That has to stop," Gideon said flatly. "The mind diving. You could have died last time."

"I've advised the same," Heather added.

"For the time being, yes. I'll stop," I said with a raised brow.

No one was going to tell me what to do except me. I was a grown woman and old enough to make my own decisions and my own disastrous mistakes. While I appreciated their concern and took their advice seriously, they were not my keepers.

I was my keeper.

"I need to speak with Michael," Heather said, grabbing her purse.

"I know not of whom you speak," I said, narrowing my eyes at her.

She slapped herself in the forehead. "My bad, Miss

Shakespeare. I need to talk to John Travolta," she amended. "Better?"

"Much," I replied.

"Do you have anything you want me to tell him?" she asked, heading for the door.

"Nope. Anything I want to tell him, I'll say to his face," I told her.

"That should be fun," Heather commented.

"A freaking riot," I agreed with a humorless laugh.

"Alrighty then," she said. "Don't you guys do anything I wouldn't do."

"And what exactly won't you do?" Gideon inquired, walking over to the couch and scratching the dogs.

"Nothing," Heather said, walking out the front door with a parting laugh.

"That certainly leaves a lot of options," I said.

Gideon glanced over at me with an expression that made me forget how to breathe. "It most certainly does."

CHAPTER ELEVEN

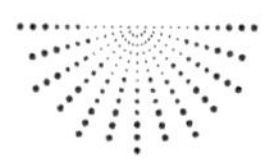

HAVING *THE TALK* WAS HORRIFYING.

Having *the talk* with someone who was a gazillion years old was downright bizarre.

Everything up till this moment had been amazing. We'd made out like teenagers then I'd filled him in on what had happened while he was gone.

I told Gideon about the luncheon, the aftermath with Missy and the alarming talk with Birdie. Like Heather, he'd never heard of a Soul Keeper. Could a Soul Keeper really exist if the Grim Reaper and the Arbitrator between Heaven and Hell knew nothing of it? Was that possible?

Everything was possible.

Even the dreaded *talk*...

"So, I think we should get a few things out of the way before we go any further," Gideon said, pulling me onto his lap.

Gideon's physical beauty still threw me at times. His lips

were sexy and swollen from our massive couch make-out session and his shirt was torn. No one should look as good as he did. My body tingled from head to toe and I was positive my hair looked like I'd been electrocuted. However, my lust-addled brain wasn't working well enough for me to care.

The man was created for kissing.

"Right," I muttered, pulling my shirt down and straightening my clothes. "Birth control?"

"Do we need it?" he inquired.

I was sure I turned bright red, but I held his gaze. I was forty and this was a responsible, albeit unsexy, conversation we were having. It wasn't as if this would be the first time I'd had sex. I'd been married for a long time. Of course, Steve was gay, but that was beside the point. "Yes to the birth control. I mean, I've never been regular, but I still get my period. And now that I know ancient Immortal swimmers can make a baby, I think we should take precautions."

"Ancient?" Gideon inquired with a chuckle.

"Bad word choice," I mumbled, wondering how many more mortifying things would fly from my lips. Probably a lot.

"Not to worry," Gideon assured me with a wink. "I won't debate the truth."

Gideon snapped his fingers and produced a large box of condoms. Tossing them onto the coffee table, he looked at me and grinned. "Done."

"Okay," I said, amused and impressed. "You think we're going to need that many?"

"Yes, I do," he replied silkily.

My face felt like it was on fire.

"Well, umm... I have a clean bill of health," I said, kind of wanting to die. "I've had my yearly check-up and I'm good to go."

"Immortals can't carry disease," he said, enjoying my discomfort.

"I know this is hilarious to you," I snapped. "However, we're grownups—you more than me—and this is what grownups do before they bang."

Gideon's delighted laugh went all through me. I craved his laughter as much as I craved the rest of him.

"I agree," he said, still smiling. "I have an important question for you, though."

"What?" I asked, racking my brain for what I'd missed. I'd read a few articles on what potential sex partners should discuss and some of it didn't apply to us. "Oh, wait. I'm supposed to ask you what you like."

Gideon leaned back on the couch and put his hands behind his head. "You," he said. "I like you."

"I meant sexually speaking." I narrowed my eyes playfully. I seriously wanted to jump him. My impulse control disappeared when he was near.

"My answer remains the same," he replied. "And you? What do you like, Daisy?"

I sighed. The truth shall set you free or make the hot man on the couch toss you off of his lap and run like hell.

"Honestly, I don't even know," I said, no longer embarrassed. I was a grown-ass woman and I would own my sexuality and my lack of practical knowledge in the sex department. I was in love with the man I was talking to, and he loved me. "At forty, I wouldn't say I'm experienced. If I think about it too hard, I get terrified that I'm going to suck at it. But when you kiss me, all I want to do is crawl inside of you and stay. I want to touch you so badly, it's all I can think about."

Gideon closed his eyes and smiled. "I have no damn clue what I did to deserve you, but I'm not letting go. Experience means little to nothing. What matters is us. Period. I love you and want to make you happy in every way possible. If something doesn't feel good, you tell me. I'll find something that feels *very* good. Trust me."

Words were some seriously great foreplay. At least, Gideon's words were.

"Will you do the same?" I asked. I was tempted to rip off his clothes and skip over the rest of the responsible adult conversation.

"I will. I promise."

I nodded and felt sexier than I had in a very long time. The talk wasn't stupid or embarrassing. It was impowering. Being honest with someone you loved and wanted to be with was so right.

"I read a few articles," I admitted with a wince.

"About sex?" he asked, sitting up.

"Yep—more of a list of questions to feel each other out."

"Hit me," Gideon said.

"Mmmkay," I said with a giggle. "Number one. What kind of relationship is this?"

"An endless one," he replied without hesitation, pinning me with a look that sent my heartbeat into overdrive. "Your thoughts on that?"

"I'll cop to liking the way you think," I told him. "Has to be exclusive."

"No-brainer," Gideon said, raising a brow. "On both sides."

"Well, duh," I shot back with a grin. "You're pretty much the sexiest person alive, Grim Reaper."

"Right back at you, Death Counselor."

Wrinkling my nose, I sighed. "I'm forty," I reminded him.

"And I'm older than dirt."

"Fine point. Well made," I conceded. "We've already covered protection. We haven't discussed fantasies and fetishes."

Gideon couldn't suppress his grin. "No fetishes. Many fantasies concerning you."

"Same," I said, falling further under his spell. "Oh... what was the important question you wanted to ask?"

Gideon sat up straighter and cleared his throat. His expression grew serious. My stomach tightened and I wondered what the heck was about to come out of his mouth.

"Would you like to examine my balls before we start?"

"Umm... no. I'm sure your balls are fine," I choked out, trying my best not to laugh.

I failed.

"You sure?" he teased.

"I'm really sorry about the ball discussion Steve and I had," I whispered. "That must have been all kinds of awkward."

"I rather enjoyed hearing you talk about my balls," he

replied with a naughty smirk. "Haven't had my privates discussed in public… well… ever."

"I'm great for things like that," I said weakly. "Gotta stand up."

"Why?" Gideon asked, tightening his hold on me.

"Because when I'm close to you, I feel like a horny teenager," I said, escaping his grasp with ease. "Can't think straight."

I wasn't lying. It was surreal. I'd loved Steve and would get little tingles when I was around him in the beginning, but it didn't compare to the enormity of what I felt for Gideon.

"How did you do that?" Gideon asked, shocked.

"Do what?"

He shook his head and looked down at his hands with curiosity. Flexing his fingers, he clapped his hands. A massive bolt of lightning flew from his fingertips and blew up the armchair.

"Oh my God!" I shouted. "Lightning in the house is off limits."

What the hell did I just say? Never in my life did I think I'd have to make lightning rules for inside the house. It was insane. However, not as insane as what Gideon had just done.

"Needed to test them," he told me as if that was a reasonable answer.

"How'd they do?" I demanded, slapping my hands on my hips and staring at my chair with dismay.

"Good news. They work."

"Bad news," I snapped. "You ruined my chair."

"Whoops," Gideon said, waving his hand and repairing the chair.

Standing my ground, I glared at the man who only moments ago I wanted to bang—well, I still wanted to bang him… "This isn't going well."

"I could have blown up the house," he pointed out.

"Not helping."

"Got it," he said, sucking his bottom lip into his mouth. "I'm sorry."

I was aware he was trying not to grin. While his apology was sincere, his actions were a little sucky. As attracted as I was to the Grim Reaper, it would get old fast if he blew up all my stuff.

"I accept… this time. Lightning belongs outside, not in the living room. You feel me?"

"I feel you," Gideon said.

"I mean, I don't want to be a downer, but I like my house."

Gideon put his hands up and grinned. "I like your house too. I'll keep all explosions outside from this day forward. I promise."

"Thank you."

"You're welcome," Gideon replied, and then looked down at his hands again. "Daisy, how did you get out of my embrace?"

"It's not that I didn't want you to hold me," I assured him. "I just can't make coherent thoughts when you do. I needed space to think."

"Not what I meant," he said, glancing up at me. "Come here, please."

"Since you asked nicely, I will. But no more lightning, dude," I said, falling on top of him and wrapping my arms around him. "Now what?"

He wrapped his arms tightly around me and buried his face in my hair. The feeling was as close to magic as I'd ever come.

"Now try to get away," he instructed.

"What if I don't want to?" I teased.

"Daisy. I'm not joking. Try to leave my arms."

Gideon was odd at times, but as he'd said, he was older than dirt. I'd play along and see where it was going. I remembered Jennifer telling a story about the games she and Dip Doody played in the bedroom. Now I wished I'd paid better attention. However, if he incinerated any more furniture, he was in deep shit.

"Fine," I said, slipping right out of his embrace and skipping across the room. "Are you going to chase me?"

Gideon's mouth was agape. He stared at me then paled as he examined his hands again.

"What's wrong?" I asked, feeling panicked that he might feel the need to *test* his hands out again. Not to mention, his reaction was wildly unsettling. "What did I do?"

"You did the impossible," Gideon said as a small grin of absolute puzzlement pulled at his lips. "No one can escape my hold unless I let them."

"Then you must have let me," I said, not following.

"I did not," he replied. "Letting you go is not in my wheelhouse. Ever."

"Good to know," I teased. "I plan on keeping you too."

"Daisy, you don't understand," he said, standing up and

approaching me. "If you can escape death, you can escape anything."

"You're making me a little nervous," I told him. "We both know I'm becoming a freak of nature. Maybe it will go away."

"Have any of your powers decreased?"

Had they? Nope. They'd become more intense. "No."

"Do you feel different?" Gideon asked.

"I don't think so," I said, looking down at my body.

Gideon paced the room, glancing up at me every so often. Shit. I'd totally ruined what was potentially going to be the best night of my life so far by escaping from his embrace. Of course, him burning my chair with a bolt of electricity didn't exactly help set the mood either.

"Can we just pretend it didn't happen and go back to making out?" I suggested. "I didn't mean to freak you out."

Gideon crossed the room in three steps, took me in his arms and spun me around like I weighed nothing.

"This is fucking perfect!" he shouted.

"Getting dizzy," I told him, hanging on for dear life.

"Sorry," he said, putting me down but keeping me close. "Fucking perfect."

"What's perfect?" I asked, eyeing him with concern.

Taking my hand and leading me to the couch, he seated me then squatted in front of me. "If you can get away from me, you can get away from *her*."

"Her who?" I asked, confused.

"The Angel of Mercy," he said, his eyes darkening with hatred. "She won't be able to hurt you."

"When you say hurt…"

Gideon was quiet for a long moment. "As in destroy you," he said flatly. "She won't be able to. You can get away."

"Or I can fight."

"Bad plan," he said. "Very bad plan. When you back an animal up against a wall and its existence is at stake, it will do anything to take others down with it."

That scenario didn't sound like a good time. The best option was that Clarissa was found by one of the Immortals before she tried to finish what she had begun with me.

"Why the hell is the Angel of Mercy—a complete oxymoron—after me in the first place?" I hissed, growing furious. "When it started, I thought it was because of you and me. However, Steve's death was long before I even knew you. She has it out for me for another reason altogether."

Gideon squinted and tilted his head to the side. "I hadn't put that together."

"Actually, I didn't until right now either," I told him.

We sat in silence and stared at each other for a few minutes. The plot kept getting stranger.

"You think she'll come after me?" I asked.

He shrugged. "I wouldn't put anything past Clarissa," he ground out. "There was a reason Tim, Candy and Heather stayed with you while Charlie, John Travolta and I searched for her."

"Thank you," I said with a small grin.

"For what?"

"For calling my sperm donor John Travolta."

Gideon laughed and kissed my nose. "It's my great pleasure to make you smile and to piss the Archangel off. It's killing him to have to answer to the name."

"Warms my heart," I said with a giggle, and then stiffened as a horrible thought dawned on me. "Shit. I think he knows."

"He knows what?"

"I think John Travolta knows why she's after me. His reluctance to go after Clarissa and his lifelong denial of being my sperm donor adds up to something very off," I said, feeling ill. "I'd bet my squatters and my newly acquired car-door-ripping skills on it."

Gideon looked at his watch and swore under his breath. "It's midnight."

"Tomorrow," I said. "I'll pay Darth Vader Daddy a visit in the morning."

"With me," he insisted.

"That's fine," I agreed. "I don't know where he lives anyway."

"We have about eight hours till it's socially acceptable to smack down John Travolta," he pointed out.

"What in the world will we do with eight hours?" I asked with a naughty grin. To hell with reality. I wanted to bang my beautiful lover. For all I knew, tomorrow could be my last day on earth… "Should we blow up more stuff? Outside?"

"I have a much better idea," Gideon said. "You up for it?"

"I do believe the question is *are you up for it*?" I shot back.

Gideon threw his head back and laughed. "I am very *up* for it."

"Very?" I asked, pulling my shirt over my head and tossing it aside.

"Very. Very. Very *up* for it," he said, taking me into his arms and kissing me until I forgot my name.

"Wait," I said, glancing around. "If we do it here, we might have an audience.

Gideon paused and then grinned. "Do you trust me?"

"Should I?" I asked.

"You should," he replied.

"Then yes. I trust you."

Famous last words.

However, I was definitely right to have trusted him.

Surprisingly, the Grim Reaper was a *very* trustworthy guy.

CHAPTER TWELVE

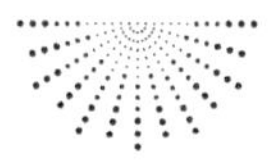

"Where are we going?" I asked, peering out of the car window as we sped through the night. The stars danced on the horizon and a sliver-thin moon floated in a cloudless sky.

Gideon drove with a sure hand and a lead foot. It didn't bother me a bit since I drove the same way. I had a general idea of our location, but we'd taken a lot of turns and I couldn't be sure.

"It's a surprise," Gideon replied, watching the road.

"I'm not great with those," I told him, noticing the big box of birth control sitting between us.

My smile grew wide. I ceased to care where we were going and just wanted to get there. While my world might be imploding, tonight was going to be perfect.

"I have a hunch you're going to like this surprise," he said, pulling off the road and cutting the engine. "We're here."

"Umm... okay. Wow." I smiled politely and tried to figure out where *here* actually was.

All I could see were rolling meadows and trees. It was thirty degrees outside and there were no buildings in sight. I had to admit the property was gorgeous bathed in starlight, but it was freaking freezing outside. He was insane if he was planning to have sex on a blanket in the icy outdoors.

"You like it?"

"Is that a trick question?" I asked, trying to gauge how to proceed.

Gideon laughed and gave me a quick, hard kiss. Grabbing the condoms, he opened the driver's side door and stepped out of the car.

Dammit. I probably should have asked a few more potential sex partner questions. However, banging outside in the winter hadn't come up on the list.

"Why don't we do it in the car," I called out, shivering as a chilly wind whipped through the interior.

"You cold?" Gideon inquired with amusement in his tone.

"It's winter," I reminded him with an eye roll. "If you think you're going to get me naked in thirty-degree weather, we need to chat."

Again, he laughed.

As always, his laugh made me weak.

However, not weak enough to bang in a bone-chilling outdoor backdrop.

"Dude. Seriously," I complained. "This really isn't working for me."

"Hush," Gideon said, opening my door and extending his hand. "You said you trusted me."

Nodding my head, I sighed. "I did," I admitted. "But if this is your idea of sexy and romantic, we have a problem."

"Come with me."

Gideon took my hand and led me away from the warm car. The sound of frozen leaves crunching beneath our shoes didn't really set the right mood as far as I was concerned, but I'd told him I trusted him. And I would keep on trusting him until he suggested removing even one item of clothing in this cold.

"How far are we walking?" I asked.

"Till we get there," he answered with a grin.

"You're one of those guys," I muttered.

"Yep," he agreed with a chuckle.

As we carefully walked down a wide tree-lined trail, the air warmed dramatically—to about eighty degrees. I sucked in a shocked breath and glanced up at Gideon.

"Trust me," he whispered.

"I do."

The trail opened up to a breathtaking garden that in no way, shape or form should have been alive this time of year. Enormous cream-colored lilies—bigger than any I'd ever seen—shone in the brilliant starlight and spilled from delicate trellises. Tall grasses swayed seductively and the warm breeze rushed over my cheeks like a caress. Flowering vines of riotous colors made a fragrant wall around the garden.

"What the heck?" I gasped. My mouth had fallen open and I wondered if we had walked into a different dimension.

"Still trust me?" Gideon asked, enjoying my reaction.

"Yes," I said, grinning like an idiot. "How?"

"A beautiful woman deserves to be surrounded by beauty when..."

"When she's about to check out the Grim Reaper's balls?" I inquired, trying to keep a straight face, but failing.

"Among other things," he shot back dryly, removing his winter coat and tossing it to the ground.

I shrugged and removed my coat as well. When in Rome —or wherever we were...

"Can I ask where we are?" I questioned, smelling one of the roses as I wandered the garden.

"You may," Gideon said, watching me.

I waited for the answer but it never came. Eyeing him with amused annoyance, I blew out an audible sigh. "I have to ask twice?"

"I think there are many things you might ask twice for this evening," he replied casually as he removed his shirt.

I almost fainted.

"Oh my god," I choked out. "That should be illegal."

Gideon was otherworldly beautiful—the ridiculous kind of gorgeous—gray-blue eyes, messy blond hair and a rock-hard body. It made me a little self-conscious about removing my own clothes.

However, the naked lust shining in his eyes did a whole hell of a lot for my ego.

Glancing away to squash the insane impulse to tackle him to the ground, I repeated my question. "Where are we?"

"Do you not like what you see?" Gideon asked, observing me bury my head in a lilac bush.

"I like it too much," I told him truthfully with my head still in the bush. "I don't really trust myself not to attack you."

"The feeling is mutual," he admitted. "Being attacked by you would be outstanding."

"I wouldn't be too sure about that," I replied, turning around and squinting my eyes. It made him appear a little blurry. However, even blurred the man was just as hot. Damn. "I knocked down a tree and pulled a car door off its hinges. If I were you, I'd be worried about my balls."

Gideon's burst of laughter was all I needed to let go of my inhibitions. It was probably a very good thing he was Immortal, since I was unsure of my own strength.

"We'll get to my balls shortly," he said. "As to where we are? We're on a piece of property I recently bought."

Glancing around, I took it in. It was magical. I still had a difficult time getting comfortable with the magic, but it didn't scare me. Magic was a part of the man I loved. I had every intention of loving every facet of him. Besides, I had my own magic. I could glue a squatter back together in no time flat. Not quite as sexy as Gideon's magic, but it was something.

"You have a house in town and one in Hell," I pointed out. "Why do you need another piece of property?"

Gideon walked me over to a bench I hadn't noticed.

"Well, you see," he said, sitting down and pulling me onto his lap. "Once upon a time, there was a beautiful woman—a funny, kind, thoughtful and very smart woman—who gave an undeserving man a gift. The gift of starting over. She wanted to build a real and lasting foundation. The man figured it might be handy to have a place to build the house."

My body began to tingle and my heart pounded in my chest.

"So, you were thinking to build the foundation right here?" I whispered.

He nodded and grinned. "Every room can be built carefully and with love. Each stone can be chosen by the beautiful woman and the man who can't live without her."

I trembled in his arms. It wasn't from the cold. The chilly air didn't exist in the enchanted bubble Gideon had created.

"That's a *huge* step," I said softly, brushing his hair off of his forehead.

"One of many hopefully."

"That was seriously hot," I said with a giggle.

"I aim to please."

"You're doing very well," I told him.

"Do you think I'll get into your pants this fine balmy evening, Death Counselor?" he inquired with a lopsided grin.

"Odds are very good, Grim Reaper."

Standing up and placing me on my feet, he led me to an archway covered in a cascade of sparkling gold flowers.

"What's beyond the archway?" I asked as my stomach tightened with anticipation.

His carnal grin sent a thrill through me. I grinned right back.

"I was thinking the bedroom could be over there," he said, pointing beyond the archway.

"Oh really? And what else do you have planned?"

"It's a surprise. You'll have to wait and see," he informed me as he walked through the archway and disappeared from sight.

While surprises weren't really my thing, this one sounded promising. Good things were supposed to come to those who waited, and I'd waited a very long time to feel like this about someone.

"Where did you go?" I called out as I followed the path he'd walked.

"I'm in my favorite room in our house," he yelled back. "You might want to check it out."

"Maybe I will." I laughed as I pushed my way past a fragrant weeping cherry tree in full bloom. Exotic flowers and shrubs that I'd never seen before lined the golden-pebbled path that led to the man I searched for. Bending down, I picked a bouquet of purple and blue glitter-encrusted daisies and tucked them into my hair.

"Are you lost?" Gideon called.

"Nope, just got waylaid by the scenery."

"Scenery is pretty damned good in here."

"On my way, Mr. Impatient," I said with a laugh as I picked up my pace then stopped dead in my tracks. I'd entered yet another garden.

The garden where carnal dreams were made.

There were daisies everywhere—every color and size imaginable. They shimmered and swayed in the breeze. Gideon had chosen the flower that matched my name and had lost his mind with the décor. I'd never been anyplace so decadent and lovely. Daisy-shaped jeweled candles hung in the air connected to absolutely nothing but magic. The best part was the massive bed in the middle of the *bedroom*—and the man who was standing next to it.

"Oh my God," I whispered, trying to take it all in. "You did this for me?"

"I'd do anything for you, Daisy."

How was it possible to love someone so much, so quickly? Would we last? Would the foundation be strong enough to rock? Because I was positive we would rock it…

Gideon's lust-filled gaze followed me as I walked around the area and touched the different daisies.

"They're breathtaking," I said.

"They don't hold a candle to you," Gideon replied.

I'd never felt so beautiful, so wanted—so powerful. Who knew a fallen Angel… a Demon, would be the man I would love with my entire soul?

The emotion was too much. I didn't know if I was about to cry or laugh or run for my life. It was perfect—too perfect. I wasn't sure I could live up to my surroundings.

"Are you crying?" Gideon asked, walking toward me.

"Happy tears," I promised, wiping my eyes with my sleeve.

He kissed away a tear I'd missed. "We should probably be naked for what I have planned next."

I nodded. "That's usually how it goes."

"And you can make sure my balls meet your satisfaction."

My laugh rang out and echoed through the garden. All thoughts of not being good enough evaporated. The Grim Reaper had my heart and knew exactly what to do to put me at ease. His sense of humor was as sexy, if not sexier, than the rest of him.

"I appreciate your willingness to be so open about your balls," I told him as I pulled my shirt over my head and stepped out of my pants.

"My pleasure," Gideon replied, removing his clothes with inhuman speed.

"Wow," I choked out in awe.

He was a Greek god come to life. Every inch of Gideon was perfect, including his *very up for it* privates… and even his *balls*. The evidence of his desire made me bold, and I removed my bra and panties with a giggle.

"You're magnificent," he said as his eyes devoured my nakedness.

"You're not too bad yourself," I shot back.

Gideon's grin widened. "And my balls?"

I felt the heat start in my chest and crawl up to my face. I was never going to live down the fact that I'd had a conversation about his balls with my dead husband. Never.

"Your balls are very *bally*," I said, walking over to him and cupping the topic of our conversation in my hand. "I heartily approve of your balls."

Gideon sucked in a sharp breath through clenched teeth. His eyes went from gray-blue to a sparkling red. His need was unmistakable.

"My *bally balls* approve of being handled," he said.

"And the rest of you?" I teased.

"The rest of me would be fucking delighted to become acquainted with you."

"That's a good thing since I plan on handling all of you."

Gideon let his head fall back on his shoulders and he groaned. "Daisy, this is going to be over before it starts if you keep saying things like that."

"That would be a shame." I walked over to the bed and lay down. "I have some parts that would like to get acquainted with you, too."

Gideon literally sprinted to the bed and jumped on it. The movement bounced me high in the air. He caught me effortlessly and straddled me over his chest. Slowly, I ran my hands over his strong body, memorizing him. His hands explored my curves. My body grew hot with need and I couldn't get enough of touching him or feeling his hands on me.

I closed my eyes and let my other senses take over. It was fun and natural… and amazingly right.

"Daisy, I want you to keep your eyes open," Gideon said, running his strong hands over my shoulders then cupping my breasts. "I need to make sure you're with me the whole time."

Opening my eyes, I smiled. "I'm here. I'm right where I want to be."

Leaning forward, I brushed my lips over his and felt the tingle shoot straight to my toes. If this was what kissing him did to me, I couldn't fathom what the rest would feel like.

"More," he insisted, tangling his hands in my hair and deepening the kiss.

Our tongues danced and my body began to move in a rhythm that was unfamiliar and wildly freeing. My insides felt molten, and I was slowly coming apart in his arms. Crawling off of him, I pulled him on top of me. All of his hard against my soft was almost enough to send me over the edge. Gideon feathered my neck and face with kisses that left me breathless. Strong waves of desire pulsed through me.

"You good?" he asked. His eyes were hooded and his voice was rough with lust.

It was all kinds of sexy.

"Yes," I said. "More please."

His smile was naughty. I wanted to kiss it off his lips.

But Gideon had other ideas.

Extremely good ideas.

Gideon's mouth and hands were weapons of sexual destruction. I had never wanted to be destroyed in my life until now. I writhed against him and ran my nails down his back.

"You have the condoms?" I asked, breathing hard as his kisses moved from my neck to my breasts.

"Yep. Don't need them yet," he said, moving lower. "Trust me."

"Oh my God," I cried out as he kissed a place I'd never been kissed.

My back arched and a shudder of pure delight consumed me. The sound of his laughter at my reaction didn't make me self-conscious at all.

"Good?" he questioned.

"Umm... yes. So good. You are amazing at that."

"Thank you," he said with a laugh.

"No, thank you."

My breasts felt heavy and swollen and every other part of me felt like a live wire. My body rocked as Gideon took me to heights I didn't know existed. Fisting his hair in my hands, I let the moment take me.

I screamed as an orgasm overwhelmed me. My entire body clenched with intense pleasure. I rode out the aftershocks as Gideon moved back up my body with an expression of smug male pride written all over his beautiful face.

"That was nice?" he asked with a smirk.

I shrugged and bit my bottom lip so I wouldn't grin like a fool. "It was okay," I teased.

"Guess I'll have to try again and do better this time," he said, raising an amused brow.

"That might kill me dead," I whispered, tracing his lips with my finger. "It was… I've never… It was perfect. Sex is so much fun."

"It's supposed to be," he said, shaking his head and grinning. "When it's with someone you love, it's far more than just sex."

This *was* the way it was supposed to be. I just didn't know it until now. "I want to touch you."

"That can be arranged," he said, rolling off of me and lying on his back.

I was a kid in a candy shop… or rather, a woman with an extreme sweet tooth in an x-rated candy shop. My excitement was obvious and Gideon's delight made me bold.

His hissed intake of air as I took him in my hand and stroked him made me giddy.

"Good?" I asked, watching every nuance of expression on his face.

"Perfect," he ground out as his body moved in rhythm with my touch. "Gonna need those condoms very soon."

"How soon?" I asked, leaning forward and putting my mouth where my hand had been.

"Now," he said, lifting me off of him and frantically grabbing the box.

Watching him put on the condom was as much of a turn-on as every other move he made. No awkwardness. No annoyance that he had to wear it. While I was sure I would find a few faults here and there, I was pretty dang sure none of them would be in the bedroom department.

"You ready, Angel Eyes?" he inquired, looking like he wanted to eat me whole.

"Are you, Demon Boy?" I challenged.

"I've waited my whole damned life to make love to someone I love. This will be a first for me."

His words humbled me, and my entire body tingled. I caved into my instincts and tackled him. His surprised grunt was followed by a laugh as he flipped me over and pinned me beneath him.

"You win," I gasped out.

"We win," he corrected.

The mood went from silly to serious on a dime. My body ached with desire. I arched my back and opened my legs. I wanted all of him—mind, body and soul. His eyes blazed red and I met his intense gaze head on. The intimacy was almost too much, but I was going into this with my eyes wide open.

"I'm in love with you, Daisy," he said in a tone that made me shiver with happiness.

"And I'm in love with you, Gideon."

Taking him in my hand, I led him exactly where I

wanted him to be. Nothing had ever felt so right. Our kisses became frenzied and with one swift thrust, we joined.

"You good?" Gideon asked, barely able to restrain himself, but needing to know I was with him.

"Yessss," I hissed, undulating beneath him. "More."

And my wish was granted.

The speed of his thrusts increased and I bucked wildly beneath him as we careened toward an orgasm so intense it would probably kill us—well, not him since he was Immortal. However, if I had to go, this was one hell of a way to do it.

My gaze locked on his and the vulnerability I felt from him overwhelmed me. His eyes were wild and the sounds he made went all through me. I now knew what it meant to love completely—to be one with another person. The Grim Reaper was mine, and I was his.

"Come with me," he demanded.

And I did.

We both cried out and color burst behind my tightly closed eyes. My back arched and a jolt of pleasure radiated through my entire body. Orgasm number two overcame me and a scream flew from my lips. I trembled and clenched him inside me as I rode out the waves. As soon as it ebbed another took hold, and I wrapped my legs around his waist and moaned.

"Gorgeous," he whispered as he kissed me with such passion I thought I might orgasm again.

"You are really, really, really good at this," I said with my hands cupping either side of his face.

"*We* are really, really good at this," he replied. "Hold that thought."

He rolled off of me, removed the condom and snapped his fingers. It vanished into thin air.

"That's a nifty trick," I said, still feeling little aftershocks roll through me. "We brought a bunch of those, didn't we?"

"We did," he replied, eyeing me curiously. "Would you like to use a few more?"

"Yes, I would," I said. "Well, that is, if you can."

"Oh Daisy," Gideon said with a laugh. "You have no clue who you're dealing with. I definitely *can*."

"And you have no clue who you're dealing with, Gideon," I told him. "Because I *can* too."

And we did.

Because we could.

Four more times.

Best damned night of my life.

CHAPTER THIRTEEN

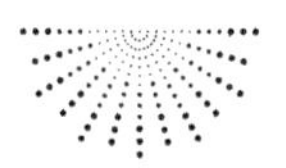

"I'M NOT DOING THIS," I SAID, GAPING AT HIM LIKE HE'D LOST his mind. "There is no way I'm doing this."

"Oh, come on," Steve begged, sitting across from me at the kitchen table with a ridiculously wide grin on his face. "Think of me as one of your girlfriends. We're just having a little breakfast and gossiping."

Pressing my lips together, I searched for an appropriate response. It was not going to happen anytime this year… or decade.

"And yes," Steve continued. "I'm fully aware that I'm your dead, gay husband. However, the *gay* part of the description qualifies me to stand in for the girlfriend role since none of them are here right now. I *am* your best friend. Plus, I feel very invested."

"In Gideon's balls?" I choked out, unable to believe the conversation.

"Yes," he said with a chuckle. "Does the Grim Reaper suffer from cryptorchidism or not?"

"Oh my God," I muttered, my chin dropping to my chest. Steve was not going to let up until he had the intel on Gideon's junk. How was this my life?

Gideon and I had slept in the enchanted garden after many aerobic rounds of the most amazing sex of my life. He'd dropped me off about an hour ago to go home and shower and change for our John Travolta smack attack. It was eight in the morning, now, and I hadn't had caffeine. Yet somehow, I was discussing the balls of the man who I'd banged last night with Steve.

Peeking up at my dead, gay best friend, I grinned. "You really need to know?"

"I do," he replied, grinning back at me.

I was working on very little sleep and my judgement was definitely off, but I was about to share shit I probably shouldn't.

"Coffee first," I said, getting up and making my special iced caffeinated confidence booster. If I was going to have this chat, I needed liquid fuel with an enormous squirt of chocolate syrup.

"Take your time," Steve said.

Shaking my head and laughing, I concentrated on my coffee. "I will. Thank you."

"Welcome." Steve was proof that one could die, but Southern manners lived on for eternity.

I would update Steve on the state of the Grim Reaper's balls, but the rest of the night was off limits.

Taking a huge slug off my coffee, I sat back down. "His

balls are fine. They are very nice balls and there are two of them. Fully descended."

"Excellent!" Steve said. "I did a little light reading on the subject so I would know what we were in for."

"We?" I asked with a laugh.

"Of course," Steve said with a wink. "You'll always be my girl, and I want the best for you. So, anyhoo, I just need to ask a few more questions."

"No."

"Great, was he able to get it up?"

"Oh, my hell. That has nothing to do with his balls."

Steve shook his head. "You'd be surprised. Just answer the question."

"Umm… yes. He did fine in that department."

Steve raised his hand for a hive five and I obliged him. Honestly, it was kind of fun to gossip a little.

"Wait," I said after sucking back another sip of iced coffee. "If he'd only had one ball, he wouldn't have been able to get it up?"

"Only in some very rare cases," Steve explained. "However, even with one ball, a man can produce enough testosterone to get an erection and ejaculate. Therefore, he can also produce adequate sperm for fertilization."

"Why did you look all of this up?" I asked, open-mouthed.

"Well," Steve said, looking quite pleased with himself. "I wanted to make sure your dreams could still come true even if Gideon was sporting one ball."

"He has two," I pointed out.

"Even better," Steve replied with a thumbs up.

"What dreams are you talking about?"

Steve sighed and floated over to me. Wrapping his semi-transparent arms around me, he rested his head on my shoulder. "I know how much you always wanted a baby," he whispered. "I wanted to make sure Gideon could give you everything you wanted, since I couldn't."

I was speechless and wanted to cry. I had wanted children for a long time, but that was my past, not my future. I was forty. While I was fully aware women were having kids into their fifties these days, having a baby with someone who resided in Hell part time wasn't exactly ideal.

And what the heck would I give birth to? An Angel/Demon/human who could talk to the dead, create enchanted flower gardens and demolish cars? The terrible twos would be horrifying.

"Oh, Steve." I sighed and leaned my head against his. "I'm responsible for my dreams. Not you. And not Gideon. As sweet and alarming as your research is, I'm no longer in the market for a baby. I have dogs."

Steve chuckled and floated to a new position. We were face to face. "Daisy, never say never to anything that results from two people loving each other completely. Of course, we are talking about sperm that's older than time, but miracles can happen. Look at you."

"Yep, look at me. I had a mother who killed herself over a dead man and a father who wants nothing to do with me," I replied. "Not an outstanding example."

Steve was quiet. There was nothing to say.

The fact that my mother fell in love with one of the ghosts she was counseling and followed him into the darkness by committing suicide was simply a sad truth of my history. I'd only been five when it happened—thirty-five years ago. I barely remembered her.

And my surprise daddy?

There was a fine reason I hated surprises. John Travolta was not a welcome addition. Thank God I was forty and not fourteen. While it still hurt, as a teenager, the knowledge would have been devastating.

"Anyhoo," I said, pasting on a smile and changing the subject. "I should probably eat breakfast, but all of a sudden I'm not hungry."

"You need to eat your dang breakfast, Daisy girl," Gram announced, zipping into the kitchen with Jimmy Joe Johnson on her heels. "You quit eatin', you're gonna get so skinny you won't be able to see your shadow."

"No need to worry about that," I told her with a laugh, happy to have a distraction from the conversation Steve and I were having. It had gotten too dark. "Would cookies be okay?"

Normally, a banana and oatmeal were my standard go-to breakfast items. However, my stomach was in knots. The day ahead left me feeling on edge.

Gram fluttered around the kitchen searching for something that might appeal to me. Not that she could actually prepare it, but old habits die hard.

"They're peanut butter cookies," Steve volunteered, always ready to defend me and my bad choices. "Peanut butter has protein."

"Fine," Gram huffed. "Four cookies, but you have to have a piece of fruit with it."

"Deal," I said, grabbing a banana and my sugary-protein morning meal. "Have you seen Birdie? I'm worried about her."

Gram sat down on the table right in front of me. "She's been hidin' in the cellar."

"I don't have a cellar," I said, confused.

"I think Gram means the crawlspace," Steve said.

I glanced over at him. "Not exactly a place I'd want to hang out."

"Ditto," Steve said. "I'll go check on her."

"Thank you," I told him as he sank through the floor and vanished.

I'd do it myself, but I had to get ready for a visit with Darth Vader and couldn't really show up covered in cobwebs and dirt. However, if Birdie was still down there when I got back, we were going to spend some quality time together in my crawlspace.

"Gram, I'm taking part in a surprise ambush on John Travolta this morning. Want to help me pick out an outfit?" I asked, grabbing another cookie and heading upstairs.

"Thought you didn't like surprises," Gram pointed out.

"Only when they happen to me. You want to help?"

"Can a fish cry underwater?" Gram asked, following me.

I stopped and stared at her. "Can it?"

"Can what?" she asked, shooing her beau away. "Jimmy, as much as I adore ya, I'm gonna have a little Daisy/Gram time."

He bowed politely, blew Gram a kiss and disappeared.

"I have it real dang bad for that dead man," Gram said, patting her heart. "Jimmy Joe Johnson just dills my pickles and then some. Sometimes the porch light is on and nobody's home, but he's awful cute. Have to be careful with him though, seein' as how he cries all the time."

Looking up at the ceiling, I smiled. Reality was a relative word in my happy home. "Awesome. However, you didn't answer my question."

"What question?"

"Can fish cry underwater?"

"Do man-eatin' sharks eat women too?" she shot back.

"That's your answer?"

"You betcha," Gram said with a cackle as she flew up the stairs to my bedroom.

"It's no wonder I turned out strange," I said to no one as I took the stairs two at a time. I needed armor and a lightsaber for my meeting this morning.

However, a spiffy outfit would have to do.

"YOU KNOW WHAT'S WEIRD?" I ASKED, SLIPPING INTO BLACK suede boots.

Gram tilted her head to the side and waited for the punchline. It didn't come.

"Was that an actual question?" Gram asked. "Cause if it was, I can think of about a hundred million things that ain't quite right."

I laughed. She was correct. The fact that I was having a conversation with my dead grandmother was definitely one of them.

"Do you have something specific on your mind, sweetie?" she inquired.

I did. Upsetting her was the last thing I wanted to do, but the question had lived in my head for many years.

"Why didn't we ever talk about my mom much?" I asked.

My words lay heavily in the air.

My head felt light and I kept on with my task of getting dressed to avoid the fact that I'd possibly just pulled the pin out of a grenade.

Checking myself in the mirror and trying to decide if the outfit was right was a mindless thing to do. I never really thought much about what I put on, but even I knew the outer layer was important today. Sweatpants and a t-shirt were sadly not an option.

I'd tried on a few dresses, and then decided on black pants and a fitted cashmere sweater instead. Gram had vetoed jeans. I kind of liked the disrespect jeans showed, but I wasn't a child acting out. I was a woman who needed answers from a man who might or might not give them to me. Looking like an adult was a smart start.

"You gonna cover those eyes?" Gram asked, referring to my sparkling gold peepers.

"Nope, and you didn't answer my question."

Gram hovered next to me and wrung her hands. "At first, we did talk about your mama, but you would cry for days on end. You didn't eat—barely talked. After a while, I stopped. Couldn't stand to see you so sad."

"I don't remember that," I said with a shake of my head. "Why don't I remember?"

Gram shrugged and gave me a hug. "Don't rightly know,

Daisy girl. You were only five. The brain does funny things to protect us from pain."

"You think I subconsciously pushed all of it away?" I asked, walking over to my dresser to choose earrings and a necklace.

It was odd how distant I felt talking about the woman who had given birth to me—Alana. Neither Gram nor I ever said her name. Maybe I *had* pushed memories away because they'd been too hard to handle for someone so young.

"Possible," Gram said, pointing to a pair of small silver hoop earrings and a thin silver chain necklace with a diamond drop. "Wasn't until the day you met Missy that you seemed to calm down and come back to life."

"Missy and I met around the time my mother died, right?"

Gram nodded. "Yep. Didn't care much for Missy's parents—they were as mean as snakes and as worthless as gum on a boot heel, but that little girl was a dang ray of sunshine. She made you smile through your tears and you've been as thick as thieves ever since. I just love that little gal."

"I do too," I said, absently putting the jewelry on and wondering why I didn't recall what Gram was talking about. "Can I ask another question?"

"Daisy girl, you can ask whatever you want," she said, kissing the top of my head. "If you'd like, we can sit down sometime and I'll tell you all about your mama."

"Say her name, Gram."

"Will that hurt you?" she asked, more serious than I'd ever seen her.

"No. I think maybe it hurts more to pretend she didn't exist."

"Alana," Gram said quietly. "Means valuable and precious. Maybe it's time you got to know her."

I nodded and something in my heart broke. Maybe it *was* time. I had no clue how long Gram would stick around and when she left, the memories would go with her. The only way a person lived on was in the memories of those who loved them. I couldn't love my mother unless I knew who she was.

"That would be good. I'd like to get to know Alana. Were you aware she was seeing Clarence Smith?"

Gram scratched her head then sighed. "Can't rightly say I was. Your mama was real private about her beaus."

"Did you know the ghost she died for?"

Gram paled and levitated. "No. I didn't. Once your mama took over as the Death Counselor, I stopped seein' the dead. Told her she didn't have to start the job since I was still kickin', but she said she wanted to. Said it gave her something to be proud of."

Being a Death Counselor made me feel proud, too. I wondered if I had other things in common with the woman who had given me life.

"How did you find out she'd died?" I asked. "I mean, about the suicide."

Gram's movements grew faster and her agitation made her flying clumsy. She fell right out of the air and landed at my feet.

"Oh my God," I cried out as I gently picked her up and held my weightless grandmother in my arms. "I'm so sorry… so sorry. I know how much this upsets you. I shouldn't have asked. We can just talk about the happy times. I'm good with that."

Laying her head on my shoulder, Gram sniffled. "No, little girl," she whispered brokenly. "You have a right to know everything. I'm the one who should be sorry."

"No. I'm sorry," I insisted.

"Nope," Gram countered. "I'm sorry."

I almost said it again then shook my head. "How about we agree that we're both sorry and table this conversation until later?"

"Works for me, child," she said, smiling. "I get all riled up when I talk about your mama's… Alana's death. I guess you never get over the loss of a child."

My heart hurt and I felt awful. "We don't have to talk about the sad parts. Ever."

"We do. Should have hashed it all out when I was alive, but it just never felt right," she said. "Now that I'm dead, I think we should give it a shot."

"We have really strange conversations," I said, relieved that she truly wanted to talk about my mother.

"That we do," she replied. "That we do, Daisy girl."

CHAPTER FOURTEEN

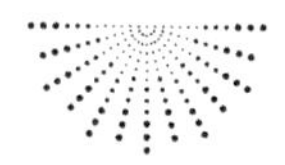

"You drive fast," I pointed out.

Gideon glanced over at me and grinned. "I've been in the car when you drive."

"Your point?" I inquired, loving that the morning after the best sex I'd ever had wasn't awkward in the least.

Everything felt natural and right—the way it was supposed to feel. I still got a little breathless when I looked at him, but I doubted that would ever go away.

"No point," he said. "Simply an observation that your driving skills make mine look amateur."

"You're saying you drive like a *granny*?" I teased.

"Not sure I would have chosen those words," he said, highly amused. "However, you definitely win that exchange."

"Thank you."

Gideon chuckled. "Wasn't exactly a compliment, but you're welcome."

I was silent as Gideon continued to navigate the country roads. John Travolta didn't live in town as I'd expected. I was sure he had a mansion on the ritzy side of town, but I was incorrect.

"So, John Travolta is a country kind of guy?" I asked, needing conversation to calm my nerves.

"One could say that."

"How long has he lived in his house?"

"About a hundred years, I'd guess—maybe a hundred and fifty," Gideon replied.

I scrunched my nose as questions flooded my brain. "In the *same* house?"

"Yes."

"How does that work? I mean, he clearly ages himself, but wouldn't people catch on? I would have thought you guys would relocate all the time so you wouldn't get busted for being, you know..."

"Older than dirt?" Gideon finished my sentence with a raised brow.

"I was looking for a nicer way to say it, but yes," I replied with a sheepish grin.

"The truth is the truth," he pointed out. "Some of us do move around, but this area has the strongest portal between Heaven and Hell in the Universe."

"So, most Immortals live around here and reinvent themselves every generation?"

Gideon nodded. "Many do. Occasionally, Immortals have to leave for a while. If we like a particular piece of property or a home, they simply leave it to a family member in their will. Then we take a quick leave of absence and return as the younger niece or nephew of the original owner."

"The original owner and the new owner being the same person."

"Yes," he said, casting a sideways glance at me. "Does the reality disturb you?"

Did it?

I shook my head. "No," I said, thinking it out as I spoke. I lived with dead people. Not much freaked me out lately. "Although, it's still surreal to me. The logistics are mind boggling. How long have you had your house in town?"

Gideon thought for a moment. "About seventy years, give or take a few."

"And have you died off and left it to a relative?"

Gideon again glanced over. "Once. Left it to my son. Gideon Jr."

"That's handy," I said with a laugh. "Do you own a lot of houses?"

"I do."

"How many?" I questioned.

Gideon shrugged. "Lost count."

"Dude," I said. "That's not right. One house should be enough for a person."

"I'll pare it down," he promised, amused.

"Wait. Do you have a house in Greece?" I asked.

Stories about Greece were something special I remembered about my mother. It was a vague and fuzzy memory, but I'd held on to it. She'd told me Greece was a magical place filled with love and that she would take me there one day. That had never happened, but the stories had stuck with me always.

"Three," he replied, looking guilty.

I laughed. "Keep one of them, please. I've never been to Greece and it's on my bucket list."

"Done," Gideon said with a smile. "I'm here to make your bucket list wishes come true."

The line was familiar. Steve had said something similar earlier. Both Steve and Gideon loved me. However, neither were or would ever be responsible for making my wishes come true. But it was a lovely thought.

"And John Travolta? Who did he leave his house to? A son? A brother? A long-lost nephew?" I asked.

"Not sure, you'll have to ask John Travolta."

"It's not really a social call," I reminded him.

"Correct," Gideon agreed. "However, that's exactly how we're going to treat it. For lack of a better way to put it, we'll call it a father-daughter get-together."

"Sperm donor and unwanted spawn slightly polite visit," I corrected him.

"Definitely more accurate," Gideon commented. "I'd suggest polite interaction unless he gives us reason to behave otherwise."

"Okay," I said, thinking going in with metaphorical guns drawn was probably a bad plan. "Does he know we're coming?"

"No. I figured since he's been fond of surprises lately, we'd give him a taste of his own medicine."

We drove on in silence. Unsure of how I was going to get the information I was after, like why he was reluctant to go after Clarissa, why she was after me, along with his life-long denial of me, I made plans A, B, C and D inside my head. With life as off-kilter as it was, I'd probably end up going with plan Z, but rolling with the changes had become my new way of life. It was that or the mental institution.

"We're here," Gideon said in a calm voice. "You ready?"

I nodded and swallowed back my fear and anger. Neither would serve me well this morning.

The tree-lined drive was impressive—manicured and lovely. However, the house made the landscaping pale in comparison.

John Travolta lived in an enormous white marble mansion. It was fascinatingly beautiful and horrible.

One could argue that the white exterior represented the purity of an Angel. On the other hand, one could say it was as cold as ice—lifeless and without character. I was of the second opinion.

Thinking about my old farmhouse, a small smile pulled at my lips. It wasn't perfect by anyone's standards, but it was loved and lived in. It had a warmth that was sorely missing here.

My stomach roiled and I grabbed the dashboard as Gideon parked in the circular drive.

Gideon's eyes narrowed with concern. "Daisy, what's wrong?"

"Having a déjà vu," I whispered, trying to figure out what it meant. "I think I've been here before."

"Here?" he questioned. "At this house or in this area?"

"This house," I said, squinting at it and trying like hell to remember. Adrenaline shot through my veins and my heart raced. Something was important, and I couldn't put my finger on it. Had something horrible happened here? "Maybe I dreamed it."

Gideon watched me as I worked through my panic. Did it matter if I'd been here? Had my mother described it to me as a child, and I just felt as if I'd seen it? Had I finally lost my ever-loving mind for real?

"Tell me what else you remember about it," Gideon said, rubbing my back for comfort. "Details. Any details you remember, tell me now before we go in."

"Have you been here before?" I asked.

"I have. What do you recall?"

Breathing in through my nose and exhaling slowly through my mouth, I closed my eyes. What would help was to run ten or twenty miles. Running let my thoughts come freely and without any filter on my part. Going for a run wasn't in the cards at the moment. Plus, I was wearing high-heeled boots and cashmere—not really running attire.

"Gold," I whispered as pictures raced across my mind. "Gold fountain. Paintings—frescos on the ceilings. Angels. Violent Angels. Pale pink clouds."

Gideon's hissed intake of breath wasn't what I wanted to hear. I was onto something.

"No rugs. Squares. White and gold square tiles on the floor."

Opening my eyes, I stared at Gideon. He stared right back at me.

"Am I right?"

"You are," he said tersely. "Do you remember when you were here? Who you were with?"

I shook my head. "No. I had to be young, but I don't remember anyone else being around. Could I have dreamed it?"

"I don't see how," Gideon said, gripping the steering wheel. "I'm not sure this visit is a good idea. I don't like how I feel right now. Too many puzzle pieces missing. It gives the Archangel the upper hand."

"Too late," I whispered.

John Travolta stood ten feet from Gideon's car and eyed us with curiosity. He didn't seem angry. Although, he certainly didn't seem excited to see us. He was more resigned than anything else. Maybe the man had known we were coming after all.

"Follow my lead," Gideon said.

"What are you going to do?" I asked.

"Not a clue," he replied. "You with me?"

"One hundred percent."

CHAPTER FIFTEEN

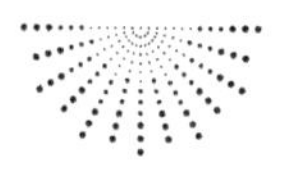

THE INTERIOR WAS EERILY LIKE THE MEMORIES I'D DESCRIBED. It did absolutely nothing to calm my already jangled nerves. It increased them. Today, I was unearthing parts of my past that I'd buried long ago. It wasn't fun.

"May I ask what brought you here today?" my father questioned as he led us through the grand foyer to an opulent office.

The office was unfamiliar. Gideon covertly caught my eye and I shook my head no. He nodded curtly.

"We were out for a drive and found ourselves in your neck of the woods," Gideon replied in a cold tone.

"I'm supposed to believe that?" the Archangel shot back equally as cool.

"You're welcome to believe what you want," Gideon said, taking a seat on a white marble bench in the office. "Not very comfortable."

"Not meant to be," my father replied with a dismissive shrug. "Ensures guests don't get too comfortable and overstay their welcome."

"Not very Southern of you," I commented, looking around.

"I'm not Southern," the Angel pointed out. "Have you heard from the Angel of Mercy?"

My head whipped up and I pinned the man with a glare. "No. Have you?"

He walked around his desk and seated himself before he spoke. "I have not."

"Did you warn her before she ran? Your reluctance to punish her is suspect," Gideon ground out as John Travolta's eyebrows shot up in surprise.

"I did not warn her," he said evenly. "Is that why you came? To ask me if I'd apprised Clarissa of the bounty on her head for her plethora of crimes?"

I narrowed my eyes at the man. "You clearly have a conflict of interest, Darth Vader."

"I thought it was John Travolta," he replied.

I shrugged. "I like to change it up."

"You're going to answer a few questions," Gideon announced.

"Am I?" The Angel raised a brow and glared at the Grim Reaper.

"You are, Archangel." Gideon smiled. It was not a nice smile. I'd have to classify it as terrifying.

"We shall see, Reaper."

This wasn't going what I would call well. Gideon and John Travolta didn't like each other a bit. It was becoming very clear that the meeting was going South—pun intended.

"Gideon," I said, wondering if I was making a gargantuan mistake. "Can you give my father and me a moment?"

Gideon jerked his head in my direction and looked at me as if I was nuts.

I was nuts.

However, I came for information and I wasn't going to get it at this rate.

"Bad plan," he hissed.

"The plan we're working with now is worse," I told him.

I was in love with Gideon, but that didn't mean he was always right. Not that I was either, but my gut said I'd get more out of the Angel if it was just him and me.

"You heard her," John Travolta said smugly. "Leave."

"Pipe down," I snapped at my father, whose expression registered shock at my rude admonishment. "I did not tell Gideon to leave at all. I'd just like to chat with you alone... with Gideon on the other side of the door."

"As you wish," Gideon said, standing up and moving to the door with great reluctance. He turned as he was about to leave and smiled once again at the Archangel. "If one hair on her body is harmed, I will destroy you. Heaven and Hell be damned."

"I'd expect no less," he answered, sounding unsurprised by the threat.

With a curt nod, Gideon left the office and closed the door behind him.

John Travolta and I stared at each other warily. He seemed as intimidated by me as I was of him. It was ludicrous since he could most likely turn me to ash with a flick of his hand.

"I will answer two questions, Daisy," he said, still seated behind his big desk. "Choose them carefully."

"Your cryptic games are getting boring," I said, approaching his desk. It felt good to be looking down at him. The man was much taller than I was, but from this vantage point I felt more in control.

He shrugged. "Not games. Parameters."

"Safe limits so you don't reveal yourself," I said with an eye roll. "Nice."

"Call it what you wish. It is what it is. What do you want to know?"

"I've been here before," I said flatly. "A very long time ago."

His eyes widened ever so slightly. It was barely noticeable, but my eyesight was killer now.

"That wasn't a question," he said mildly.

"Correct," I agreed. "It wasn't. Say her name. Say my mother's name."

"Not a question," John Travolta snapped as a brief flash of sadness passed his handsome features.

"It was a demand," I said. "You owe me a few things."

He sat silently and stared at me. I held his gaze. The length of the stare-down went far past what was considered socially polite, but it was an unusual situation. Under normal circumstances, I would have dropped my gaze.

Not today.

"You look so much like her," he whispered.

"Her name. Say it."

Michael the Archangel closed his golden eyes and said the name of the woman he'd impregnated to the child they'd created together—the child he hadn't wanted. "Alana. Her name is Alana."

"Was," I corrected him. "Her name *was* Alana. She's dead."

"Yes."

"Did you love her?" I asked, and then shook my head in disgust.

It wasn't one of the questions I wanted to ask. I'd just wasted a request on a child's need to know her daddy loved her mommy.

"I did. With everything I am," he replied. "Second question?"

If I could have kicked my own ass, I would have. I was an idiot and he was a liar. If he loved my mother, he had a shitty way of showing it. Taking back control was necessary. Statements and demands were in order.

"Clarissa is after me and I don't know why," I began, then held up my hand as he started to speak. "That wasn't a question. It was backstory so you'll be able to answer to my satisfaction."

John Travolta sat back in his chair with an expression I thought might be pride. I had to be mistaken. Wishful thinking would screw me up. The man didn't give a crap about me.

"Please continue," he said.

"I will," I shot back. "I thought it had to do with my relationship with Gideon, but Clarissa was the cause of Steve's death long before I knew Gideon. There has to be another reason behind her actions."

"Are you sure it's you she's after?" my father asked.

The question was absurd, but he'd left himself open. Today I would miss no openings.

"If you ask a question, I get an extra one," I informed him.

He sighed then chuckled. "As you wish."

I had two questions again now. "Yes, I'm sure it's me she's after. She killed my husband and tried to send him wrongly into the darkness. Pretty heavy evidence that she's trying to destroy me."

"There are shades of gray around every corner," he replied, as cryptic as ever.

I was tempted to ask him to be more specific, but that was a question. His idea of specificity could be more cryptic than the statement I wanted clarified.

"Ambiguity is such an unfortunate personality trait," I said. "Doesn't really look good on you."

It didn't look good on me either, but at least I was working on it. Maybe I'd inherited it...

"Be that as it may, facts change when you live as long as I have," he pointed out. "Vague statements tend to hold true far longer."

I called him Darth Vader, but I should switch to Yoda with the *truisms* he was spouting. I did not want to leave this meeting more confused than when I came in.

"Whatever," I said rudely. It was a little difficult to be rude on purpose, but I was seriously annoyed. "I believe that you know exactly why Clarissa is after me."

"You have proof?" he asked.

"Nope, but I did just earn another question," I shot back. "I have three now."

John Travolta arched a brow in surprise. "I'm not on my game this fine morning. So be it. Ask your questions."

"Why is the Angel of Mercy out to destroy me?"

"She's not out to get you," he replied. "Two more questions."

"Were you born an asshole and a liar or did living forever make you that way?" I shouted.

"That was two," John Travolta said. "I'm not lying. As to being an asshole, it would depend on with whom you're speaking."

Shit. I'd wasted another question and got a lie in return. Fine. There was no cryptic way around the next question.

"If it's not me, then who is she after?" I hissed, wanting to headbutt the Archangel.

He eyed me for a long moment. Again, I held his stare.

He was the first to look away.

"Answer me. You made the rules. Play by them," I ground out.

"The Angel of Mercy's ire is directed at Alana. It has been Alana the entire time."

"Repeat yourself," I demanded. "Now."

"Clarissa wants to destroy your mother—not you."

I came as close to an out-of-body experience as I'd ever had. The ringing in my ears was high-pitched and made me grind my teeth. My hatred for the man who was a lying sack of shit grew to a proportion I was unable to control.

My instincts took over and it wasn't pretty. In the

moment, I felt no shame. I had no clue how I would feel later, but I didn't give a damn.

There was no shade of gray lurking around the corner.

This was a black-and-white situation. The lies had to end.

"Liar!" I screamed, diving across the desk with the intention of rearranging John Travolta's face.

Gideon burst into the room just as I got one solid, bone-cracking punch in. I felt the sensation reverberate all the way up my arm into my shoulder when my fist connected to his face. My father's head jerked back, but he didn't lift a finger to defend himself.

If I wasn't crazy—and that was entirely up for debate, considering I'd just delivered a powerful left hook to the face of an Archangel—I would have said he looked relieved that I'd punched him. Unfortunately, Gideon pulled me off of the Angel before I could test the theory.

My behavior horrified me, but I wasn't ready or able to stop.

"No, Daisy," Gideon said as he held my live-wire body tight against his chest. "What the fuck did you say to her?"

My father gingerly touched his nose, which was broken if the gushing blood was anything to go by. I knew I could slip from Gideon's embrace easily, but it was a good idea to stay put right now. My rage was still at a boiling point and my fists wouldn't unclench.

"The truth," John Travolta said, tonelessly. "I told Daisy the truth."

"Bullshit," I hissed. "My mother is in the darkness. You know that as well as I do. Why Clarissa would be after a dead woman living in Hell is beyond me. It's the stupidest excuse to protect the Angel of Mercy I've heard yet. You disgust me!"

My father's expression deserved an Academy Award. His confusion at my statement was so truthful and honest, I laughed. He was one hell of an actor.

"Alana is not in the darkness," he said, shaking his head.

"Again, I call bullshit," I snapped. "What is wrong with you? She committed suicide. That's a guaranteed trip to Hell, from what I understand."

Gideon's hold loosened, and he turned me around in his arms so we were face to face.

"Daisy, your mother is not in the darkness," he said.

This could not be happening. Was it Lie to Daisy Day?

Twisting out of Gideon's grasp, I heard a grunt of surprise from John Travolta. I was sure letting him know my strength wasn't in my best interest, but he should have gotten a clue when I'd broken his nose so easily.

My own violent streak shocked me, but to be told something I knew as truth was a lie—something as serious as my mother's *death and afterlife*—short-wired my tenuous grip on sanity.

Pacing the office and wanting to peel the skin off my body, I did breathing exercises. They weren't helping, except they did stop me from speaking. I had nothing nice to say. Usually, in that situation I said nothing. However, I was sorely tempted to say all kinds of awful things right now.

I was ready to tell both of them to take a hike. My new plan was to round up Heather, Tim and Candy. We could go after Clarissa ourselves. Maybe Charlie would join my new team. He was an insane badass.

However, when we found her... she was mine.

Gideon and John Travolta were out.

And now I needed to get out.

Slipping off my high-heeled boots, I held one in each hand. I was sure I would cut my feet up running fifteen miles barefoot, but the pain would be refreshing after the lie-fest.

"Daisy," Gideon said carefully. "What are you doing?"

"I'm leaving."

"I'll take you home," he said.

John Travolta still seemed to be absorbing all I had said.

"Gonna run," I replied. "Need a little *alone* time."

"Please be seated," my father said, eyeing both Gideon and me. "I'm perturbed by this conversation, and we need to get to the bottom of why Daisy believes Alana is in the darkness."

"Nope," I said, walking to the door. "I'm good. Had about all the bullshit I can take today."

The door slammed shut by itself and a strong wind laced with gold flecks picked me up and set me on the bench next to Gideon. I was literally glued to the damn bench.

John Travolta was cheating, and I was having none of it.

Slicing my hand through the air, I cut through whatever spell he'd cast and stood back up.

"That was all kinds of rude, Darth Vader," I snapped as he stared at me like I had three heads. "I will not be kept anywhere against my will. Ever. You feel me?"

"Dear God," he gasped out, looking down at his hands in utter disbelief. "How?"

"She can also escape my embrace," Gideon said, watching me with the same surprised awe as my father.

"She can escape death?" my father choked out.

"*She* is right here," I snapped at both men. "And I really don't see the big deal. I don't like to be trapped. No-brainer."

"Yet you have no footprint," John Travolta said, perplexed.

"Correct," I replied with an eye roll.

The men silently stared, and I began to grow uncomfortable.

And guilty.

Shit.

Closing my eyes, I dropped my boots to the floor and joined them. I wanted to curl into a ball and cry like a child. While John Travolta made a practice of lying to me, Gideon did not. Hell was large, I would think. Was it possible he didn't know all the residents?

"My mother is in the darkness," I said softly. "She fell in love with one of the dead she was counseling. I don't know what sins he committed in life, but he went into the darkness. In order to follow him, she killed herself so she could join him in Hell."

The room was silent. I didn't make eye contact with either man.

"How do you know this?" my father inquired, sounding older than time itself. "Who told you this?"

Glancing up at him, I felt bad that I'd busted his nose. Why? I had no clue. He'd deserved it, but...

"Gram," I said hollowly. "Gram told me."

Gideon sat down on the hard marble floor next to me. He extended his hand and I warily took it. "How would Gram have known this? Did your mother leave a note behind?"

I was stunned. He'd made an interesting point—and one I'd never even considered. How *did* Gram know? She'd told me she wasn't familiar with my mother's beaus—not even John Travolta, who'd knocked my mother up. Gram couldn't see the dead after my mother took over as the Death Counselor, so there was no possibility that she knew the ghost my mother had fallen in love with and followed into the darkness.

"She must have left some kind of note," I whispered, wondering for the first time if the information was incorrect. "She had to have left a suicide note. No other way Gram could have known."

"She fell from a bridge," my father said. "She did not jump. Alana would not have left a suicide note since it wasn't a suicide."

My bullshit detector was exploding in my brain. The damn thing was probably broken. It flashed so fast and bright, I had to close my eyes. "And you know this how?" I asked in an icy tone. "Were you there? Or maybe you pushed her?"

"I loved her," he said. "I would have never harmed her."

"But I'm fair game?" I asked emotionlessly.

John Travolta said nothing. At least he didn't lie this time.

I looked at Gideon. The pain in his expression matched what was raging inside me. I trusted the Grim Reaper. I loved him and I knew he loved me.

"She's not in the darkness?" I whispered.

He shook his head. "She is not in the darkness. I promise you."

"No chance you might have missed her?" I tried again. I wanted to believe him so badly, I could taste it.

"Not a chance," Gideon replied.

I nodded and sighed. "So, she's in the light?"

Gideon and I both turned our heads to the Archangel. He met our gazes evenly and without hesitation.

"Answer me," I insisted.

"Alana is destined for the light. That's all I can say."

If looks could kill, John Travolta would be dead. Hate didn't begin to describe what I felt for the man.

Gideon stood and helped me to my feet. "You ready to leave?"

Turning to my father, I tried one last time. "Are you going to answer any more of my questions?"

"I can't," he replied.

"You won't," I contradicted him.

The man said nothing. I'd expected the response. I'd hoped I was wrong.

I wasn't.

"I'm ready to leave," I told Gideon then turned my attention to the evil behind the desk. "I despise you."

My father nodded. His face was devoid of emotion. "As you should."

His answer was as horrible as anything I'd heard him say. It was a knife to my gut.

Without another word, I turned and left. Gideon followed.

"Where should I take you?"

"Home," I said, feeling so tired I just wanted to sleep. "I need to have a chat with Gram."

CHAPTER SIXTEEN

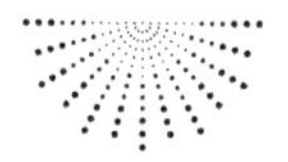

Gram's grayish complexion paled considerably. My stomach cramped and guilt ate away at me. Upsetting the woman who I loved unconditionally by asking her to talk about her only child's death went against every instinct I had. Her confusion threw me, but doors that were once closed and locked slowly began to creak open.

"It's the truth," Gram insisted, her expression perplexed and her eyes huge. "It has to be."

Staying calm was key. I sucked up the need to freak out. It would get us nowhere fast. The pieces of the missing puzzle were important. I could feel it in my bones. But did all the pieces go to the same puzzle? I was pretty sure I was close to at least a couple damned pieces that might fit together, but the picture I was creating was anyone's guess right now.

"Okay," I said. "But tell me how you know she took her own life. Did Alana leave a note?"

Gram tsked and waved her finger at me. "Daisy girl, it's disrespectful to call your mama by her first name. I won't be havin' a conversation if you can't mind your manners."

Looking down at the whitewashed slats on the front porch, I counted to ten and remained even-tempered. Gram wasn't making it easy. She was grabbing at straws to avoid answering my question.

"Sorry," I said, to keep her calm. "You're right. I was rude, and I was brought up better than that. I understand this is difficult, but I need you to answer me, please."

Gram nodded and wrung her hands nervously. "Feelin' kind of sick," she muttered. "Darnedest thing, since I'm dead. You'd think you wouldn't get a bellyache after you kicked the bucket."

"That is strange." It was odd that she felt a physical ailment. None of the others, even with the frequent loss of body parts, had ever complained of normal human aches and pains.

She fluttered around the porch and shook her head so fast, I thought she might be having a seizure.

Shit. This was a terrible idea. I sure as hell hoped the outcome was worth it.

"Come on over here," I said, sitting down on the swing and patting the seat next to me.

We were the only two on the porch. Gideon had gone in the house with Steve and a few other squatters when we'd arrived, and I'd stayed outside with Gram. Jimmy Joe Johnson had wanted to hang around, but I'd asked him politely for some privacy.

He'd cried for about ten minutes, but eventually

departed. I didn't enjoy hurting his feelings, but the Unofficial Mayor of Squatter Town was quite the cry baby. I never knew what might set him off.

"Come sit, please," I coaxed her with a smile.

Gram floated over warily and seated herself next to me.

"Take my hands," I requested, reaching out to her.

"Oh Daisy," she whispered sadly as she placed her cold hands in mine. "I'm scared. I lost her, and now I feel like I'm gonna lose you, too."

"It's okay, Gram," I promised. "I'm right here. I'm going to tell you a few things that I learned—not sure I believe them yet, but that's where you come in."

"I'm puttin' on my big girl panties," Gram said, holding her chin high. "Not that I change my panties anymore."

Despite the serious nature of what I was about to share, I couldn't help myself and grinned. "That's kind of gross," I pointed out.

"Darlin', it's a perk of being dead," she informed me with a wink.

She was relaxed and more herself. I needed her to stay that way.

"I love you, Gram."

"Love you more, sweetheart."

"You going to stay with me?" I asked cautiously.

She nodded. "If I freak, just yank me out of the air and slap me upside the head."

"Mmmkay," I said with a small smile. "I don't think my mother is in the darkness."

Gram eyes lit up with joy for the briefest of moments

and then dilated strangely. Her body jerked and trembled. The reaction was bizarre.

"Can't be, Daisy girl," she whispered woodenly. "Your mama killed herself to follow her lover into the darkness. Suicide. Guaranteed ticket to Hell."

"Can I see the note she left?"

"What note?" Gram asked, confused and still sounding robotic.

"Her suicide note," I clarified. "She had to have left one or you wouldn't have known the circumstances of how she died."

"Your mama killed herself to follow her lover into the darkness. Suicide. Guaranteed ticket to Hell," she repeated like a broken record.

"You met her lover?" I pressed.

"No," Gram said, tilting her head to the side and squinting at me. "Did you?"

"No, I couldn't see the dead when I was little," I reminded her. "Ohhh, of course you didn't meet her lover. You couldn't see the dead then, either. Right?"

"Yep," Gram said. "Once your mama took over, the dead went away just like they did when you took over. Your mama never brought her beaus around."

"Right," I said, nodding slowly. "So, you don't even know for sure if she *had* a lover who went to the darkness."

"Your mama killed herself to follow her lover into the darkness. Suicide. Guaranteed ticket to Hell," Gram said in a monotone, growing agitated and paler.

If she wasn't already deceased, I would think I was killing her.

Something clicked in my brain. What if getting her to admit she might be wrong could destroy her?

The thought was horrendous, but it was possible.

Anything was possible...

Change of plans. One where Gram would stay safe and I could possibly find out the truth. Which meant speaking to Heather was on the top of my list.

"You're right, Gram. I guess it's just wishful thinking on my part," I said, squeezing her hands gently. "I'm so sorry. I don't know what I was thinking."

Her relief made me want to cry. "No worries, Daisy child. Everyone gets confused."

"How about we watch a marathon of *The Price Is Right*?" I suggested as her eyes went back to normal and a bit of color came back to her papery cheeks.

"That sounds like a right fine idea," she said with a grin. "Haven't spent any time with my boyfriend Bob in a few days.

"Jimmy Joe Johnson isn't jealous of Bob?" I asked with a smile of relief that she was no longer in a robotic state.

"Nah," Gram said with a cackle. "Jimmy Joe has him a crush on Vanna White. Works out just fine."

"I'm sure it does," I said with a tiny eye roll and a laugh as I followed Gram into the house.

"*Price Is Right* in Daisy's bedroom," Gram hollered to the ghosts as she flew around the living room and headed for the stairs. "You comin' darlin'?"

"Go on up," I said. "I'll be there in a few."

I felt Gideon's eyes on me as I paced the living room and muttered to myself.

"You okay?" he asked warily as Steve floated next to him, equally concerned.

"Can you call a meeting together while I watch an episode of *The Price Is Right* with Gram?" I asked.

Gideon nodded.

"Great," I said, giving him a quick kiss then starting up the stairs.

"Daisy?" Gideon asked.

"Yes?" I looked back at him.

"You want to give me a few more details?"

Smacking myself in the forehead, I groaned. "That would probably be helpful."

"It might," Gideon agreed with a grin.

"I need Tim, Candy Vargo, Charlie, Heather, you and Darth Vader to be here." I checked my watch and debated if I should wait till tomorrow.

Nope. The ball was rolling and I wasn't going to drop it.

"What time?" Gideon asked, pulling out his cell phone.

"Two," I replied. "But ask Heather if she can be here at one-thirty please."

"Am I giving a reason for the gathering?" he inquired, curious himself.

I paused and stared at the man I loved. "No. Just tell them to be here."

"Roger that," he said, looking at me strangely. "Go watch the show. I'll take care of it."

My heart sped up and I wanted to tell him what I had planned, but something stopped me.

"Thank you."

"Always, Daisy," he said. "I will always have your back."

I nodded, afraid I was going to word vomit everything inside my head. I couldn't take the chance he would talk me out of it. With one last smile, I turned and mounted the stairs.

I knew Gideon hadn't done it. Actually, I would bet my life on it. He was with me when I'd told the story to John Travolta that I'd always believed. However, while I trusted Gideon completely, everyone else was guilty until proven innocent.

"How hard is it to reverse a thought planted in someone's mind?" I asked Heather. "And what would it do to the person? Would it hurt them?"

"Hello to you, too," she said, entering the house.

"Sorry. Hi," I said, taking her coat and hanging it in the foyer closet. "Can the magic be reversed?"

"Why?" she asked, perplexed. "I don't think the thoughts I put in Jennifer, June and Missy's heads are harmful. I mean, I was stupid to have done it without asking you first, but—"

"Not what I'm talking about." I took her by the arm and led her to the kitchen where we would have privacy. I didn't need Gram overhearing. She still wasn't quite right in the head. Actually, none of us were quite right in the head, but she wasn't completely back to herself yet.

Gideon had run out to Smithee's Wine and Cheese Shop to pick up some snacks. Smithee's was normally out of my price range, but Gideon had insisted on paying. For a second, I wondered how much money he had, but stopped myself just short of asking. The answer would probably make me pass out, and I didn't have time for that.

The meeting wasn't exactly a party, but in the South, food was required at any gathering longer than a half hour.

"Explain to me why you want to know that," Heather said, opening the fridge and searching for a bottle of water.

"First answer the question," I said.

Heather found the water, took a long swallow and eyed me with concern. "I've never reversed it," she said. "I've only planted thoughts twice."

"In Jennifer, June and Missy?"

"Yes, and once a few hundred years ago," she confirmed. "I'm not exactly proud of any of it, but both times it was to help someone I loved."

A feeling of relief washed over me. I didn't think Heather had planted the false story of my mother's death into Gram's mind, but since I was aware she could do it, I couldn't rule her out… until now. Hopefully. A little more insurance was needed.

"Who is the person you would die for?" I asked.

"What kind of question is that?" Heather demanded.

"A very serious one."

"Daisy," Heather said, wildly confused. "What is going on?"

"Please just answer."

Heather ran her hands through her hair and sucked her bottom lip into her mouth. "Missy. I would die for Missy."

"Would you be willing to swear on Missy's life that those

two times were the only two times you planted new memories?"

"Swearing on the life of someone I love is harsh," Heather said slowly. "However, whatever it is you're not telling me is clearly important. Correct?"

I nodded and waited.

Heather took another sip and sighed. "Yes. I would swear on Missy's life that the two instances I told you about were the only times I've planted memories."

Blowing out the breath I didn't know I was holding, I sat down at the kitchen table and closed my eyes. "Thank God," I whispered.

"You believe in God now?" she asked, sitting down across from me and handing me her half-drunk bottle of water.

"I believe enough to say thank you," I said with a weak smile and took a sip.

"Okay," she said, clearly still confused. "You going to tell me why we're having this discussion?"

"I am," I promised. "But I need you to explain something else first."

"Shoot," she said, resting her elbows on the table and leaning forward.

"If the thoughts were reversed—back to the truth—what would happen?"

Heather grew pensive and rubbed her temples. "Honestly, I don't know."

"You have to know," I insisted. This was not part of my plan. Heather was a gazillion years old. She *had* to know.

"I'm not comfortable reversing anything I planted in

Missy, June or Jennifer," she said firmly. "While what I did wasn't exactly ethical, it didn't harm them in any way. And it got you out of having to explain the unexplainable."

"I'm not asking you to do that," I told her.

"Then what are you asking me to do?" Heather asked, growing frustrated.

I didn't blame her, but I needed to understand as much as I could before I laid all my cards on the table.

"Hypothetically speaking... could you reverse the thoughts planted in someone's mind if you hadn't planted them?"

She stared at me like I was crazy. That was already a given and didn't bother me a bit.

"No," she said, standing up, walking back over to the fridge and pulling out a full-sugared Coke.

Heather didn't drink soda. Ever. I'd clearly rattled her.

"Only the person who put the thoughts in the mind can reverse it... that is, if it can be reversed at all," she said, wincing as she took a sip of the soda.

"If you drink that you're going to be wired," I pointed out.

"Already am," she said. "Daisy, if you need my help, you have to tell me what's going on."

"Fine. I agree," I said, taking the Coke from her and finishing it off in one enormous swallow. "I think someone implanted the wrong cause of my mother's death in Gram's mind. She's always believed that my mother fell in love with one of the dead she was counseling and followed him into the darkness by committing suicide."

"Oh my God," Heather said, scanning the kitchen counter. "Where are the cookies June made?"

"In the cookie jar," I said.

"Of course they are," she muttered, bringing the entire jar over to the table and digging in. "So, tell me this. How do you know that's not true?"

"Because my mother isn't in the darkness," I said as Heather practically choked on her cookie.

"Did you ask Gideon?"

I nodded and grabbed a cookie. "And John Travolta."

"Is she in the light?" Heather asked, trying to piece together the story.

"Daddy Dearest said she's destined for the light. Kind of sounds like she might be in limbo somewhere."

"Pardon my sailor mouth, but that's fucked up," Heather said flatly. "Never heard of that."

"You've also never heard of a Soul Keeper," I reminded her.

"True," she agreed. "Did you try to tell Gram the truth?"

"As much of it as I know," I confirmed.

"And?" Heather pressed, curious.

"She went kind of robot-zombie on me—got incredibly upset and kept repeating the exact same phrase—*Your mama killed herself to follow her lover into the darkness. Suicide. Guaranteed ticket to Hell.*"

"Holy shit," Heather muttered. "And that's why you called the meeting? To figure out who implanted the wrong information?"

I nodded, feeling all kinds of guilty. "I'm—"

"Daisy, don't," Heather said, touching my hand. "I'm

going to hope you didn't think I would do something like that, but I also understand how much Gram means to you."

"I'm sorry," I said, wishing I hadn't just downed a soda and five cookies. My stomach roiled.

"Nope. No apologies," Heather said. "None. If I'm being honest… *and I am,* I'd do the same."

I still felt wonky, but I did what I had to do and one of my best friend's wasn't furious with me. So far so good.

"Do you know who else can plant memories? Can John Travolta?" I asked.

Heather was silent for a long moment. "I don't know. But I sure as hell can help you find out. You think this will get us closer to finding Clarissa?"

"I don't know," I conceded, twisting my hair in my fingers. I watched Donna the Destroyer chase her tail around the kitchen and hoped I wasn't doing the same thing. "However, it gets us closer to *something.*"

"Your logic is…" Heather started.

"Flawed," I finished for her. "However, it's a puzzle piece. I'm starting to believe everything might be connected in some kind of farked-up way."

Heather took in what I said then nodded. "I've got your back, Daisy."

"I love you, Heather."

"Right back at you."

CHAPTER SEVENTEEN

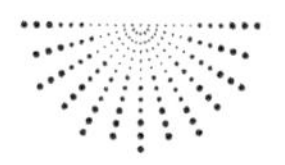

IMMORTALS WERE PROMPT. THEY WERE NOT A MINUTE EARLY and they were not a second late.

Heather and Gideon were already here. At two sharp, everyone else I'd invited had arrived on my doorstep. One was bearing a gift and one came with needles. I wasn't thrilled about the needles, but it would save me a trip to the lab.

"I brought a dish," Tim announced with pride as my dogs sniffed the air then slunk away.

Donna and Karen's reaction didn't bode well for Tim's culinary skills. My dogs would eat anything—including poop. Tim didn't notice that the aroma had offended my dogs. He kept right on talking.

"Found the recipe in a cookbook I failed to deliver due to the recipient calling me an unsavory name. This particular individual, who shall remain nameless, also cheats on her taxes, has procured an illegal cable box and lives in the blue house with the overgrown lawn three doors down from the park on South Street. I felt justified in keeping the cookbook... among other things. The wonderful part of the story is that I just so happened to have all of the ingredients in my pantry."

"Wow," I said, taking the enormous tin-foil-covered platter from his hands while breathing through my mouth so I couldn't smell it. There was a whole hell of a lot wrong with his *story*, but I refused to take the bait. I'd deal with it another time. "Thank you."

Tim winked. "I'm working towards an A," he whispered. "I also refrained from rehoming three of the twelve vibrators that went through the mail system this week."

It was tempting to ask him what he had done with the other nine, but I didn't want to know. Tim had now dropped from a B- to a D+ with a little extra credit for bringing food to the meeting. It was irrelevant if it was inedible.

"For the most part, I'm proud of you," I told him, praying he wasn't the one. In a very short time, Tim had wedged his way into my heart and I was completely fine with it. I enjoyed him—even with his penchant for outlandish illegal activities.

"Thank you," he replied, pulling a piece of paper from the pocket of his uniform. "I wasn't sure what kind of party this was going to be, so I prepared some trivia."

"Umm... it's not really that kind of gathering," I told him.

Tim's chin dropped to his chest and he made a squeaky noise that brought my guilt roaring to the forefront. The man was crushed.

Shit.

"However, a bit of trivia could lighten the mood," I said, sure I would regret trying to spare his feelings.

"I wouldn't eat that crap," Candy Vargo announced, pointing to the platter and waltzing around my house like she owned it.

"Candy Vargo, you're makin' my butt itch," Gram snapped, appearing from out of nowhere and getting up in Candy's face. "You're gonna need to slap that yap trap shut. I don't see you bearin' any hostess gift. Tim here is workin' on his manners. It's not goin' real well, but he's tryin'. It don't matter that what he brought smells like a wet dog after a polecat bath."

"Thank you," Tim said to Gram while making a face at Candy.

It was shocking to watch people who were older than time act like fourth graders.

"She just said your dish smelled like a skunk's ass," Candy pointed out gleefully to Tim.

"That's it," Gram shouted as Candy realized she'd gone about ten steps too far and dove behind the armchair to avoid Gram's wrath. "I'm gonna jerk your tail in a knot and cancel your dang birth certificate. You apologize to Tim right this second."

"Are you serious?" Candy asked, appalled.

Gram's eyes narrowed to slits. "Do I look serious to you?" she demanded.

"I'm going to go with a yes," Candy muttered, terrified.

Gram was dead. She was a ghost. Candy was Karma. She

controlled fate. The exchange fascinated me. Bottom line... don't screw with fate and *never* screw with Gram.

"Can't hear ya," Gram said, putting her hand up to her ear.

"I have to do it now? In front of everyone?" Candy asked, feeling the situation out.

Charlie and John Travolta wandered into the house after chatting on the porch and watched the standoff with interest. Heather and Gideon came out of the kitchen to see what the fuss was about and ten ghosts floated down the stairs for the show.

"Yep," Gram snapped, slapping her hands on her hips. "I'm doin' this for your own good, Candy Vargo. You've been alive far too long to have such crappy manners, bless your heart. But now you have me, and I'm gonna fix you if it's the last thing I do."

"Good luck," Heather said, putting an array of fancy hors d'oeuvres on the coffee table.

"I'd suggest you apologize," Charlie said, grinning. "Gram means business."

"No one asked you," Candy shot back and walked over to Tim. Sucking in a huge breath, bouncing on her toes for a few minutes and then finally letting out a pained groan, she did as she was told—kind of. "Gram says I have to say I'm sorry."

The dead squatters applauded Candy's shitty apology, but Gram was having none of it.

"What the ever-lovin' hell kind of apology was that?" Gram hissed.

"It was fine," Tim said with a chuckle. "For Candy, it was

exceptional. I accept."

"Daisy," Charlie said, placing a leather case on the sofa. "Do you mind if I draw some blood before we get started?"

Now was as good a time as any. John Travolta seated himself on the armchair that Candy had been hiding behind and watched silently. He was uncomfortable being here, and I didn't care. In the *Land of Make Believe,* I'd dreamed of having a father. In the *Land of Reality,* it sucked. I didn't want him in my home. Missy had given me sage a while back and I planned to put it to good use later this afternoon.

My gut said Darth Vader hadn't planted the false information in Gram's mind, but my gut had been wrong many times. If it had served his purpose to do it, he would.

"Normally, I'd do this at the lab," Charlie said in his kind way. "But since I was coming by, I thought we could get it done lickety-split."

"Sure," I said, handing Tim the odiferous platter then rolling up my sleeve. I was happy I'd downed a soda and ate a bunch of cookies. Giving blood made me light-headed. I had no clue how much blood Charlie would need to take. "What will you test for?"

Charlie pulled out some needles, syringes, tubes and antiseptic wipes. "Irregular DNA and other abnormalities. I was able to pull your file from last year's physical so I have something to test the new data against."

"Is that legal, Enforcer?" Candy queried with a grin.

Charlie turned his attention to Candy and gave her a look that wiped the grin right off her face. "That is the pot-calling-the-kettle-black kind of question from you, Karma," he said, sharply. "I'd suggest you rethink speaking. It won't end well... for you."

I was relieved Charlie didn't blast Candy with a bolt of lightning. I'd already had the discussion with Gideon about electrocution being off limits in the house. I was not looking forward to having the same conversation with Charlie.

Refocusing on me, Charlie smiled politely. "Daisy, is there anything you'd like me to check while I'm at it?"

"Umm... I think you have it covered," I said, digesting the word *abnormalities*. I could tell Charlie right now I was abnormal—no blood test needed.

"After Charlie drains you dry, I have sustenance for you, Daisy," Tim said, walking over to the coffee table.

"That's a joke, right?" I choked out.

"It is," Tim said proudly. "Not many get my jokes like you do."

"I didn't," I muttered under my breath as Charlie chuckled.

Shoving the snazzy hors d'oeuvres over, Tim made room in the very center for his edible offering. I held my breath as he removed the foil. I was pretty sure I was going to have to eat one of whatever he'd brought.

"Tada!" Tim said as everyone stared in confusion at the platter.

"What in tarnation is that?" Gram asked, hovering over the table to get a better look.

"I'm glad she asked before I did," Candy mumbled.

"Is it s'mores?" Heather asked politely.

"No. I don't think so," Gideon said, squinting at it.

"There's bread on it and something I believe was pinkish at one point."

"My bad," Heather said quickly. "I thought the burnt part might be marshmallows. I just *love* burnt marshmallows," she added, realizing she'd just insulted the hell out of Tim.

Thankfully, Tim's lack of social skills made it very difficult to insult him.

"It's Pigs in a Blanket," he informed the group. "I might have overcooked them a bit, but I'm sure they're still delicious. My cat loved it, and she's quite picky."

"They look wonderful," I lied.

Pulling out his trivia notes, Tim gave us a quick lesson on charred, bread-wrapped hotdogs.

"Pigs in a Blanket are also fondly known as Devils on Horseback, Kilted Sausages and Weiner Winks."

"I call 'em cocktail weenies slapped in a biscuit," Candy offered as she grabbed one and shoved it in her mouth. "A little crunchy, but edible."

Tim was thrilled with Candy's assessment and felt the need to further enlighten us. "Very easy to make," he went on. "It's simply a small frankfurter wrapped in croissant dough. The wieners are typically small in size, but a hotdog can be used in a pinch. Some people use Vienna Sausages, but my cat hates those and I don't keep them in the house."

"Okay then," Charlie said with a polite smile and a nod to Tim. "I'll just take a bit of Daisy's blood and then we can move on to the agenda."

"Works for me," I said, sticking out my arm and turning my head away. Needles were not my thing.

Unfortunately, my father was directly in my sightline.

He wasn't looking at me. He stared at the photo on the side table. It was a picture of Gram, my mother and me. He slowly raised his hand and touched it so reverently, I felt like I was seeing something I shouldn't.

Gideon saw it was well and caught my eye.

Raising a brow, he silently asked me if I was okay. I smiled and nodded. I didn't think he could read my mind, but he was so in tune with my feelings it was eerie… and hot… which led to inappropriate thoughts. Of all the things I shouldn't be thinking of, my mind went to the daisy-filled magical bedroom. Again, I was fairly sure the Grim Reaper might be able to read my mind. He grinned at me in a way that made my breath catch in my throat.

"Almost done," Charlie said, capping a tube full of my blood and hooking up another. "You have wonderful veins."

"Thank you, Charlie." A compliment was still a compliment even if it had to do with announcing to a room that I had big veins.

"My pleasure, Daisy," Charlie said, capping off the last bottle, removing the needle and putting a Band-Aid on my arm.

Charlie was sincere and sweet. It was difficult to remember he was the Enforcer and that when he was pissed his eyes turned silver and his fingers sparked.

My father checked his watch and cleared his throat. "Is there a reason we're gathered? I have business to attend to."

"You're lackin' some manners, too," Gram said, giving him a nasty look. "However, I don't like you enough to crawl up your ass. You don't deserve the time of day from me."

John Travolta had the decency to look embarrassed. "You are correct. I'm sorry."

"Lots of mea culpas going around this afternoon," Heather said, pouring lemonade into glasses. "Why don't we just try to tolerate each other for a bit?"

"Excellent plan," Tim agreed. "I have more trivia if anyone is interested."

"Hold that thought," I said, rolling down my sleeve and glancing around the room. "Gram, where is Steve?"

"He's in the cellar with Birdie," she said, shaking her head. "She's not doin' so good."

"You have a cellar?" Heather asked, handing me a drink.

"Crawlspace," I told her, then realized this was a good out. I was worried about Birdie and she was next on my list, but I didn't want Gram here for the meeting. "Gram, could you go to the cellar and help Steve cheer Birdie up?"

"It's a crawlspace, Daisy girl," she corrected me.

"Umm... right," I said, shaking my head. "Could you go to the crawlspace and give her some Gram love?"

"You bet your bippy I can! Dead folks," she called out. "Let's go take care of our gal. Birdie is not right in the head and thinks it's funny when body parts fall off. I figure we can all rip our arms off and put on a little show to turn her frown upside down."

The squatters squealed and zipped around the living room with excitement at the thought of dismembering themselves and then playing Whac-A-Mole with their appendages.

I really needed to buy some stock in superglue.

"I'd like to go to the crawlspace," Candy Vargo said. "That sounds like an excellent time."

"Later," I told her. "You can go after the meeting."

Candy rolled her eyes and piled a plate high with Tim's Wiener Winks.

"Let's get this show on the road," Heather said, sitting down on the couch.

The clock was ticking and I needed answers.

CHAPTER EIGHTEEN

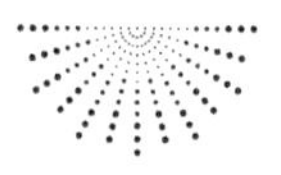

I CIRCLED THE ROOM AND MADE SURE EVERYONE HAD something to eat. It was ingrained in my *abnormal* DNA that I feed people. It also gave me something to do since my entire body tingled with nerves.

"I'd like to get to know everyone better," I said, clasping my hands together and pasting a smile on my lips.

"That's why we were called here on such short notice?" John Travolta asked, surprised.

The smile left my lips. My father made it hard to be civil.

"Yes," I said flatly. "You have a problem with that?"

"None at all," he replied.

"Call me crazy," Tim said.

"Crazy," Candy supplied quickly.

Tim shot her a look and Candy rolled her eyes.

"Gram would make me say I'm sorry for that," she grumbled.

"I accept," Tim replied, ignoring the fact Candy hadn't

apologized. "As I was saying, call me crazy, but you already know us, Daisy."

"Wrong," I corrected him. "I know you as Tim my mailman and friend who rehomes sex toys, not Tim the Immortal Courier between the darkness and the light. I know Candy as the cashier with bad manners and an endless supply of toothpicks from the Piggly Wiggly—not as Karma. I know Charlie as June's beloved husband who adores her as much as she adores him, not as the Enforcer."

"And you know John Travolta, aka Clarence Smith, aka Darth Vader, as your former boss, not Michael the Archangel," Tim added.

"Don't forget he's also your dad," Candy reminded me, as if I needed reminding.

"I prefer sperm donor, and I couldn't forget if I tried," I said flatly.

John Travolta didn't blink an eye. His poker face was exceptional.

"Alrighty then," Heather said, steering the conversation back on track. "Daisy knows me as one of her dearest friends, not the Arbitrator between Heaven and Hell."

"That begs the question as to how well the Death Counselor *knows* the Grim Reaper," Candy Vargo said, waggling her brows. "Have you seen his nut sack yet?"

Gideon laughed. "That is none of your business, *Karma*."

"While this is true," Candy said, grinning, "I do have to admit I'm curious how many snapper slappers you have."

"Two," I volunteered, then closed my eyes in mortification. Would I never learn? How many times was I going to discuss Gideon's junk in front of the same people? "Sorry," I choked out, trying not to laugh.

"Not to worry," Gideon said with a wink. "While I find your comfort level with talking about my balls in public slightly alarming, I also find it alluring."

"This is degenerating into a conversation I'm not comfortable with," Tim said with a shudder. "With Daisy's permission, I'd like to offer up some trivia to get things back on track."

"Umm, no," I told him. "We'll save that for the end. Cool?"

"Certainly." Tim nodded and put his trivia list back into his pocket.

"I'll start with Karma," I said, feeling nervous and somewhat ridiculous. I was a forty-year-old person attempting to chat with people who had seen centuries—tons of centuries. In all reality, I was a child compared to them. Yet, at the same time, it wasn't all that strange.

Which meant I might be insane.

"I don't like going first," Candy complained. "I want to go third and get a feel for what's going on so I can make a decision if I'm going to lie."

At least she was honest...

"It's not a test," I said with an eye roll. "How long have you lived in this town?"

Karma shrugged her shoulders. "Time means little to me," she said. "Tim, how long have I been here?"

Tim's brow wrinkled in thought. "Sixteen years," he said. "You moved here in December sixteen years ago and have been a rude thorn in everyone's side ever since."

"Thank you," Candy said. "Hate to think I was slacking."

"Oh, you're not," Tim told her.

"Why?" I asked. "I mean, I know about the strong portal between Heaven and Hell, but is that why you came here?"

"Hell no," she said with a laugh. "I don't use the portal unless I have to. The earthly plane is my territory. I came because I had a few warrants out for my arrest and needed a little legal assistance."

"A few? More like twenty-seven in twelve countries," Heather mumbled.

"Zip it," Candy snapped. "I paid you, didn't I?"

"That you did," Heather replied dryly.

"Didn't expect that," I said, shaking my head. "Had you visited before?"

"Never," Candy said, waving her hand dismissively. "People are too damned polite in this part of the world. Only came here because I knew I could use the portals if I couldn't get the Feds off my ass."

I couldn't help myself. The answer wasn't pertinent to anything, but now I was dying to know. "Do I want to ask why they were after you?"

"You really don't," Heather said. "Really."

"Roger that," I said. "So, Candy, just for clarification, you've never set foot in Georgia before sixteen years ago?"

"Correct," Candy replied. "Do I get a prize?"

"No. You don't," I said, realizing this was going to take too long. "I'm going to cut to the chase."

"Thank God," Candy said. "If I have to listen to Tim tell his backstory, I'll have to eat my own arm."

"First of all, I'm telling Gram you said that," Tim

announced. "Secondly, it would grow back. You're Immortal. And third, eating your own body parts is disgusting and it tastes awful."

"And you know this how?" Charlie inquired, glancing over at Tim in horror.

"Don't ask if you don't want to know," Tim said primly. "It's not a pretty story."

The chat had taken a left turn and was careening in a direction that was going to make me hurl.

"As I said," I announced loudly before anyone could ask Tim to expound on self-cannibalism. "I was wrong. I don't think I want to know any of you *that* well. Who here can plant thoughts in humans' minds?"

Everyone was silent… and surprised, except Heather. I wasn't sure if they were surprised that I knew about it or if it was bad manners to have asked.

"I can," Heather said. "And I'm sure some of the other's here can as well."

"I can't," Gideon said, looking at me. His expression was filled with curiosity.

I shook my head and prayed it conveyed that I knew he hadn't done it.

His expression didn't change. Dammit, why the hell hadn't I told him? I was an idiot.

He thought I suspected him of planting the false story in Gram's mind. My chest tightened and I hoped he'd forgive me after the fact—not for suspecting him, because I didn't—for not sharing my thoughts. He'd asked me to trust him and I hadn't… again. Shit. I was already rocking the foundation and the house wasn't built yet.

Turning away from him, because I wasn't about to have that conversation with him publicly, I focused on the Immortals who had not yet spoken.

"And the rest of you?" I asked.

"Only those with Heavenly Angelic blood can implant thoughts," Charlie said. "That would preclude Tim, Candy and myself. Gideon lost the ability when he fell from the Heavens. Heather, you're an anomaly."

"Wait. That can't be correct," Heather insisted, confused.

"Yes, it can," my father said.

Heather's head whipped to the Archangel and her eyes narrowed. "How?"

He sighed and looked down at the floor for a long moment. A very long moment.

I could literally hear Heather's teeth grinding. "If by some chance we're about to have another Luke Skywalker/Darth Vader moment, we should probably take this outside," she ground out.

"As you wish," John Travolta said, standing up.

The gasps were loud, but the sounds of Heather's furiously shouted profanity then her fist connecting to Darth Vader's face were positively horrifying. I was sure his head must have flown off. I idly wondered if an Immortal could grow another head or if it could be superglued back on. Tim would probably know.

Faster than a human eye could follow, Gideon dove into the fray and pulled a murderous Heather off the man who clearly got around with the ladies. Charlie stood between Heather and John Travolta with his hands held high. His eyes sparked a blinding silver and his entire body glowed.

I said a quick prayer that my house would still be standing in the next few minutes, but I kind of doubted it.

Candy Vargo sat down on the couch next to Tim. They both started shoving burnt Wiener Winks into their mouths like they were eating popcorn as they watched the shitshow unfold.

"This is turning out to be a great fucking party," Candy said with a mouthful, elbowing Tim who, in between grabbing another burnt weenie, elbowed her right back.

The Archangel Michael made no move to attack Heather, just as he'd made no move to retaliate against me when I'd broken his nose. I could only believe he was getting no less than he thought he deserved.

"I was created!" Heather yelled.

"Some of us were," Charlie agreed, eyes still shimmering bright. "Some of us were not."

"I have no memory of you," Heather hissed at the Archangel, trying to break Gideon's hold and failing. "You lie."

"No," Michael said. "I omit. I do not lie."

The meeting had gone very wrong. I'd found out who could plant memories, and a whole hell of a lot more. "Lying by omission counts as lying. You have no sense of responsibility. You're vile."

"Be that as it may," he said, glancing at me then turning his attention back to Heather, "it came from a higher power than myself that I was to sire you and then leave you to the Universe."

Heather shook like a leaf. "I have a mother?" she demanded.

"I am unaware of who she is," he said emotionlessly.

"That seems a little off. Were the lights out?" Candy mused aloud.

Tim stood and scratched his head. "I know of this. It's appalling. There was a group created—kind of like thoroughbred horses—no sexual intercourse involved. It was done to streamline the species. Very unethical, if you ask me."

"No one asked you," John Travolta said so coldly, I stepped back. "And yes, it was unethical, but we are all aware there are shades of gray around every corner, especially for those who can't die. There are many circumstances of which we have no control. I didn't know that you were one of the products of the experiment until a century ago, and I was forbidden to reach out."

"What made you change your mind?" I asked, unable to stop myself. I was sure his answer would be cryptic like it always was.

"Because it was wrong," he said. "Because Heather asked. Because she has a right to know."

"Will there be consequences for you if they become aware you told me?" Heather asked.

Michael shrugged. "I have ceased to care. It should not have been a secret."

Heather stared at him for a long moment. She calmed herself with effort. She paced the room and gathered her thoughts. "So, basically I'm a horse. An Immortal horse."

No one said a word. While Darth Vader was her father in a very indirect sense of the word, he was more of a sperm donor. Literally.

"I wonder how many exist?" Tim questioned aloud, and then zipped it when Charlie glared at him.

"Five, from what I understand," Michael said.

"Identical to me?" Heather asked.

"No," he replied.

"Unbelievable." With a huge sigh of resignation, Heather slowly crossed the room and extended her hand to Darth Vader. "I'm sorry for attacking you. Sadly, and unsurprisingly, you were a pawn as much as I was."

And yet another turn of events I didn't see coming. I'd expected a little more bloodshed and possibly a few tears. It had been wildly anticlimactic.

"Hang on," I sputtered in shock. "That's it? You're not going to punch him again?"

"No. I'm not," Heather said, sounding old and tired.

"Do you want me to punch him?" I offered, wanting to have her back since she always had mine. It wasn't mature. It wasn't becoming, but it felt right.

Heather took a deep breath and then exhaled audibly. "No, but I appreciate the offer. There are things you don't understand, Daisy—hopefully will never have to understand. We're all pawns in a larger game. It is what it is. I bear the Archangel no ill will. However, the one punch I got in was satisfying."

The Archangel took the Arbitrator's hand and shook it. "I am truly sorry, Heather."

"Me too, Michael," Heather replied.

"Wait. We're sisters," I said as my brain raced and my mouth followed.

Heather's laugh was hollow. "That's the only good thing

to come out of this mess," she said, and then calmly turned back to the man who'd sired her. "So that leaves you, Archangel. You planted the incorrect cause of Alana's death in Gram's mind, because I sure as hell know I didn't do it. And apparently no one else here could have."

"That's certainly bad form," Tim said, shaking his head. "I'm surprised at you, Michael."

"I didn't do it," Michael said.

"Then who did?" I demanded of my father.

His lips compressed and his color heightened. "It was not me," he said, pinning me with a hard stare. "Think. Please think. The words cannot come from my lips. Too much is at stake."

And another puzzle piece fell sickeningly into place.

"Clarissa," I said. "Clarissa did it."

My father didn't confirm or deny, but I saw a brief moment of great relief in his eyes.

"Why?" I demanded. "No more cryptic bullshit. We are so far past that point. The guessing games are over."

Everyone looked at the Archangel.

"To cover her tracks," he replied reluctantly.

"You will have to expound on that, Archangel," Charlie instructed. "Now."

Glancing around the room warily, he motioned for us to gather close. Waving his hand, a shimmering bubble surrounded us.

I looked over questioningly at Gideon.

"Insurance," he said. "Soundproofing."

"Because?" I pressed. "I don't think the ghosts are going to blab."

"Not the dead. Other Immortals," Candy said.

"Exactly how many Immortals are in town at the moment?" I snapped.

All eyes went to Tim.

"Right now, just those of us in the room," Tim said. "However, other's bop in and out occasionally."

Dropping my chin to my chest, I bit back all the questions I wanted to ask that had little to do with what we were discussing. I wanted to know how many Immortals existed. I wanted to know if they all knew each other. I wanted to know how many shitty ones there were like Clarissa. Instead, I zeroed back in on my father. I'd ask Gideon the questions later.

"Start talking, please," I said.

"That was polite," Candy commented.

"Can't be helped," I said. "It's the way I was raised."

"I can help you undo that," she offered.

"I'll pass."

Charlie cleared his throat and aimed his attention at my father. "Continue, Michael."

The Archangel nodded curtly. "What I'm about to say could destroy someone I would willingly die for," he said so softly, I leaned in. "I believe the Angel of Mercy is near. There's a reason we couldn't find her. We've searched in all the wrong places."

Gideon ran his hands through his hair and made a disgusted sound deep in his throat. "I agree. Charlie and I believe Clarissa is most likely hiding in plain sight."

"I'd thought the remnants of her footprint were left over

from her time here," Charlie explained. "However, now I believe they're more recent."

"I concur," Tim whispered, looking over his shoulder and shuddering.

"Umm... that might have been good information to have shared," I hissed, glaring at all of them.

"It was just discussed this morning," Gideon assured me. "You have never been alone without Immortal protection in that time."

"And you will not be left alone," my father promised.

"Okay," I said, my mind racing. "Spit out the reason we're huddled together and whispering."

"Clarissa has Alana's soul," he said, as my heart lodged in my mouth.

"Not possible," Karma said, shaking her head.

"She has it," my father growled. "When Alana wasn't in the darkness or the light, I confronted Clarissa. She told me she was keeping Alana's soul as leverage. She's used the abhorrent fact against me since the day Alana died."

"That's why you've ignored me?" I asked, not following. "Because of my mother's soul?"

He nodded.

"Nope. Not buying it," Gideon ground out. "She was five when her mother passed. In all that time, you never acknowledged Daisy. Holes. Too many holes, Archangel."

"We tried to hide Daisy's existence from Clarissa since the day she was born, to protect her. It was Alana's choice," my father admitted with great sadness.

Many things were clicking together now, but many of the pieces were still missing.

"What are you omitting?" I pressed. "And no bullshit or shades of gray."

My father sighed dramatically and raised his eyes to mine. His focused attention made me forget anyone else was in the room. His power was immense.

"For thousands of years, Clarissa and I were lovers on and off," he said.

"Jesus, you get around," Karma muttered.

"Enough," Charlie chastised Karma, who zipped it quick.

I had the same thought, but never would have voiced it. John Travolta was thousands of years old. He was bound to have had many lovers during that time, and insulting him was counterproductive. I still needed to know more.

"Go on, please," I said.

The Archangel nodded. "I never loved Clarissa. It was simply two people who had lived for eternity and were bored. Or that's what I'd believed."

"She loved you," I whispered. "She loved you, and then you fell in love with my mother."

Again, he nodded. His expression was pained. "We made every effort to hide it from everyone."

"I never knew," Charlie said.

"That was the point," he said.

"But Clarissa found out and lost her mind," Gideon surmised.

"She did," my father said. "She threatened Alana's life. As long as I stayed away from Alana, she was satisfied."

"But you didn't stay away from my mother," I said, knowing the end of the love story was tragic, but somehow thankful that my mother had true love.

Michael shook his head. "We were as necessary to each other as breathing," he said. "We were so secretive of our love, not even your grandmother knew."

Gram's words about my mother being private about her beau's echoed in my mind.

"But Clarissa knew?" Gideon asked, not wanting the Archangel to leave out anything important.

"For several years, Clarissa suspected nothing. She would pop in and out to make sure I'd kept my word."

"You didn't," Charlie said.

"No. I didn't," my father agreed.

"She worked for you when I did. She posed as your daughter," I said.

"She insisted on it," he replied, and then paused. "She did it to keep an eye on me and an eye on you."

"That's scary, but I'm still confused," I said, trying to make linear sense of all I was learning. "Why does Clarissa have my mother's soul?"

"Everything was fine until you were about five. We'd stayed hidden well," he said. "You were correct that you have been to my home. It was *your* home as well, up until your mother died."

My mouth dropped open. "Why don't I remember?"

"Clearly, you did," he said with a small smile. "I tried to erase the memories from your mind to save you unnecessary pain, but since you're of my blood, it didn't completely take."

"Wait. Where in the heck did Gram think we lived?" I asked.

"A few hours away," he said. "You and your mother visited her weekly."

"Yet we were only a few miles from her," I said.

My father nodded.

"Holes," Gideon repeated, taking my hand in his. "Fill them, Archangel. Now."

"Clarissa was gone from this part of the Universe for the first several years of your life," he told me. "When she came back and discovered your existence, she wanted you dead. What I believe is that your mother traded her life for yours, and Clarissa trapped and kept her soul."

"So, she killed herself?" I asked, thinking maybe the suicide part was correct but the reasoning as to why was flawed. "That would mean she was destined for the darkness."

"No, if she had been destined for the darkness, that is where she would be," Michael said as his eyes went a sparkling gold filled with fury and regret. "I believe she was pushed off the bridge."

"By Clarissa," I said. Something inside me broke. I'd avoided feeling anything for the woman who bore me. I'd pushed all memories away because I thought she'd left me for someone else. She'd left me for me... The guilt raging inside made me breathless. "That's why you don't want the Angel of Mercy destroyed," I said as tears rolled down my cheeks. "Because it will destroy Alana, too."

My father said nothing. He didn't have to.

The rules had changed.

The game was no longer simple—not that it was to start

with, but now it was far different. "You all truly believe Clarissa is in the area?"

"I do," Gideon said.

"New plan." I swiped my hand through the air and disintegrated the bubble surrounding us. "We stop looking for her."

"What the hell?" Tim asked, looking at me with an expression of shock. "How did you do that?"

"Don't know. Don't care," I said, realizing everyone was staring at me—even my father. "We will draw her to us."

"That's the new plan?" Candy Vargo asked, squinting at me like I'd lost it.

"Yep." I informed them. "To me. We will draw her to *me*."

"I don't like it," Gideon said tersely.

"Not real fond of it, either," I told him as a feeling of confidence—or insanity coupled with a death wish—blossomed in my chest. It felt right and damn good. "However, this has to end. I want what belongs to me. I'm the Death Counselor. My mother is dead. She's mine. She belongs to me and then to the light."

"I will stand by your side," my father said.

"That's part of the plan, John Travolta. I *want* you by my side," I said.

The Archangel's eyes grew wide, but he said nothing.

"Damn this was a fucking out-of-control shindig," Candy said, heaping another pile of Wiener Winks onto a plate.

"Are we almost done here?" Tim asked as I held my father's gaze.

"We are," I replied.

"Excellent." Tim pulled his trivia sheet from his pocket. "I shall leave all of you with this... the space between your eyebrows is called a glabella. Illegible handwriting is called griffonage, and *to testify* was based on the Roman court swearing to a statement by swearing on the longevity and health of their testicles."

"As I said," Candy announced with a cackle. "Excellent fucking party."

CHAPTER NINETEEN

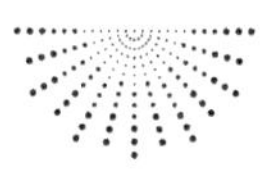

No firm plan had been made by the time everyone left. We'd agree to talk tomorrow after everyone had a chance to sleep on it. My father was not in favor of using me as bait, but even he agreed I was probably the one who could pull her out of hiding.

"Come with me," Gideon said, pulling my coat from the foyer closet and handing it to me.

"I have to clean up," I told him, pointing to the plates and glasses littered around the living room.

"I've got it," Heather said. "I need something mindless to do for a little while. Go with Gideon."

"You sure?" I asked.

"Positive," she replied. "I'll straighten up, take the dogs out to do their business and then go home."

"Thank you, Heather."

"You're welcome… sister," she said, trying the word on for size.

I grinned, as did she.

Heather shook her head. "And the Universe keeps getting stranger."

"And better," I added, giving her a quick hug.

"And better," she agreed. "Much better."

"You ready?" Gideon asked.

"Born ready," I replied. "Or something like that."

Gideon grabbed my hand and led me to his car.

"Where are we going?" I asked as he got in and started the ignition.

"To *our* house," he replied. "We need to have a little chat."

My heart sank. I hated that he was upset with me. I should have shared my thoughts about someone planting the wrong story in Gram's head with him privately, but I hadn't. My protective instincts for Gram took a front seat. However, trust was a two-way street and I was driving on the wrong side.

"Gideon, I didn't think you did it."

"I know."

"You're not mad?"

"I'm not mad."

"I was an idiot not to tell you what I was thinking."

He nodded. "I'd have to agree."

Shit.

We drove the rest of the way in silence—lost in our own thoughts. My brain came up with a hundred ways to apologize for not coming clean with him before the fact, but they all kind of sucked. Gram was my world—even dead, she was my world. However, Gideon was my world, too, and I hadn't been fair to him.

"It's okay, Daisy," Gideon said. "Stop beating yourself up. I know Gram and I are both your world."

"Oh my God." I gasped and punched his arm. "You can read my mind?"

Gideon chuckled. I didn't think it was funny.

"Only when you think very loud. Like now," he assured me.

"Shit," I muttered. This was not welcome news. "Wait, could you tell I knew you hadn't planted the thoughts?"

"I could."

"So, you're *really* not upset with me?"

He shook his head. "I'm not upset, but I think we have some work to do."

My relief was overwhelming. And he was correct. We had work to do, and I was willing to do it. However, I was curious about something. "Can I read your mind if you think loudly?"

"I don't know," Gideon said, pulling off the road at the same spot we'd parked before. "You've surprised me repeatedly. It wouldn't shock me to know that you could read my thoughts."

"Can I try?" I asked, feeling silly.

"Yep," he said, turning to me and staring straight into my eyes.

His face was expressionless. No clues there. His body was still and there was no sign of nervousness. What I could see visually wasn't helping. Looking for physical clues was messing me up. Closing my eyes, I almost laughed. If I was going to try, I was *really* going to try. I could mind dive into the dead. How hard could reading the Grim Reaper's mind be?

The images were fuzzy at first. I was sure my own imagination had taken over. Wishful thinking was some powerful stuff. As the images grew clearer, I saw me. But not the image that greeted me in the mirror every morning. Nope. I was a freaking goddess. My eyes sparkled gold and my skin glowed. I was also completely naked. My wild dark curls blew around my head and the smile on my lips was so carnal, I giggled.

"You see it?" Gideon asked, amusement in his voice.

"Umm... I see me."

"You're seeing you the way I see you," he said softly.

"That's what you see?" I asked. "Because if it is, you might need glasses."

His laugh rang out in the tight interior of the car, and I grinned.

"There's more, Daisy. Keep searching."

I did.

Oh my God, I did.

I felt the heat on my cheeks and put my hands on my heart to calm the fluttering. His thoughts were x-rated and hotter than anything I'd ever witnessed.

"Umm... we didn't do that the other night," I said in a whispery voice an octave higher than usual.

"No," he agreed. "Something to look forward to."

Opening my eyes, I gaped at the man sitting across from me. The man was beautiful, and he found me beautiful too.

"I read your mind."

"That you did," Gideon said. "As I said, it doesn't surprise me at all."

"You have very naughty thoughts." I bit back a grin. As crazy as life was, it was also wonderful.

"Only where you're concerned."

"Mind reading can't be great for relationships," I pointed out, wrinkling my nose.

"Then we have to promise not to do it unless it's necessary… or sexual," he suggested with a lopsided grin.

"Why did we come here?" I asked as the blush crept up my neck and landed on my cheeks. "Are we going to… you know…"

Gideon leaned in and kissed me. "That can be arranged," he said. "However, we came for another reason."

"Okay," I said, following his lead and getting out of the car.

The sun was bright and the wind was low. It was cold, but not as chilly as the other night. We walked the familiar path hand in hand and a calmness filled my soul.

"I have something to show you."

I eyed him and raised a brow. "Is that a euphemism for something naughty?"

"Nope," he said with a laugh. "It's more of a metaphorical lesson of sorts."

Shit. That sounded iffy.

"Awesome," I said, hoping I sounded sincere. "I'm ready."

I WAS NOT READY. I WAS NOWHERE NEAR READY.

"Holy crap," I shouted as we came to the clearing where the garden had been. It was no longer just a garden. The garden was still there, but there was more—much more.

Where there had only been flowers and a huge bed, was now the most beautifully graceful farmhouse I'd ever seen. Rocking chairs and a swing dotted the wraparound front porch, and I spotted a massive chimney on the far-left side of the roof. The house stood two stories. It was large, but not grossly so. It screamed to be loved and lived in.

"Do you like it?" Gideon asked casually.

There was nothing casual about the question. He knew it and I knew it.

"It's lovely," I said truthfully. "How many bedrooms?"

"Four, but that can be changed," he replied.

I nodded and kept staring. "I thought we were going to build it together."

"We are."

"But…" I said ,then gasped.

With a wave of his hand, the house collapsed in on itself. Gone was the elegant home. A pile of rubble remained atop a large concrete foundation.

"I didn't mean for you to do that," I said. "I just thought…"

With another wave of his hand, a new house took its place. It was a gorgeous fieldstone home with pillars flanking an impressively carved teak front door. As magnificent as it was, it was still homey and inviting.

"Do you like it?" he inquired.

"What's not to like? It's beautiful."

"Knock it down, Daisy," he urged.

"Are you serious?" I asked, shocked.

"Very," he replied.

"Umm… not sure I can," I told him, feeling a strange tingle of adrenaline shoot through me. "I'm good with trees and ripping off car doors, but I don't know if I can demolish a house."

Gideon gently pushed me forward. "Knock it down, Daisy. See what happens."

"You're nuts."

Gideon grinned. "I thought we were going to stop discussing my balls."

"Only in public," I shot back with a laugh. "In private, your balls are fair game." All of this was absurd. "Should I punch it?"

"I'd hate to see you break your hand," Gideon said. "Try using something else."

"My head?" I suggested, thinking it wasn't any better of an idea than my fist.

Gideon's laugh rang out and the sound made me feel pretty damned good. But I still thought headbutting a stone house wasn't going to end well.

"Use your mind," he said softly. "Your magic."

Rolling my eyes, I groaned. "Just because I can get out of your hold and bust through John Travolta's bubbles does not mean I can demolish a freaking house."

Gideon shrugged. "You'll never know until you try."

Direct challenges were difficult to pass up.

"Fine," I huffed. "But if you laugh at me when I fail, I'll take it out on your fully descended balls."

Again, he laughed.

Again, I felt delight.

"Screw it," I said, slashing my arm through the air and sending my thoughts at the lovely house.

The rumble caught me off guard. A stone house falling down was much louder than a wooden one.

"What the hell?" I shouted as I watched the destruction in shock.

Gideon's arms encircled me from behind and he held me close. "What's left of the house?"

"Not much worth saving," I said, still unsettled and strangely excited I'd been able to do it.

"Ahh, but there is. The most important part of the house is still there."

Leaning back on him, I eyed the huge mess and then smiled. He was correct.

"The foundation," I whispered. "The foundation is still there."

"Yep," he said, kissing the top of my head. "The house can fall many times, but a strong foundation is all we need to rebuild."

"This is your way of telling me it's okay that I didn't tell you about my suspicions?" I asked.

"It is."

"Kind of dramatic," I said with a little giggle.

"Possibly," Gideon agreed, "but you'll never forget it."

He had that right.

"Gram loved you with all she had for your entire life," Gideon said. "Her wellbeing is your responsibility. I feel the same way about you."

"Thank you, Gideon."

"You're most welcome, Daisy."

Looking up at him, I smiled. "Do you think there's a bed underneath all that rubble?"

"I do believe there might be a bed to be found," he said in a tone laced with amusement. "Are you sleepy?"

"Not at all." I grabbed his hand and marched him toward our foundation. I wanted to try out the position I'd seen in his mind. "Are *you* sleepy?"

"Nope. I could stay up all night with the right incentive."

"Pretty sure I know what the right incentive might be," I said.

His laugh filled me up. I craved it.

"I'm positive you do."

CHAPTER TWENTY

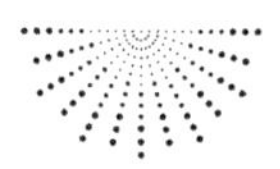

"GO HOME AND GET YOUR CLOTHES AND SOME OTHER STUFF," I said as we pulled up in front of my farmhouse. "I'll be fine."

"Is that Heather's car?" Gideon asked, scanning the driveway.

"Yep, it's a rental since I totaled her other one," I replied.

It was dark out now. The stars were small glittering dots in the distance and the moon hung low in the sky illuminating the yard with a warm yellow glow.

"I'm surprised she's still here," Gideon said.

"Me too. We've been gone for *five* hours," I said with a wide and very satisfied smile on my lips. "I don't think it would have taken Heather five hours to straighten up and take Donna and Karen out to do their business. My guess is she stayed to talk or fell asleep on the couch."

Gideon's smile was as wide as mine. The position I'd seen in his mind had been even better in practice. I'd be searching his thoughts for more of those kind of things...

"It should only take me a half hour." He checked his watch then kissed my nose. "How about popcorn and a movie when I get back?"

"Perfect," I said.

Tomorrow would get here soon enough. Plans for finding Clarissa and getting my mother's soul back would be made in the morning with people who had far more experience than I did with the Immortal world. Tonight was mine and Gideon's… and Gram's and Steve's… and the squatters and Heather's, if they were up for a movie.

"Do you like *Happy Gilmore*?"

"I don't know him," Gideon replied. "Is he a friend?"

I laughed. "Nope. It's a movie. It's a hot mess and it's hilarious. Gram loves it because her boyfriend Bob Barker is in it. I promised to watch it with her. Do you mind?"

"Not a bit," Gideon said. "Sounds excellent."

"If your expectations aren't too high and you think poop jokes are funny, then excellent fits," I told him.

Gideon shrugged. "As long as I can sit next to you on the couch, I stand by my statement."

"You're going to have to fight off Donna and Karen for the honor," I told him as I got out of the car.

"Those girls love me," he said as he slowly pulled away. "Not a problem. Be back soon, and I like extra butter on my popcorn."

"Got it," I said with a laugh. "Go so you can come back. Donna, Karen and I will be waiting."

My fur babies did love him. They had very good taste.

~

"Crap," I muttered as I pulled the handwritten note off the front door and read it.

Rental car wouldn't start.

Transported home.

Dogs did their business. Twice.

Living room is clean and I ran the dishwasher.

Will pick up car tomorrow.

xoxo Heather... your sister (I'm still digesting that one LOL)

I considered calling Gideon and asking him to turn the car around and come back but decided against it. He'd be back in a half an hour. Besides, I'd just demolished a house for the love of everything unreal. I'd be fine on my own for a freaking half hour.

Fishing my keys out of my purse, I grinned when I thought about the past several hours at *our house.* In between orgasms—his and mine—we'd discussed the kinds of houses we liked. Neither of us wanted anything fussy or traditional. Open floor plans, lots of natural light and wood, a gourmet kitchen—for him, since he was the far better chef —along with a really big master bed were at the top of our list.

The idea of customizing something specifically for us from the foundation up excited me. Creating a home from scratch with Gideon would be a first. I'd never done anything like it. Steve and I had fixed up the farmhouse, but we hadn't built it. Although, I wasn't sure I was ready to sell the farmhouse. Maybe, I'd rent it out or turn it into a bed and breakfast.

Entering the house, I froze as a feeling of foreboding

took hold of me. I flipped on the light switch and glanced around in horror.

The couches were slashed and stuffing was strewn everywhere. Pictures and paintings had been ripped from the walls and torn to shreds. The tables were overturned and broken and my overstuffed armchair looked as if it had been incinerated. Shards of glass covered the floor and not a ghost was to be found.

"What the hell?" I choked out.

Hindsight was 20/20. Not checking that Heather was actually at the house was unwise. Insisting Gideon leave was a shitty plan. Deciding not to call him when I realized Heather wasn't here might have been my final mistake.

Dropping my purse and slamming myself up against the wall so no one could come at me from behind, I inched along the wall back towards the front door.

My house was trashed, and my dogs definitely hadn't done it.

My stomach plummeted. Where were my dogs?

Where were my babies?

"Donna? Karen?" I called out in a shaky voice. "Do you guys want a treat?"

Both of my furry girls bound out from behind the couch and practically knocked me over. My relief was so intense, tears pooled in my eyes. They were panting hard, and Karen shook like a leaf. Donna sat at my feet facing away, baring her sharp teeth and growling at the vandalized room.

"Oh my God," I said, squatting down and trying to calm them. "It's okay. I'm here. I've got you. Although, we're getting the hell out of here. Now."

Turning toward the front door, I screamed and jumped back at the sight that greeted me.

"Is that any way to greet an old *friend?*" Clarissa inquired, tilting her head to the side and examining me from head to toe with displeasure.

I returned the favor.

She looked unhinged. Her outfit was sloppy and dirty. Her eyes were dull and lifeless. I'd never once seen the woman when she wasn't completely groomed from her toenails to the top of her dyed head. The Angel of Mercy had turned into a hot mess.

"I'd hardly call you a friend," I said, keeping my voice steady.

Donna continued to growl. Karen took a cue from her buddy and growled along with her.

"I think it's soooo cute that you have a Hell Hound," she said, waving her hand and creating a bubble that surrounded the trashed room.

I sucked my bottom lip into my mouth and bit down on it so I didn't squeal with relief. If I could break through John Travolta's bubble, there was a fine chance I could break through Clarissa's. I needed to stay close to the door so I could make a run for it when the opportunity arose.

Please let the opportunity arise.

"Hell Hounds are quite *tasty* from what I hear," Clarissa purred with a smile that made me want to headbutt her. "Just roast them with a little salt and pepper and you have a rare delicacy."

"If you try to eat my dog, it will be the last thing you do," I informed her coldly.

"Ohhhh, so brave," she said with a brittle laugh that made the hair on my neck stand up. "Where have your manners gone, Daisy? That's no way to talk to a guest in your home."

"I wouldn't go so far as referring to yourself as a guest," I shot back, wondering if I could keep her talking for the half hour it would take for Gideon to come back. "More like an intruder."

"Semantics," she said with a shrug. "It just breaks my heart that you're not happy to see me."

"If you had a heart, then I'd feel bad. Since you don't, I don't," I replied in a polite tone that belied my words.

That's when I noticed Steve, Gram and Jimmy Joe Johnson. They floated on the outside of the bubble and looked terrified. I didn't want them anywhere near this.

When Clarissa briefly turned away, I mouthed *get Gideon*. Steve nodded and disappeared. *Get the ghosts out of the house,* I mouthed to Gram and Jimmy Joe, and to my relief, they vanished, too.

Clarissa really did look rough. She'd always been a redheaded, overly made-up she-devil, but she had a desperation about her now that made her extremely dangerous. I used to think she was pretty in a hardened way, but those days were over. What she'd done to my mother and father and Steve destroyed any beauty she ever had.

"It's not in your best interest to be ugly," she warned. "I can make your life very difficult."

"Are you serious?" I demanded with a humorless laugh. "You've already done a fine job of making my life difficult so far."

"Thank you," she said.

"Wasn't a compliment," I shot back.

"Yes, I know," she hissed. "However, I'm insulted by your rude reception. I don't like it."

"You tried to send my husband wrongly into the darkness after you caused his death," I said evenly, judging how far I was from the door. My damn purse with my cell phone in it was on the floor and out of reach. My best bet was to break the bubble, grab my dogs and run. I was faster than hell on my feet and wildly happy about that right now.

"Everyone makes mistakes," Clarissa said, shaking her head dismissively. "He'll be fine in the darkness."

"Steve's not going into the darkness."

Her body stiffened and her eyes narrowed to slits. "Of course he is."

"Nope," I said. "It wasn't a suicide. Funnily enough—which actually isn't funny at all—he was run off the road by a deranged Angel."

Her eyes widened in shock for a hot second. She made pouty lips and spoke to me like an adult using baby talk to speak to a dog. "How very, very, very sad. Delighted you got it figured out."

Riling her up wasn't the best plan, but if I threw her off enough, I might be able to figure out where she'd hidden my mother's soul. However, that was a delicate subject, and I would tread lightly. Risking my mother was not in anyone's best interest.

"Yep, I'm glad we got it figured out too," I said, playing the idiot. I gave her a thumbs up.

"Is something wrong with your hand?" Clarissa inquired rudely.

"No," I said. "Hand's fine. As I was saying, once it was revealed Steve's death wasn't a suicide, it was decided he belongs in the light."

"They went off the word of a dead man?" she asked as her eyes flashed with fury.

"Stop playing games, Clarissa," I snapped. "It's not a good look on you. You're on the run because you're in a shitload of trouble. I know you caused Steve's death, and so does everyone else."

The Angel of Mercy grew agitated, pointed her finger at the staircase and blew it sky high. The walls around the staircase were loadbearing. The house creaked but didn't fall apart. I was tempted to use my newfound demolition skills to bring the entire house down around us so I'd have a head start in getting away from her, but I worried about my dogs. Donna would probably be fine, since she was a Hell Hound, but endangering Karen was not part of my plan.

"Everyone else does *not* know, you stupid child," she snarled. "You have no proof. Just a dead man's word delivered by a Death Counselor who was married to him. It's a very clear case of conflict of interest. I win."

Did she truly think she'd gotten away with it? She couldn't. Why was she on the run if she thought she'd gotten away with it? She had to be after something else.

How much did she know? How much should I tell?

It wasn't smart to let her know how the others got the proof. There was a chance she'd go back into hiding or permanently disappear if she was clued in that I knew who my father was. I'd never get my mother's soul back.

"Anyhoo, I have things to do and places to be," she said, sounding bored. "I do believe you have something of mine. I'd like it back. Now."

"I have nothing that belongs to you," I said. "Nothing."

"Ahh, but you do," she contradicted me and shot a bolt of lightning from her fingertips that landed dangerously close to my head and took a chunk out of the wall. Karen yelped and Donna growled. "For years I thought the old lady had it, but I was wrong. Should have known you would have been able to find it."

What the hell was she talking about?

"You're going to have to be a little more specific," I said, buying time. We had to have been talking for about fifteen minutes. If I could get her to monologue for a few more, I'd have backup. Bad guys loved to monologue—at least they did in the movies.

Another bolt of lightning came even closer to my head. Donna and Karen's growls intensified as the smoke curled from the scorched wall behind me. The unmistakable aroma of singed hair—mine—made me cringe. "If you blow my head off, you won't get what you want."

"Good point," she said, turning her deranged attention to the front of my house and setting it ablaze. "However, after I get what I want, you'll probably perish in the fire. Sorry about that."

It was instinctual. I didn't realize I'd done it until after it was done.

Swiping my hand through the air, I put out the fire. It still smoldered, but the flames were gone.

Clarissa's scream of fury was so shrill, I slapped my hands over my ears.

"How?" she demanded. "Explain!"

"No."

She eyed me with hatred and paced the room like a madwoman. The glass crunched beneath her stiletto-clad feet as she muttered obscenities.

On a dime, she shifted. Her fury was replaced by a sweetness so repulsive, I almost laughed.

I didn't. I was smarter than that.

"Okay, Daisy," she said, seating herself on the edge of the broken coffee table. "I'm looking for a troublesome old soul. A woman. She's wanted in Heaven, and I can't seem to locate her. I think you have her."

"A ghost?" I questioned as I braced myself against the wall due to the fact that my knees had turned to jelly. If this was going where I thought it was going, then this was a really bad time to pass out.

Clarissa tilted her head to the side and got lost in thought. "I suppose she could be in ghost form, but last time I saw her, she was more of a blob."

"A blob?" I asked, squinting at her.

She nodded and rolled her eyes. "Are you hard of hearing?" she snapped. "A soul looks like a blob. A ghost looks like a ghost."

"Umm… I just have ghosts, and ghosts look like ghosts," I said, still feeling light-headed. I wanted to scream with joy, but I wasn't sure I was correct. "No blobs. Can you tell me anything else about this blob?"

"Are you making fun of me?" she asked, raising her hand to destroy more of my house.

The Angel was deranged and unpredictable, which made her incredibly dangerous. Her behavior was batshit crazy. It was going to be hard to take her down if it couldn't be determined what she would do next.

Shit.

"Not making fun of you at all," I insisted, trying to keep my tone light and the hatred buried deep. "I'm actually fascinated by your knowledge. As the Death Counselor, I've never actually witnessed a soul blob, just ghosts."

She nodded and bought it hook, line and sinker. "When a human perishes, the soul shoots out of the body—looks like a blob. It's disgusting. If the soul has unfinished business, it becomes a ghost."

"I see," I said. "So, you saw this soul right after it died and then lost it?"

"Something like that," she said, staying vague. "Have you seen it?"

"No. If it had unfinished business, it might have come to me as a ghost. I can ask around," I told her. "How long ago did this human die?"

I held my breath and waited.

Her smile was positively nightmare-inducing. "Playing me is a very bad plan, Daisy the Death Counselor. You know exactly who I'm looking for, and I think you're hiding her. It makes sense, and I'm a very logical Angel. Families tend to stick together."

The bitch did *not* have my mother's soul. I was sure of it

now. Where it was, I had no clue. But if Clarissa didn't have it, her punishment wouldn't affect my mother.

She'd lied to Michael. She'd killed my mother and made sure my father disowned me. She'd also killed my husband to try to destroy me. She was the worst kind of abomination—and I loathed her with every fiber in my being.

How much should I tell her?

A whole bunch. It was time to mess with her and make her sloppy.

"Does the soul happen to have died thirty-five years ago?" I asked. "Is her name Alana?"

Clarissa's face reddened and her eyes literally sparked with menace and hatred. "Give her to me," she snarled.

"I don't have her," I said calmly. "However, since we're coming clean here, I know who my father is. Michael touched me when I went into Steve's mind and *everyone* saw what you did when he sent it to the other Immortals. Your ass is grass. Your guilt has been recorded and you are fucked."

"You lie!" she shouted, diving forward.

Barely dodging the bolt of lightning she threw at me, I reared back and delivered a left hook to her face that sent her flying across the room. Her crazed grunt of fury didn't bode well for me living into the next hour, but if I was going down, I was going down fighting.

"My nose," she hissed as blood ran down her lips and onto her dress. "You broke it."

"Looks better that way," I told her with an insanely inappropriate laugh. Slashing my hand through the air, I disintegrated the bubble, pushed my dogs out of the front door and shut it behind them.

Donna howled like the world was ending, but they were not going to die tonight. Only problem with what I had done was that Gram and Jimmy Joe Johnson had shown back up, and Gram was free to make her presence known in a big way. She wasted no time.

"Son of a bitch," Gram screeched as she whipped around Clarissa like a crazed tornado. "You will not come into my girl's house and mess with her."

"Watch me," Clarissa growled.

With a flick of her hand, a vicious, gold-flecked wind picked me up and slammed me against the wall with such force, I saw stars. With a silent thank you to John Travolta for using the wind on me earlier, I broke the spell, shook it off and tackled Clarissa to the ground.

"Bust her ass," Gram yelled. "Hit that bitch!"

I'd never heard Gram talk like that in my life. The woman was riled up, but I was a good granddaughter who obeyed my elders.

"On it," I yelled, kneeing Clarissa in the stomach, which earned me a slap across my face that would probably leave a permanent mark.

"I'll kill everyone who means anything to you," she threatened, trying to throw me off of her. Her failure to toss my ass across the room shocked me almost as much as it shocked her.

Laying into her already broken nose, I nailed her again. "I wouldn't do that if I were you. You have enough problems without more death on your hands."

"You should have never been born," she screeched, raking her nails down my cheek. The Angel was insane and talking bullshit. "He was mine. Michael loved me until that whore came along. Funny thing, it was a whore who helped the whore get away. Ahh, the irony."

All of her words made me sick and I wanted her to stop talking. Using my elbow, I paid her back for disrespecting my mother. The sound it made connecting to her crushed nose sickened me, but no one calls my mother a whore.

"No, actually he didn't. Ever. Michael never loved you. He told me." My torn cheek felt like it was on fire and blood seeped into my mouth.

Gram and Jimmy Joe hovered around me and tried to create a distracting wind. It was working. Clarissa's hair was in her eyes. Only problem was, mine was too.

"You will pay," she choked out through the blood spurting from her nose.

"I already have," I told her. "It's your turn now."

"Hog-tie her," Gram shouted. "Tie her up like a stuck pig!"

I had no clue if tying her up would work. It was a long shot, but it was something. Rolling off of Clarissa and running to the far side of the room, I tore the floor-to-ceiling curtains from their rods.

The crack of lightning was horrible. Gram's scream was even worse.

The plan failed. Not because the curtains wouldn't hold her. I never got that far.

The plan failed because Clarissa disappeared.

However, she'd left me a parting gift.

Jimmy Joe Johnson was in pieces amidst the shattered glass on the floor. He was almost invisible and fading fast.

"No," I cried out, desperately trying to gather up his parts. "No, no, no. Gram what happened?"

Gram's sobs racked her body and she held the head of her beau in her shaking hands. "Jimmy Joe Johnson saved me," she choked out through her tears.

"I don't understand," I said, trying to find his midsection and having no luck.

"She went for me and my man jumped in front and took the hit. Jimmy Joe Johnson sacrificed himself for me—was willin' to die for me."

I didn't have the heart to remind her that both of them were dead already. What Jimmy Joe had done was truly beautiful and may have cost him dearly. I wasn't sure if I could glue him back together since I couldn't find all of his parts.

"Daisy girl," Gram whispered.

"Yes?" I answered, glancing over at her from my spot on the glass-covered floor.

"I need you to help my Jimmy Joe," she said, gently kissing the forehead of his detached head. "We owe that to him."

"I will, Gram," I promised, closing my eyes for a quick second. "I will."

I hoped to Hell and back I wasn't lying.

CHAPTER TWENTY-ONE

"GODDAMMIT," GIDEON ROARED AS HE MATERIALIZED IN THE middle of the living room and took in the carnage with wild eyes and a vicious expression. "Where is she?"

"Gone," I said, holding back tears with effort.

My adrenaline had spiked and now I was coming down hard. However, I still had work to do. Most of Jimmy Joe was unrecognizable. The promise I'd just made to Gram was looking impossible.

Nothing is impossible. You just have to believe.

Gideon's eyes blazed red and his dark side took over. Shimmering ebony wings erupted from his back and a golden glow surrounded him. The span of his wings had to be six feet and the glowing light made them sparkle. He was beyond furious. As his ire mounted, he began to growl and speak in the language I'd heard him speak in Hell.

"She harmed you," he hissed, carefully picking me up off the floor and examining me.

"She didn't look so good when she left, either," I said, trying to make light of one of the scariest episodes in my life thus far.

"I will destroy her," he snarled, gently touching my torn cheek.

The Grim Reaper was a sight to behold. Gideon was still Gideon, but he was also a beautiful, deadly winged beast. His gentleness with me was in direct juxtaposition to the fury simmering below the surface.

"Kind of hurts," I said, trying to remove his hand from my bloody face.

"Stay still," he whispered, and continued to cup my cheek.

The sensation of tiny, searing-hot needles piercing my skin in quick succession made me want to scream. However, the look of concern and love in Gideon's blazing red eyes made me grit my teeth and bear it.

"Stay with me, Daisy," he said. "I'm trying to do this quickly."

"Tattoo my face?" I asked with a grimace, trying to make a joke.

It fell a little flat. It was difficult to be funny when my face was on fire.

"No," he said, with a tight smile. "I'm healing you. The pain will be gone soon."

"How soon?" I asked through gritted teeth.

"Done," he said, removing his hand and pulling me against him with care.

"Thank you," I said into his chest.

My face still throbbed, but the burning sensation was gone. I had no clue if I'd be scarred for life physically, but I was pretty sure there would be some mental baggage left over.

"Where is Heather?" Gideon asked in a terse voice, holding his anger in check with effort.

"She wasn't here," I admitted. "Her rental car wouldn't start so she transported home. She left a note."

Gideon expelled a frustrated sigh and I felt his body tighten. "And you didn't call me," he stated flatly.

"I didn't call you," I confirmed. "That fact is at the top of the list of the stupidest things I've done in my life."

"Correct," Gideon said, holding me tighter. "You will *never* do anything like that again. Am I clear?"

Although, I was tempted to fire back that I was the boss of me, I didn't. He was correct—a little alpha dude with the delivery, but correct. The man loved me and I loved him. If the tables were turned, I'd want to kick his ass.

"I will never do that again," I promised.

"Ever?" he pushed.

"Never ever," I assured him.

Gideon's body relaxed somewhat, but his hold did not. "You could have died."

I simply nodded.

"That's unacceptable," he said, sounding pained.

"I didn't," I pointed out. "I'm here. Where's Steve?"

"I sent him to get the other Immortals in case Clarissa was still on the premises," Gideon replied.

Gram floated over with Jimmy Joe's head cradled in her

arms. "My Daisy girl kicked that nasty bitch's ass. The nose on that heifer won't ever be the same."

"You broke the Angel of Mercy's nose?" Gideon asked with a tiny trace of amusement in his voice.

"Busted it good," Gram confirmed. "Nice wings, Gideon —real shiny. Can you fly with those suckers?"

Gideon chuckled. His wings retracted and rested on his back. "Thank you, Gram. And yes, I can fly with these suckers."

"Love to go on a ride sometime," she said, and then looked down at her beau's head in her hands. "Jimmy Joe would have loved it too. Might've cried a little cause he's afraid of heights and all, but I just know he would have loved it."

"I have to fix him," I said, moving away from Gideon's warm embrace and getting back down on my hands and knees.

The Grim Reaper joined me. "What are we searching for?"

"Jimmy Joe Johnson," I said, glancing around in despair. "He's all over the place. I have to find all of him and put him back together. He saved Gram's life."

"But she's dead," Gideon whispered so Gram wouldn't overhear.

"I know that," I whispered back. "But Clarissa tried to destroy her and Jimmy Joe dove in front of her and took the hit. Blew him to smithereens. So, while my statement isn't technically correct, it's literally correct in a broad sense of the definition."

Gideon stopped searching and stared at me.

"What?" I asked.

"Clarissa did this to Jimmy Joe?" he asked, his brow wrinkled in thought.

I nodded and went back to work. Help would have been nice, but I was fine without it. The ghosts were my responsibility. Jimmy Joe was my hero because of what he did and I wasn't about to leave any of him on the floor.

"Why was Jimmy Joe still here?" Gideon asked. "Do you know what his unfinished business was?"

I shook my head. If I spoke, I would cry. I had no clue why Jimmy Joe Johnson was still here. My norm was to let the dead come to me when they were ready to move on. Pushing hadn't felt right, and I didn't want anyone to feel unwelcome or like I wanted them to leave.

God, had my manners left my squatters in a limbo of sorts? Should I have a freaking schedule? Honestly, I didn't care how long they stayed. My life was fuller with all my dead friends.

"I can hear you," Gideon said, smiling.

Why was he smiling at me? "I'm getting ready to cry," I told him, pushing some of the glass away and sitting down. "I really don't think my thoughts are funny right now."

"They're loving and sweet," he said.

"Loving and sweet certainly didn't help Jimmy Joe."

"Do you know that as fact?" he questioned, waving Gram over.

"The more I know, the less I know," I muttered, closing my eyes and trying to make everything disappear.

"Daisy girl," Gram said. "You've got nothin' to feel bad about. You've been busier than a moth in a wool mitten. You're handlin' the dead much better than your mama or I ever did. Jimmy Joe, bless his heart, has had a wonderful stay."

I opened one eye and looked at her. "I'm doing a good job?"

"Yep. I'm right proud of you. I want you to quit goin' round your ass to get to your elbow."

Squinting at her, I let out a pained laugh. "Is that even possible?"

"No! And that's my point, child," she said, hugging Jimmy Joe's head to her. "We're all just doing the best we can. That's all we can do."

"Gram," Gideon cut in. "Do you know what Jimmy Joe's unfinished business was?"

"Yep."

We waited.

And waited.

"Are we supposed to guess?" I asked with the beginnings of a real smile.

If Gram knew, I could hopefully solve it and he could rest in peace and move into the light.

"My poor Jimmy Joe Johnson just felt awful that he died with credit card debt," she said, shaking her head sadly.

I was kind of shocked that someone had stayed due to credit card debt, but Jimmy Joe was an odd one. However, this was an easy solve unless he owed hundreds of thousands. I had Steve's life insurance money in the bank. Which meant I could easily give Jimmy Joe peace.

"How much?" I asked Gram.

"I'll pay it," Gideon offered.

"No," I said firmly. "I'll pay it."

"I'd really like to pay it," Gideon insisted.

"Umm… nope. Jimmy Joe was my guest. I can pay it," I said, giving Gideon a look.

Gideon sighed and, if I wasn't mistaken—and I wasn't—he rolled his eyes.

"Daisy, I have *a lot* of money," he informed me.

"Irrelevant," I told him, so tempted to ask how much, but I didn't want to know.

"Y'all need to hush," Gram hissed. "If anyone is gonna pay it, it's me."

"You're dead," I pointed out.

Gram looked surprised for a second, and then laughed. "Yep, but I had a life insurance policy that's comin' your way, Daisy girl," she said. "So technically I could pay off my man's debt. But I'm not gonna do that."

"Mmkay," I said. "Not following that logic, Gram."

"Jimmy Joe told me the check was in his briefcase at his house, in the crawlspace—addressed, stamped and ready to go," she explained. "He didn't want to tell you yet because we were havin' so much fun courtin'."

I shook my head and grinned. "So, this will consist of a breaking and entering into a *crawlspace?*"

I'd done it before for my dear dead buddy Sam. I could do it again. I just hoped the house was empty this time.

"Kind of," Gram said with a wink. "You won't have to break at all, just enter."

Gram was getting as cryptic as the Immortals.

"There's kind of a lot going on right now," I reminded her. "A few details might be helpful."

Gram laughed, floated down to the floor and sat herself next to me. She held Jimmy Joe's head in her lap and patted it lovingly. "Can I ask you a question?"

"Do I have a choice?" I shot back.

"Nope."

"Ask away," I replied as Gideon chuckled, grabbed a ripped-up pillow and got more comfortable.

"Who'd you and Steve buy this house from?" she asked.

I looked down at my hands for a moment and sighed. Was Gram losing it? "The bank," I said, humoring her. If she got too off track, I'd pull her back. "The owner had passed away and the bank sold the house for the out-of-state relatives."

"Correct! And do you recall who actually owned the house?"

"Nope," I replied with a shrug. "Is that important?"

"Sure is, darlin'," she said with a wink.

My mouth fell open and I stared at the head in her lap. "Jimmy Joe Johnson? He was the owner of my house?"

"Bingo," Gram yelled, tossing Jimmy Joe's head in the air, catching it and kissing the top of his head.

"He died a long freaking time ago," I said. "He stuck around forever."

Gram nodded. "For a real long time, he was terrified of leaving the house—cried like a baby and got lost every time he tried. That's why I never ended up meeting up with him when I was the Death Counselor. My man had no balls."

The temptation to bring up Gideon's junk was strong.

However, the timing was way, way off. I stuck with the matter at hand. "So, he lived here with me and Steve the entire time?"

"Darn tootin'. He just loves y'all and was ready to get counseled by you, but…"

"But?" I pressed, still blown away by the story.

"But then I kicked the bucket and he wasn't in such a hurry to leave," she explained.

"Unreal," Gideon said with a laugh. "The briefcase is in the crawlspace?"

"Yep," Gram said. "He showed it to me yesterday when we were cheerin' up Birdie. Kind of dusty, but right where he left it."

Shit. Birdie… She needed me, and I hadn't been there for her. Even with everything going on, I shouldn't have left her hanging. No time like the present to fix that. I now had two excellent reasons to get filthy and check out my crawlspace.

"I am really glad I didn't knock my house down when Clarissa was here," I muttered, standing up and extending my hand to Gideon to help him to his feet.

"You were going to do that?" he asked, raising a brow.

"Considered it," I told him. "Thought it would be a good distraction to give me a head start in getting away from her."

"Why didn't you?" he asked, brushing pieces of glass off of my pants.

"It could have killed my dogs," I replied.

"You're serious," Gideon said flatly.

"Totally."

"If I ever get another life, I'm coming back as one of your dogs," he said with a laugh.

"Crap," I muttered. "Speaking of... they're still outside."

Moving quickly to the front door, I let my furballs back in. Donna barked and wagged her tail. Karen simply chased hers. Life was a mess, but it still had lots of little silver linings.

"Who's coming to the crawlspace?" I asked.

"Wouldn't miss it," Gideon said.

Taking his hand in mine, we walked out of my trashed house and around to the crawlspace door.

"The credit card check is over a decade old," I said, unlatching the door. "Is it still good?"

"Probably not," Gideon said. "However, I don't think it matters. Jimmy Joe will be at peace as long as it's sent."

"I can do that," I said. "But I didn't put him back together. Can he move on without all his parts?"

"Would it insult you if we worked as a team on this one?"

"Explain, please," I said.

Gideon leaned on the side of the house and crossed his arms over his chest. "Clarissa broke another sacred law by destroying one of the dead."

"One of many," I said.

"True," he agreed. "However, something like this falls into my territory. I can make the call of where to send a broken one who was unjustly harmed."

"And the call you would make for Jimmy Joe Johnson?" I asked.

"The light. I call the light."

My smile was so wide it hurt my face. "I would be honored to work with you, Grim Reaper."

"The honor would be all mine, Death Counselor. You ready to find a very old credit card payment?"

"Yes, I am, *partner*," I replied with a giggle.

"I like the way that sounds, *partner*."

"Me too," I said, getting low and crawling in. "Me too."

CHAPTER TWENTY-TWO

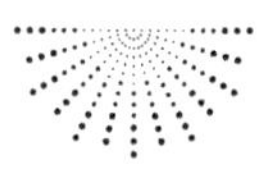

"YOU'RE SURE?" MY FATHER DEMANDED IN A VOICE SO FULL OF pain, I had to look away.

"I'm sure," I replied. "Clarissa doesn't have my mother's soul. She's looking for it and thought I had it."

Rage and confusion contorted his face. "If she doesn't have Alana's soul, where the hell is it?"

I said nothing. I didn't have the answer.

"Excuse me for a moment," he said tersely then walked out the front door of my house and slammed it behind him.

I looked over at the others in confusion.

"Did he just leave?"

"Hell no," Candy said, moving quickly to the window. "He just needs to let off a little steam. That was some big fucking news."

"Understatement," Tim said.

Charlie, Heather, Tim, and Gideon joined Candy at the bay window.

Luckily, Steve and Gram were keeping the ghosts entertained upstairs in my bedroom. They were all restless and upset since Clarissa's terrorizing visit, with the exception of Birdie, who was in seriously bad shape and resting on my newly restored couch thanks to a little magic from Candy. I could see through most of my dead buddy now and she was unable to fly. She'd weighed practically nothing in my arms when I'd carried her out of the crawlspace and back into the house. And I almost cried with joy when she'd called me a hooker and weakly flipped me off.

I put an afghan over her before I joined the others at the window.

"Everyone be ready to duck," Gideon warned.

"Are you serious?" I asked, peering out at the pissed-off Archangel in my yard.

"Very," Gideon said.

Michael glowed such a brilliant gold, it was hard to look directly at him. He lit up the yard like a blazing sun in the middle of the night. Raising his hands in the air then jerking them down violently, he created an explosion that caused the house to shudder on its foundation. His roar of agony and fury would live in my mind forever.

My instinct was to go to him, but the rules for my father and myself had not been decided. Would I even be welcome? The thought broke a piece of my heart.

"Follow your instincts, Daisy," Gideon whispered in my ear.

I glanced up at him.

"You're thinking very loudly," he said, giving me a gentle push.

"I'm going to have to figure out how to stop doing that," I muttered as I opened the front door and looked out at the father who'd loved my mother with his entire being.

Michael turned as if he felt my eyes on him and stared right back. His body still glowed but it wasn't as blinding, or maybe I was getting used to it. I had no idea what to say. Words seemed insufficient. I decided against them.

Walking down the front porch steps, I approached him. My father looked at me, his expression questioning. Keeping my gaze pinned to his, I slowly extended my hand. His beautiful eyes widened and he glanced down at my hand. I simply nodded and kept it extended.

He approached me warily, as if I would yank my hand back as he came closer. I had no intention of doing that. My gesture was from my heart. It was real and it felt right.

He took my hand. The feeling of his hand in mine was one I'd longed for my whole life. It had taken forty years to get here and a tremendous amount of shitty stuff to happen, but we'd arrived. Hopefully.

"I destroyed your yard," my father finally said, still staring at our joined hands. "Sorry about that."

I laughed. His statement was unexpected, but somehow perfect. "No biggie, I knocked down a huge tree not too long ago with my fist," I told him.

His smile lit his face and my breath caught in my throat. "Like father, like daughter," he said softly. "I'm so sorry, Daisy."

I wasn't sure if he was apologizing for the yard or for being absent my life. My guess was both.

"I'm sorry too," I said. "Come back inside."

"As you wish," he said, squeezing my hand.

The emotions rioting through me were thrilling and freeing. It filled me with something I'd been missing—something that had been stolen from me.

And it gave me yet another reason to hate Clarissa.

As we reentered the house, everything inside me felt new and shiny. However, I wasn't ready to scream with joy and call John Travolta dad. We had a long road ahead. And while I would no longer think of him as Darth Vader, John Travolta had a nice ring to it.

"Do you think the authorities will show up?" Heather asked, still looking out of the window at the massive crater in my yard.

"Oh crap," I said. "We're pretty much in the middle of nowhere, but that was a big explosion."

Tim pulled a police scanner from his pocket and checked it. "Nope. All clear."

Tim had many strange things in his plethora of pockets…

"Back to business," Gideon said.

"I agree," Heather said, turning away from the window. "Clarissa said she would kill everyone who means anything to you?"

Heather had been mortified that leaving her car here had led to me being unprotected—hence a visit from Clarissa. I'd told her ad nauseam that it was my fault, not hers, but she wasn't having any of it. With the way she'd been trailing me since she arrived, I was worried she wasn't going to leave my side for the rest of my life.

"Yes," I replied with a shudder. "I think it would be an

excellent plan to get Jennifer, June and Missy out of here for a while."

"I agree," Gideon said.

"As do I," my father added.

"I'm sending them away immediately," Charlie said, running his hands over his balding head. "Nothing will happen to June or the other women on my watch."

"Won't they be safer here with us to protect them?" Tim inquired as he swept the glass up off the floor in my living room.

"I'll take them somewhere and watch over them," Candy said. "I need a vacation anyways. I'll get those gals out of town and show them a great time." She clapped her hands and restored the blown-up staircase. "And I'll kill the shit out of anyone who tries to harm them. I've been itching for a fight lately. Annihilating someone would seriously work for me."

"That sounds a little iffy to me," I said. Candy could barely get through the luncheon with my friends without sticking her foot in her mouth and pulling it out of her butt. I couldn't imagine a vacation with the foursome.

"Nah, it's a great plan," Candy said. "I'm excellent at bumping off shit. Plus, I can share a room with the gals. Tim would have to be in a separate room, leaving them open to danger."

"When did I get volunteered to go?" Tim asked, perplexed.

"You didn't," Candy said. "I was just making a fucking point."

"Candy Vargo, you have a mouth like a sailor, but I have

to agree that you could protect them gals," Gram said, zipping into the room and fluttering around Birdie with concern. "I just don't want to hear you were picking your teeth in public when y'all get back."

My head jerked to Gram and I watched her closely. If she'd heard us talking about my mother, she could go zombie on me again. Fortunately, she wasn't behaving robotically. I expelled a sigh of relief that she hadn't overheard anything. I was ready to veer the conversation away from talk of my mother with Gram in the room. Hurting her was not on the agenda. Ever.

"What if I have food in my teeth?" Candy asked, trying to win back the rights to her disgusting bad habit.

"Then you carry a dang toothbrush in your purse and excuse yourself to find a bathroom," Gram told her.

"Oh my God," Candy groaned. "I have to carry a purse?"

I laughed and shook my head. Gram was going to be the death of the old Candy Vargo and the creator of the newer, more refined version. How was that for *karma*?

Gram was surprisingly fine about Jimmy Joe Johnson moving on. We never did find all of him, but Gideon had used some strong magic that rocked the house. Literally. The golden glow had come for Jimmy Joe, and he'd been restored to his former self even though his ghostly body had been in pieces. He'd promised to wait for Gram up in Heaven and then cried as expected. He'd thanked me in advance for sending off his very tardy credit card payment, and also for taking such loving care of his house. Steve had been delighted with the story and told Jimmy Joe he'd meet up with him in the future.

The thought of Steve leaving didn't tear at me as much as it had when he'd first come back. We'd worked out so many of our issues and both of us were happy and at peace. I would never stop loving him and would always miss him. But when he was ready to move on into the light, I would let him go.

"We should get the women out of town immediately," my father said, plugging in the vacuum and turning it on.

"Absolutely," Gideon agreed as he picked up the torn paintings and photographs, repairing them with a snap of his fingers.

It wasn't strange at all to see Gideon help with the cleanup. It was natural and right. However, watching John Travolta vacuum was all kinds of weird. I almost told him he didn't have to help, but figured it would be insulting because everyone else was pitching in. He and I were making new rules. If he wanted to fit in, I was all for letting him.

"Heather," Charlie said, scrubbing his hand over his face and wincing. "I need to ask a favor. I will owe you one in return."

"An unethical favor?" Heather asked, clearly reading his intent by his facial expression.

Charlie took a deep breath then nodded. "Yes. I want you to plant the idea for a vacation in June, Jennifer and Missy's minds."

Heather stared at Charlie for a long moment then pressed the bridge of her nose. "Fine. Where are they going and when?"

"Italy," Gideon suggested. "I have a villa in Tuscany. It's

private and safe. The staff there is discreet and Immortal. I will advise them Karma is coming along with three human guests."

"I wanna go to Tuscany," Gram griped.

"So do I," I said with a laugh.

"Done," Gideon said. "I shall take you and Gram to Tuscany soon."

"Hot damn," Gram squealed. "Can we fly on your back? I'd love to see them shiny wings in action."

"Umm… no," I said, shaking my head. "Kind of a long flight to bareback it."

"I'd have to agree," Gideon said with a chuckle as he walked around the house and continued to repair the damage Clarissa had caused.

Watching them was fascinating. "I don't know why most of you guys are lawyers. You could make a fortune in construction."

"Because we don't use magic as lawyers," my father explained. "Law is good for the mind."

"Correct," Charlie added. "I was a lawyer last century. I quite enjoy the hospital work this century." He turned his attention back to Heather. "As to where to send the women? I like Gideon's idea of Italy. June has always wanted to visit. As to when? Tonight. There's an international flight leaving from Atlanta at midnight."

"Kind of quick considering they haven't packed yet," Heather pointed out. "It's nine now and we're over an hour away from Atlanta. If I drive well over the speed limit, they'll still probably miss the plane."

"Not an issue," Candy said. "Plant the idea. We'll transport them to Atlanta."

"If you're going to transport them, I'd suggest transporting them straight to the villa in Tuscany," John Travolta said.

"Is that safe?" I questioned.

"Much safer than flying," Tim assured me. "Plus, the risk of having your rectum sucked out on an airplane vacuum toilet is greatly minimalized."

That shut everyone up for a few minutes.

Heather took my hand and led me to my newly repaired armchair. "Daisy, I understand all of this sounds unusual and possibly awful to you, but Clarissa doesn't make threats idly. Normally, we don't get humans involved in our shitshows."

"This time we do," Charlie said as his eyes turned silver and his fingertips sparked. "June is my happiness. *Nothing* can happen to her."

Heather put her hand on Charlie's back to calm him. "Nothing will happen to her. And nothing will happen to Missy or Jennifer. Candy, move your ass. We're leaving."

"Wait. What about clothes?" I asked then rolled my eyes. This kind of talk was becoming far too common for me. I simply shook my head and plowed forward. I'd joined the crazy club and I may as well participate. Plus, I didn't want my friends to have only one outfit the entire time. Jennifer would crap her pants. "They can't travel without necessities."

"Everything they need will be waiting for them in Tuscany," Charlie said.

"Holy hell on a Sunday," Gram said with an appreciative whistle. "You ancient freaks know how to travel in style."

"Gram," I chastised her. "That's rude."

"But accurate," Gideon said with a laugh. "Daisy, you don't have to worry. The girls will have a safe and wonderful time. My staff will make sure they're entertained as well as protected. Like Heather said, this isn't our norm, but the circumstances are anything but normal."

"I'm ready," Candy announced.

"Gimme your toothpicks, girlie," Gram demanded, holding out her hand.

"I don't have any," Candy lied, avoiding eye contact.

"Candy Vargo, you're talkin' with your tongue out of your dang shoe," Gram snapped. "You think I'm so dumb I could throw myself on the ground and miss?"

"I didn't understand any of that," Candy said, scratching her head.

"I did," Tim announced with pride. "She said you're a liar and that she's not stupid. I'd suggest you give up your toothpicks immediately."

"All of you suck," Candy grumbled as she pulled about thirty toothpicks out of her pocket and handed them to Gram.

Of course, they went right through Gram's ghostly hand, but Tim was quick with the broom. He swept them up and sprinted out of the room.

"You watch that mouth," Gram warned Candy. "I expect ladylike manners out of you."

"That would constitute a miracle," Tim pointed out, coming back from tossing the toothpicks.

"Miracles happen and *karma* can be a real bitch," Gram said with a cackle as she floated back up the stairs. "Daisy girl, do you need me? The squatters and Steve are watchin' *The Price Is Right*. I'd kind of like to kick everyone's behind in the Big Showcase."

"Go kick away, Gram," I told her, glad that she was leaving of her own accord. The conversation coming wasn't one I wanted her to be present for.

"Move it, Candy," Heather said, grabbing her purse. "We have work to do."

As they made their exit, my father turned off the vacuum and looked around. "Does anyone mind if I expedite the process?"

"Be my guest," Charlie said. "We need to talk."

Before I could ask what *expedite the process* meant, my father clapped his hands and everything in the house went back to what it was before Clarissa had destroyed it. Donna and Karen barked and ran zoomies around the room and Birdie weakly flipped everyone off.

"That was nifty," I said, looking around.

"You could probably do it too," he told me.

I said nothing. If I could, I didn't want to know. So much was changing so fast, I didn't want to lose myself. Cleaning like a regular person was calming and normal. I needed some normal.

Tim put the broom back in the closet and sat down next to Birdie. "Did the Angel of Circe leave any other clues?"

"Mercy," Charlie corrected Tim.

"Play on words," Tim said, raising a brow. "Circe was a sorceress who detained Odysseus on her island and turned his men to swine. Thought it was a fitting replacement… and it rhymed."

"I like it," I told him. "And no, I don't think so. Clarissa talked a lot, but some of it was bullshit."

"Never assume anything is bullshit or useless," Charlie advised. "Immortals speak in cryptic clues naturally. Can't help it. Living forever does things to a person. Games become reality without conscious effort."

"That kind of sucks," I said before I could stop myself.

"That's one way of putting it," Charlie agreed with a smile.

"Speaking of outliving society in general," Tim said. "Did you get results on Daisy's bloodwork?"

Charlie nodded. "I did."

"And?" I questioned as my stomach turned summersaults. I had no clue what he was going to say or what I wanted him to say. Being Immortal didn't sound great. However, leaving Gideon at some point sounded awful.

The fact that I was having this internal debate was insane.

"Inconclusive," Charlie announced. "The DNA is not exactly human, but lacks many of the elements of Immortals. I'll have to draw again and do more testing, Daisy. Sorry about that."

I had no clue if I was disappointed or relieved. I'd deal with that when I had to. "It's fine," I assured him. "I've got great veins."

"That you do," Charlie agreed with a chuckle. "Let's go back over the exchange with Clarissa. Shall we?"

"Hoooooooookaaah," Birdie whispered, reaching out for me.

Moving quickly across the room, I sat down next to her and put my hand on her for comfort. "Yep, I know you're a hooker," I said soothingly.

I was tempted to hug her and hold her close, but I couldn't risk going inside her mind. Besides, I wasn't sure I was ready to experience the final BJ just prior to her death. Birdie's hooker history was going to be something else.

Oh my God.

My body went cold and hot at the same time. I stared at Birdie. She flipped me off. Another piece of the puzzle fell into place.

A whore helped the whore get away.

"I know," I choked out, gaping at Birdie. "I think I know where Alana's soul is."

"You do?" my father asked.

I shook my head. "No. I mean, I don't know where it is, but I'm pretty sure I know who does."

Birdie wheezed. I knew it was a laugh, but it sounded bad. "Yausssss, hoooooooookaaah dieeah foooor yooouah."

I leaned in close and kissed her partially missing cheek. "Can I hug you, Birdie?"

"Yausssss," she replied, raising her middle finger at me.

"No," Gideon said. "It's far too dangerous."

Glancing up at Gideon, I smiled. "While I love and appreciate your concern, it's more dangerous for all of us if I don't."

"Please give me a better explanation than that," Gideon said, wanting to trust me, but terrified to do so.

"I have to trust you just as much as you have to trust me," I told him. "I'm not reliving Birdie's death. She died of a heart attack after… well, that part isn't relevant. However, I believe she knows how to find my mother's soul."

"Why do you believe this?" Charlie inquired.

"The bullshit," I told him. "There was a clue in the bullshit."

Gideon raised a brow. "You're sounding cryptically like an Immortal," he pointed out.

I laughed. He was correct. "You win," I said. "Clarissa called my mother a whore, which earned her a severely broken nose. However, she also said a whore helped the whore get away."

"I'm following none of this," John Travolta said. "If this is dangerous for you, I'm with Gideon."

My father's concern delighted me, but I wasn't caving when I knew I was right. "Birdie was a lady of the evening in life. The clues have been in front of me for a while, but I needed Clarissa's to piece it all together. Birdie is the *whore* who helped the *whore* get away."

"Yausssss, hoooooooookaaah."

"Birdie, when you told me someone died for me, you meant my mother, yes?"

"Yausssss."

"Are you the one who helped Alana get away?"

"Yausssss."

"Need more proof?" I asked the men.

"No," Gideon said with great reluctance. "No more proof needed."

I nodded and smiled at him. "I love you, Grim Reaper."

"I love you, Death Counselor."

Looking to my father, he nodded as well.

"Would you touch me while I go into Birdie?" I asked him. "I want to make sure I don't miss anything important."

He sat down next to me and put his hand on my back. "It would be my great honor to assist you."

"Thank you... Dad." The word felt odd rolling off my tongue, but it also felt incredibly right.

The Archangel's answering smile was blinding.

My decision was correct.

CHAPTER TWENTY-THREE

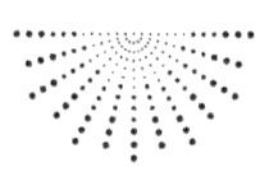

THE COLD. THE COLD WENT ALL THE WAY TO MY BONES AND TORE through my body like sharp, frozen daggers made of ice. Trying to catch my breath, I gasped for air but stayed calm.

My head pounded violently and every single cell in my body screamed for oxygen. I knew it was momentary, but it still sucked.

My mind went numb and my limbs felt like jelly.

Closing my eyes, I welcomed the icy chill that permeated my skin and seeped into my blood. It was proof that I was exactly where I wanted to be. I would never enjoy the sensation, but I'd become accustomed to it.

"Birdie?" I called out.

"Hooker?" she replied with a cackle.

"Nope, you're the dang hooker," I said, opening my eyes. "Oh my God. You're so pretty."

Birdie stood about five foot five and had black curly ringlets and beautiful dark skin. She was curvy in all the right places and had a killer smile that lit her lovely face... and fantastic boobs.

"Damn straight I am, sweetie," she replied. "I was very successful in my line of work. The knockers are the real deal. Wanna touch them?"

"No," I said, with a laugh. "However, they're terrific knockers."

"Thank you, Daisy," she said, adjusting her ample bosom with pride.

"Welcome, Birdie," I said, reaching out to hug her. "You've been a pain in my ass."

"It's my specialty," she informed me with a delightfully naughty grin. "Well, that and blow jobs."

"TMI," I told her, hugging her tight. "You really like being called Birdie?"

"Way better than Ethel," she said, cupping my cheek in her hand.

"Can I ask you a question?"

"I figure you have a lot of questions, child," she said.

Birdie and I stood opposite each other in a cavernous room of emptiness. There was no floor. No walls to speak of—more of a vast landscape of nothing. We floated in a silvery mist.

"Why did you call me a hooker all the time?" I asked.

Birdie shrugged and smiled. "Two-fold, darlin'. I was trying to let you know what I did and it just tickled me to see the shock on your face every time I called you a hooker. And by the way, I wasn't a hooker. I was a highly paid escort."

"Was that... umm..." I wasn't sure how to ask.

"It was my choice," Birdie said, raising a perfectly plucked brow. "I called the shots and enjoyed the hell out of my profession. Died right after delivering the best BJ of my life. Went out at the top of my game."

Birdie left me speechless as one of my dead squatters and

speechless right now. I wasn't about to judge the nutty woman who I'd grown to adore. She was who she was and clearly had no issue with it.

Neither did I.

"One more piece of advice before we get to the important stuff," she said, leaning in close.

I was slightly terrified. I should have been.

"The best BJ technique I can pass on is to not ignore the balls. You grab that hot man of yours and suck on those balls like they were lollipops. It'll blow his head right off—pun intended," she said with a cackle as she bent over and slapped her leg.

"I'm sorry. What?" I wheezed out, blushing furiously knowing that, yet again, Gideon, Tim, Charlie and my dad were listening in on another discussion about Gideon's junk.

"Honey, just take my advice and don't be afraid of the balls."

"I'm not afraid of the balls," I said. "I think the balls are nice... and bally."

Birdie looked at me like I was a bit crazy, which was the pot definitely calling the kettle black. However, I'd taken note of her advice.

"Alrighty," she said. "Wanna tell you a few things, and then I need you to watch something that's gonna be real painful for you, darlin'."

"Okay," I said, taking her outstretched hand and holding it tight. I felt a little light-headed and took a deep breath to calm myself. I needed to be focused and sharp. Too much was at stake.

"I knew your mama, honey, but not till I was dead," Birdie told me. "Your mama was my Death Counselor."

I was quiet and waited for more.

"I just loved your mama," she said, reaching out and touching

my nose. "You look just like her. You were an adorable child, and you turned into a beautiful and loving woman. Alana would be so proud."

My eyes welled up with tears. "Thank you."

"Welcome, Daisy," she said. "So, your mama solved my issue right off. Honestly, I can't even remember what it was." She laughed and shook her head. "I was having such a fine time spending my days with your mama, I stuck around for a while. Didn't know why... until I did."

"What do you mean?" I asked, not quite following.

"I was there when your mama died," she said softly. "Sad, sad day. I knew at that moment why I hadn't moved on yet. Your mama helped me, and it was my turn to help her."

"I need more details," I told her, dreading hearing them, but knowing I had to. My words came tumbling out so fast I wasn't even sure they made sense. "Was she murdered? Was it Clarissa? Did my mother trade her life for mine? Do you know where she is?"

"All in good time, sugar," Birdie said sadly. "Close your eyes, little girl, and I will show you."

"I'm scared," I said.

"I know," she answered. "Work through that. Your mama needs you now. A little fear is good. Keeps you on your toes."

"Birdie?"

"Yes?"

"Will you please flip me off one last time?"

Birdie's laugh echoed through the nothingness. The sound of it warmed my heart.

"With pleasure," she said as she lifted her middle finger with gusto. "Close your eyes now, child. It's time."

Taking another deep breath, I did as I was told.

Pictures raced across my vision so quickly, I couldn't make them out. As always, it was like an old, static-filled black-and-white TV screen was inside my head. Catching glimpses of my father's home, I gasped.

I inhaled and exhaled slowly... and I watched.

I saw all the gold—gold fountain, gold and white floor tiles. The paintings—frescos on the ceilings. Angels. Violent Angels. Pale pink clouds. The house had seemed cold when I'd visited my father. When I observed it now, it felt warm and full of love.

A little girl raced across the room, screaming with laughter. She was being chased by her mother and father, who laughed with the child as she stopped in front of the fountain and began telling them a story about a princess who rode a pink donkey with ten legs. The father took the mother's hand and gently pulled her to the floor so they could be a proper audience for their silly little girl.

I knew the little girl. She was me.

The screen went to static again, and I yearned to see more. Pictures flitted by of Alana and Michael waltzing and me singing at the top of my lungs for them. Images of riding on my father's shoulders as my mother grinned and painted her toenails. Quick snapshots of being put to bed by two people who adored me.

My eyes welled with tears behind my closed lids. My heart was completely filled and devastatingly empty at the same time.

The pictures faded and morphed into my mother with the ghosts. She was compassionate and kind to the dead. They adored her.

"Alana," Birdie warned. "You need to stay away from that woman. She's bad news."

Birdie zipped around my mother like a little tornado as my mother slid into a car and put a key in the ignition.

"Ethel, I know," my mother whispered, glancing around warily. "She's got my Daisy. She said she would make a deal."

"Bullshit," Birdie hissed as she flew through the roof of the car and sat in the passenger seat. "Where's Michael?"

"Away," my mother said through clenched teeth. "He can't know about this. She said he'd be cast out of Heaven."

"And you believe her?" Birdie demanded.

"No," Alana said. "She's a despicable liar, but she has Daisy, and I'm getting her back no matter what I have to do. Clarissa made it very clear if Michael showed up, she would slit Daisy's throat."

"I don't like this one damn bit," Birdie hissed.

My mother rested her head on the steering wheel and choked back a sob. "Neither do I."

My stomach crashed to my toes and I wanted to scream for my mother not to go. I wanted to beg her to call Michael. I wanted to save her.

I couldn't. She was about to save me.

The images came faster now and the sound was warped.

My mother arrived on a bridge. I sat on the ground crying. The Angel of Mercy stood above me with an ugly sneer on her face. The moon hung low in the sky and sent an eerie glow over the dark water below.

The argument was garbled between the women and making out the words was difficult, but not impossible. However, the action was tragically clear.

"Send her home," I heard Alana scream.

"She has no home," Clarissa hissed. "She should have never

been born. Michael is mine and you tempted him away. He loves me. He always has."

Alana simply nodded to appease the insane Angel.

Clarissa bent down, grabbed me by my dark curls and yanked my head back. I screamed and cried harder.

"Send her to my mother. Please," Alana begged. "She is an innocent in this. I'll give you anything you want."

"The child's the product of a whore," Clarissa snarled. "Say it. Say it and I will send her to your mother instead of choking her to death while you watch her die. However, there's another price to be paid."

"My daughter is the product of a whore," my mother whispered with tears streaming down her face. "Send Daisy to my mother."

"And what can you give me in return?" the deranged Angel demanded.

"What do you want?"

"You. I want you dead. It's the child of the whore or the whore herself. Your choice."

Alana answered without a second of hesitation. "Send my baby to my mother. That's my choice."

"Are you sure?" she asked, her eyes wild with insanity.

"I'm sure," my mother said, blowing me a kiss. "I love you, Daisy, and I love your daddy with all my heart. I always will. Do not forget."

Clarissa waved her hand and laughed manically. In a golden flash of light, I was gone.

My mother and Clarissa remained.

The next few minutes were some of the worst of my life. Clarissa's wings burst from her back and swept my mother into the air. She made no sound at all as Clarissa beat her almost to the point of death and then hurled her broken body over the side of the bridge.

My scream of agony was involuntary. Birdie squeezed my hands gently. I had to remind myself this had happened a long time ago. It wasn't happening now.

I knew my father had erased my memories, but he was never aware of this one. That I knew for sure. I also knew it was never fully erased. Gram's story now made sense, how I cried for days when she tried to speak of my mother. So many sad and tragic puzzle pieces were clicking together.

"Birdie, I still don't know where she is," I whispered with my eyes still closed.

"I'll show you, darlin'," she promised. "Stay with me."

Birdie hid below the bridge. My mother's body hit the water with a sickening crash. Her soul, a beautiful golden orb, left her body.

Clarissa flew like a bat out of hell to steal it.

However, Birdie was faster.

My mind went back to static for a brief second and then we were in a home—a home that I'd been in many times in my life.

Chills skittered up my spine. "Oh my God," I said. "I know where we are."

"Of course you do," Birdie said. "Watch."

An old woman came into the room with a young girl. I smiled when I saw the child. I would know my best friend anywhere. The little girl who'd stopped my tears. Missy. And the old woman looked just as Missy had described her. The very same woman who had told her the story of the Soul Keepers.

Missy held her beloved great-granny's hand and had no clue that the old woman was conversing with a ghost who carried my mother's precious soul in her hands.

Looking down at the child, Missy's great-granny smiled. "This little one is the strongest Soul Keeper of them all. My tiny gal has the magic and the love." She focused her attention on Birdie and the glowing remnant of my mother. "Missy will keep the two of you safe. I'm goin' to my maker soon, or else I'd let you hitch a ride in me. She will accept you both, and you will be respectful of my baby." The last part had been directed at Birdie.

Birdie nodded her ghostly head and kissed the gnarled old woman on the cheek. Missy played with her great-granny's colorful skirt and giggled as Birdie and my mother slipped in and hitched a ride.

"Missy," I whispered. "My mother is still inside Missy."

I opened my eyes and looked at Birdie. "That's why you were so excited to see Missy."

"Indeed, it was," Birdie said. "She's a rare and beautiful one. I was sad when I had to leave, but I knew it was my time—just didn't know why, until I met up with you."

I shook my head and tried to take it all in. "Could you see me? I mean, could my mom see me through Missy's eyes?"

"No, darlin'," Birdie said. "Nothing like that, but your mama could feel you. When you and Missy were together, Alana could feel your spirit."

"I think I felt her too," I said, marveling at the magic. "Missy's the one who stopped my crying when we met. She's been my best friend forever."

"Forever is a long time," Birdie said with a chuckle.

I nodded and then shivered. "I have to get to Missy."

"Yes, you do," Birdie agreed. "Don't wait for me to go into the *light. I can get up to my Heavenly maker just fine. When you leave me, go to Missy. Find her before the evil one does."*

"Birdie," I said, throwing my arms around her. "I love you and I will never be able to thank you enough."

"Find your mama and send her into the light. That is thank you enough, hooker."

I laughed through my tears and flipped her off. "I'll miss you, hooker."

"Right back at you," she replied with a beautiful middle finger salute. "Go now, Daisy. May God be with you. Or at least that hot man you're banging."

CHAPTER TWENTY-FOUR

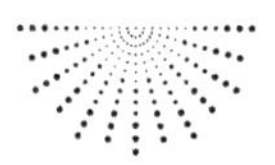

As I came to, Gideon held me cradled in his arms with his forehead pressed to mine. We were on the couch and Birdie was gone. Staying in his protective embrace would have been heavenly, but I'd just learned too many hellish truths.

"How long was I out?" I was worried that hours may have passed.

"Only ten minutes after you left Birdie. An hour total," he said, tucking my hair behind my ear and looking so relieved, I laughed weakly.

"Did Birdie move on?" I asked, looking around the room. I'd be sad if I missed it, but she'd promised me she'd be fine on her own.

"She did," Tim confirmed. "Birdie flipped all of us off and laughed like a loon when she went into the light. Told Gideon his balls were in for a treat."

"Of course she did," I said with an embarrassed groan. "Sorry."

"Nothing to be sorry about," Gideon said with a smile. "Looking forward to it."

I was about to comment, but instead, rolled out of Gideon's arms and jumped to my feet. I had just witnessed my mother's death… which meant my father had, too.

"Where's Michael?"

"Outside," Charlie told me. "You will need us to re-landscape for you in the next few days. Michael has decimated your property."

"That's fine. If I had time, I'd join him," I said, testing my arms and legs. I was good to go. "Missy's house is about twenty minutes away. If I drive, it's ten."

"We're not driving," Michael said flatly as he reentered the house looking haggard and years older than he had just an hour earlier.

"Well, we're certainly not walking," I said, moving to the foyer closet and pulling my coat off the hangar.

As I turned back to the group of men, I ran smack into my father's broad chest. His arms encircled me, and he hugged me like he would never let me go. All of my pent-up emotions drained from my body and I held on to him as tightly as he held me. The moment was beautifully tragic, heartbreaking, and long overdue.

"I'm so sorry, Daisy. I didn't know," he whispered brokenly in my ear. "I'm so damned sorry."

"I am too, Dad," I said, letting my tears flow freely.

His large body shuddered in my arms and a need to protect him from his pain consumed me. Holding him tighter, I tried to absorb his agony. But I had no more room. My anguish equaled his. The only thing left was to help each other heal, but that would be impossible if we didn't find my mother's soul.

"Missy's house," I said, pulling back and wiping my tears away with my sleeve. "Now. We have to get to Missy."

"Yes," my father agreed.

"I texted Heather," Tim said, tucking his phone back into his pocket. "She's with Missy. She hasn't planted the vacation in her mind yet, but she knows not to leave her."

"Did you tell her everything?" Gideon asked.

"No," Tim replied. "Just that we were on our way over and for her to watch out for Clarissa."

Picking up my purse, I started out the front door. "Guys, we're wasting time. I'll drive."

No one moved. What the hell was wrong with everyone?

"Am I not speaking in a language you understand?" I asked, getting angry. Time was of the essence. Birdie had said so.

"We understand English quite well," Tim replied.

I ran my hand through my hair in frustration and glared at them. "Great. Let's go. Now."

"Take my hand," Gideon instructed.

"Why?" I asked, walking to him and automatically doing as he asked.

"We're not driving. We're transporting," he told me.

My mouth dropped open. Apparently, I'd missed the memo. "I can do that?" I asked. "By myself?"

"I'm sure you could if you tried," Michael said, taking my

other hand. "However, we'll test the theory another time. Right now, we'll transport you."

"This is nuts," I muttered.

Tim shook his head. "Not nuts at all. Transporting is an excellent mode of transportation. The safety record is outstanding. Ninety-nine percent of the time there is no issue."

I refused to ask about the other one percent. I didn't want to know.

"Will it hurt?" I asked.

"Not a bit," Gideon promised. "Close your eyes, Daisy. The only side effect is dizziness. If you close your eyes, it will abate faster."

"Are we ready?" Charlie asked.

"No, but that's never stopped me before. Let's do this."

My father squeezed my hand. "As you wish."

I'd had no idea we'd all materialize at the same time in Missy's small living room. Missy's scream of alarm and horror made me feel like the worst friend in the world. It reverberated through my body and I felt it from my fingertips to my toes. It was ear-splitting.

I was relieved that I wasn't in the one percent that Tim had mentioned, but if I'd known where we were going to land, I would have insisted on driving. Although, I had to admit transporting *was* much faster than driving, even with me at the wheel. However, the fact we may have traumatized Missy for life was not worth it.

The comfort of being in a place I loved was erased by what I'd just potentially done to someone who I loved like a sister. Missy's house was a place where I'd logged many hours over the years. It had been a second home of sorts. The décor was bo-ho chic and fit my best friend perfectly—crystals and wild bursts of color in the fabrics and on the walls accented the comfortable furniture. It was a serene and mystical place.

But not right now.

"Are you people serious?" Heather shouted, wrapping her arms around a terrorized Missy. "You couldn't have arrived outside and then knocked for the love of everything wildly stupid and inappropriate?"

Missy's eyes were huge and her body trembled visibly. She peeked up at us and her gaze landed on me. "Daisy?" She looked paler than any ghost I'd ever seen.

"It's me," I said, unsure what to say or do to help her understand the unbelievable.

"How?" she asked. "How did you do that?" She turned her attention to Heather. "And why aren't you surprised?"

Heather's eyes narrowed in fury at us as she led Missy to the scarf-covered sofa. "It's a long story that you will find difficult to believe," she said, placing her hands on either side of Missy's face lovingly.

"Try me," Missy said, still shaking and glancing over at everyone who had *literally* popped in.

"Do you have wine?" I asked.

She nodded. "In the kitchen."

"Would you like a glass?" Gideon inquired politely.

Again, Missy scanned the room. "Will I need it?"

"Yes," I said with a weak smile.

"Then yes," she replied to Gideon. "No glass needed. I'll drink from the bottle."

"Excellent call," Tim said approvingly.

"I'm good like that," Missy replied, still guarded. She turned her attention to me. "Start talking, dude."

I nodded and sat down.

I started talking… and talking and talking. We all did.

There was a whole hell of a lot to tell.

"YOU LOOK SHELL-SHOCKED," I SAID, IMPRESSED THAT HER head hadn't exploded. It had taken me a while to come to terms with the otherworld that existed under my nose. Missy had truly taken it much better than I had. It was a lot to absorb that the collective age of the Immortals in the room was a number so high it could fry a brain.

"Understatement," Missy replied dryly. "I'd add gob-smacked, amazed, dumbfounded, astonished and freaked out. I'm not sure if I'm dreaming or if I've lost my damn mind."

Tim chimed in. "You're wide awake and your vocabulary is impressive. And your sanity is completely intact."

"And what you've learned—albeit against normal protocol—is the truth," my father said.

Missy squinted at him. "Not real sure *normal* should be a word in your vocabulary," she pointed out.

"Touché," Michael said with a small smile.

While Missy had taken in the information about all of us

fairly well, I still hadn't told her about what she was and why we were here. Quite honestly, I hadn't been sure she'd believe a single word of what she'd been told, but, at least, she hadn't passed out or tried to leave.

There was that...

Missy took another swig off the bottle of red and shook her head. "Scarily enough, some of your stories sound familiar," she said, offering me the bottle.

I happily took a sip. "Not following."

"Remember when I told you about my great-granny?"

My body tingled and I almost choked on the wine. I'd met her great-granny in a roundabout way a little over an hour ago. "I remember. Why?"

Missy sat back and let her head fall back on the couch. She sighed and then got lost in thought.

No one said a word. I think they were as surprised and relieved as I was that Missy wasn't on the floor in a fetal position and babbling.

Missy sat back up and slowly and deliberately made eye contact with each and every person in her home. "My great-granny told me these stories—or at least versions of them. I thought she made them up. I loved the tales—begged her to repeat them to me all the time." She shook her head sadly and looked down at the floor. "It was when she was telling me the story of the Death Counselor for the hundredth time that my parents walked in on us and caught her. They sent her away the next day to a home, and I never saw her again. They said she was crazy and had the Devil inside her —told me if I wasn't careful, I'd have the Devil inside me, too."

"They were sick people," Heather said, taking Missy's hand in hers.

Missy leaned into Heather and rested her head on her shoulder. "True. I always thought it was my fault they sent her away. I still blame myself for it."

"Can I share something with you?" Michael asked Missy.

"Will it freak me out any more than I already am?" she shot back.

Michael smiled. "No. I don't think it will."

"Then have at it," Missy said with a small laugh. "Wait, what do you call him, Daisy?"

I grinned. "At first it was Darth Vader, then John Travolta and now Dad," I said. "You can call him Clarence or Michael if you're more comfortable with that."

"I'm going to go with John Travolta," Missy announced. "It fits."

My father chuckled, walked across the small room and seated himself next to my best friend. "I will answer to many things. Whatever you choose is fine," he assured her, and then grew more serious. "Your great-granny resides in the light—in Heaven. She watches over you as your Guardian Angel, and her love for you will never die."

Missy's eyes widened and filled with tears. She gaped at the Archangel and watched in amazement as he let his own eyes turn a sparkling gold.

"You wouldn't lie to me?" she asked.

"John Travolta doesn't lie," I offered. "He omits occasionally, but we're working on that."

Michael smiled. "I neither lied nor omitted just now, Missy. What I told you is the truth."

Missy absorbed the information then leaned back onto Heather for comfort. "Okay," she said, looking around suspiciously. "While all of this has been life-altering and possibly nightmare-inducing, I'm not following why you felt the need to blow my mind. What exactly is going on? Why do I need to know all of this?"

"You ready for more?" I asked, hoping not to get shot down. I wasn't sure how much more she could take.

"Do I need more wine?" she asked, holding up the empty bottle.

Charlie stood up. "Probably," he said in his kind way. "I'll go get another bottle."

"Wait," Missy said, tilting her head in thought. "Does June know? About you?"

Charlie smiled and shook his head. "She does not. For me, June is my once in a very long lifetime love. I will age with her, and when she passes on, I'll pretend to pass on for the sake of our children. I'll move away for a generation or two and then come back to watch my great-grandchildren grow from a distance."

"I'm confused," I said as a thought occurred to me. "I thought it was rare for an Immortal to have a child. You and June have four." Maybe my birth wasn't as rare as I'd thought. If that was the case, Gideon needed to use something a little more reliable than condoms.

"Adopted children," Charlie said with great pride and a wide smile as he patted his heart. "The lights of June's and my life."

"Oh Charlie, it makes me sad that June will die and you won't," Missy said softly.

"No," Heather said. "It's rare and beautiful. So few of us get to experience what Charlie has. He'll have memories of June for the rest of time."

Missy turned and stared at Heather for a long moment. Heather stared back. It was as if they'd both forgotten anyone else was in the room.

Missy broke the stare first and touched Heather's cheek gently. "I understand. Charlie, I would like that wine, please, and I'd like to know what you people have omitted."

"Long or short version, dude?" I asked.

"Short," Missy said. "Brain's too full as it is."

I nodded. "You're a Soul Keeper. It's not a myth. It's not a wives' tale."

Missy grinned. I was floored and relieved.

"I am?" she asked with a laugh. "I'm a freak like the rest of you people?"

"That you are," Gideon said with a chuckle.

"Amazing," Missy said. "An hour ago, I thought I was having a nervous breakdown. Now, I'm kind of digging it."

"Highly unusual and quite remarkable," Tim said, smiling at Missy. "You are uniquely suited to be part of the club."

"Thanks," Missy said with a wink. "And let me tell you right now, Courier between Heaven and Hell, if you rehome the vibrator I just ordered, I will mess with your shit."

Tim looked taken aback for a moment then he sheepishly grinned. "Duly noted. Your toy shall arrive unscathed."

Missy hopped up and began to pace the small room. Charlie handed her a new bottle of wine as she passed him and she took a slug off it. Gathering her thoughts, she stopped then pinned me with a stare.

"Okay, I'm ready," she said. "It still makes no logical sense why I'm being told this if there's not a reason, so hit me with it."

"Brave and beautiful," Heather said with pride.

"Back at you," Missy said to Heather. "Out with the rest, Daisy."

"Clarissa killed my mother," I told her, trying not to let the fact send me into a fit of tears or rage. It would do no one any good if I lost my shit when I needed to keep it together. "She tried to steal her soul, but one of Mom's ghosts got to it first. Her name was Ethel, but she liked being called Birdie better because of her penchant for flipping people off."

"Is that important?" Missy asked.

"Not really," I said, shaking my head. "But you'll want to know her story at some point."

"Why?" Missy asked.

"Getting there," I promised, feeling on edge and unsure if I was ready for what was about to go down. "Birdie knew your great-granny and what she was. She went to her with my mother's soul. Your great-granny told Birdie that you were the strongest Soul Keeper alive—full of love and magic. Both my mother and Birdie hitched a ride in you for many years."

"But you said Birdie was a ghost," Missy pointed out.

"I did," I agreed, marveling at how well Missy was following. "She left you recently and came to me."

"And?" Missy pressed, growing antsy and excited.

"And before she went into the light, she told me my mother's soul was still inside you."

Missy took another long swallow and handed the bottle to Heather. Taking a deep breath, she walked to the middle of the room and slapped her hands onto her hips.

"Fine. How do we get her out?"

Everyone was speechless—even me.

"Isn't that why you're here?" Missy demanded. "I sure as hell don't want Clarissa showing up and trying to rip your mother's soul out of me. So, I'd appreciate a little cooperation. You people feel me?"

"Umm… yes, I ahh," I stuttered, standing up and feeling way over my head.

"How do we do it?" she asked.

I shrugged. "I have no idea, dude."

Both of us looked around at the group of people who'd lived thousands of years longer than we had. They seemed more confused than we did.

Crap.

"We'll wing it," Missy said.

"Is that smart?" Tim asked.

Missy rolled her eyes. "You have a better idea, Tim?"

"Umm… no, I don't. Winging it sounds like a good plan," he said.

"You ready?" I asked my best friend.

Taking my hands in hers, she took a deep breath. "I'm ready."

CHAPTER TWENTY-FIVE

MISSY'S HANDS WERE WARM IN MINE. SHE SMILED AT ME, AND I smiled back.

"We've always been connected," she said.

"Always," I agreed.

"And we always will be," she said, closing her eyes. "Just call to her, Daisy. She'll come."

A lightly jasmine-scented breeze blew through the room and an ethereal lavender glow surrounded Missy. Breathing in the scent, I closed my eyes and connected with Missy in a way I never had before.

"Alana," I called out tentatively. "Come to me. It's safe now."

I waited.

Nothing happened.

Missy squeezed my hands. "Don't be scared. Did you call her Alana when you were a child?"

"No," I said with a little laugh, my eyes still closed.

"Call her what she will recognize," she suggested.

"You think that will work?" I asked.

"I know it will," Missy replied. "I can feel it."

I'd always known Missy was special. It wasn't until this moment I understood the meaning of the word.

"Mom? Mama?" I tried again. "It's me, Daisy—your daughter. I'm here to lead you into the light. You'll be safe with me. I love you so very much and... I want to save you like you saved me. Please come to me."

The wind picked up and my eyes shot open. Missy's eyes rolled back in her head and a beautiful golden soul orb appeared on her shoulder. I quickly wrapped my arms around Missy so she wouldn't fall to the floor then I gently kissed the soul on her shoulder.

It wiggled and glowed. It was the most beautiful thing I'd ever seen.

"Did we do it?" Missy asked, holding on to me for balance as she came back from wherever she'd just gone."

"We did it," I said softly, carefully taking my mother's soul into my hands and leading Missy to the couch.

"Will she stay in that form?" Missy asked, marveling at the orb.

"No," my father said, approaching me with tears streaming down his handsome face. "Alana, take another form. Come and say hello to your family."

The Archangel waved his hand and the room filled with an enchantment so strong, I found it difficult to breathe. Shimmering gold flecks rained down from above, creating a sparkling backdrop to the magic that was happening before my eyes.

My father put his arm around me, and we watched in awe as the golden orb morphed into the woman I'd been missing my whole life. Her smile undid me, and my father continued to cry.

"I am so sorry, Alana," he whispered hoarsely. "So sorry."

She floated over and circled us a few times. I worried she didn't recognize me. I'd been five when she'd died, and now I was forty.

"I'm Daisy," I told her as she hovered in front of me and studied my face.

"I know," she replied. "I'm your mother."

I giggled. "I know."

"You're stunning," she whispered.

"So are you," I said.

She tilted her head to the side and laughed. The sound hit me in the gut and went straight to my heart.

"Silly girl," she said, touching my nose then looking at the man she'd loved more than any other. "Michael."

"Alana," he replied.

My mother's attention was now completely focused on him. The love between them was undeniable. I was heart-broken that he wouldn't be able to feel her touch like I could. Only a Death Counselor could experience the touch of a ghost.

"I'm sorry, Michael," she said. "I did what I had to do."

He nodded and reached for her. His hand went through her, but he kept it extended. "I would have done the same in a heartbeat."

She smiled. "I know."

"Mom," I said, hating to interrupt them, but worried that

Clarissa might show up unexpectedly. I was desperate to spend time with her and get to know her, but risking her afterlife for my needs was not going to happen. "Are you ready to go into the light?"

"No, Daisy. I'm not," she said.

Her answer terrified me and made me want to sob with joy.

"Alana," Michael said, clearly as torn as I was. "It's not safe for you here."

Again, she tilted her head and smiled. "It's never been safe," she replied. "And that has never frightened me. What frightens me is that Daisy isn't safe. Until the time she can live without looking over her shoulder like we always had to do, my place is with my family. Period."

I grinned. My mom had lady balls—like me and like Gram.

And that's when my happy story went horribly wrong.

"There you are, Daisy girl," Gram shouted with glee as she flew through the wall of Missy's house with Steve in tow. "I've been lookin' all over tarnation for you people. Got worried when I went downstairs and no one was home."

I glanced over at Steve in alarm. He shrugged helplessly. "She wouldn't take no for an answer, so I came along for the ride to make sure she could find her way back home."

I nodded in the direction of my mother. Steve's ghostly eyes went huge. He got the picture, and he got it fast.

"Gram," I said quickly. My world was about to spin off its axis. I had no clue what Gram seeing my mother would do to her, but I was pretty sure it wouldn't be good. "I need you to go home."

"Oh my God," Missy said in shock. "I can see Gram and Steve."

"You can?" Gram squealed with delight. "That's just fandamntastic, Missy! Daisy, I'm pretty dang sure we had an earthquake or some prehistoric moles out in the yard. We got holes you could drop swimmin' pools in, and I know them dogs couldn't have dug 'em."

"Yep," I said, moving to stand in front of my mother. "Saw that. Maybe we should put in a pool."

"Gram," Steve said, trying to run interference. "I'm pretty sure *The Price is Right* is having a marathon this evening. We should get back home. Don't want to miss the Big Showcase."

"I think you're right," she told Steve, scratching her head. "But Missy here has a TV. Don't you, darlin'?"

I shook my head at Missy. She read me correctly even though she had no idea what I was doing.

"Oh, Gram, my cable is out," she lied. "I have a repair person coming tomorrow."

"Bummer," Gram said—right before she froze.

"Mama?" Alana said, floating out from behind me with a timid smile on her lips.

Gram gasped with delight and began to shake. "Alana baby?" she choked out.

"It's me, Mama," Alana said. "I've missed you so much."

Gram's smile turned into a pained grimace and her body began to brutally convulse. She became more transparent, and ghastly keening noises came out of her mouth from low in her throat.

"No!" I shouted as I pulled Gram from the air and held

her tightly in my arms. "It's okay, Gram. You're fine. You were dreaming. You're fine."

"Your mama killed herself to follow her lover into the darkness. Suicide. Guaranteed ticket to Hell," Gram said in a monotone as her thin body continued to jerk and contort in my embrace.

"What's happening?" Charlie demanded. His eyes had turned silver and he became the badass Enforcer I'd witnessed several times.

"Mom," my mother said weakly. My father quickly motioned for my mother to hide herself behind him. She followed the directive immediately.

"Your mama killed herself to follow her lover into the darkness. Suicide. Guaranteed ticket to Hell," Gram repeated like a broken record.

"Yes, she did," I told Gram, rocking her like a child in my arms. "That's right."

"Your mama killed herself to follow her lover into the darkness. Suicide. Guaranteed ticket to Hell." Her voice was robotic and dead-sounding.

"What is happening?" Charlie repeated, alarmed.

"As we established, Clarissa planted the false narrative years ago. This is what happens when someone who has believed a vicious lie for decades is confronted with the truth," Heather said.

"Can it be reversed?" I heard my mother whisper.

Gram heard her, too, and began having seizures in my arms until she literally passed out. What had been one of the best moments of my life was turning into the worst.

"It can only be reversed by the person who planted it,"

Heather replied.

"Incorrect," Michael said, looking down at the unconscious ghost of Gram in my arms. "Planted thoughts done in malice can't be reversed. Unless…"

"Unless what?" I demanded, staring at the woman who'd given up her life to raise me. The woman who'd loved me unconditionally. Steve floated over and quietly sat beside me. His steady presence calmed me.

"Unless the one who planted it is destroyed," Michael finished.

Clarissa was Immortal. Was that even possible? Was Gram going to be a freaking zombie now all the time? Could I even send her into the light if she never came back to me?

"Define destroyed," my mother said, looking down at her own mother with utter devastation written all over her ghostly face.

"Completely turned to ash," Gideon said, putting his hand on my shoulder for comfort. I reached back and placed my hand over his. "It's not possible."

"Nope, not buying it," I said, letting go of Gideon and gently pushing Gram's hair off her face and tucking it behind her ears the way she liked it. "You're the one who keeps reminding me everything is possible if you believe."

My mother observed Gideon's and my gesture of ownership with each other and gave us a small smile. "I've had a lot of time to think over the past thirty-five years. Clarissa has been on my mind quite a bit," she said. "I think I know how it can be done."

Charlie shook his head. "The destruction of an Angel—

true destruction—has dire consequences for the destroyer."

"I concur," Tim said. "It's a death wish."

"I'll do it," I said. "I don't care what the price is."

"Absolutely not," Gideon said firmly. "I have the best chance of surviving. I will annihilate her."

"Let's not forget how much Karma enjoys assassination," Tim pointed out.

Heather eyed Tim with annoyance. "Tim, volunteering Candy Vargo for a death mission is a shitty thing to do."

Tim shrugged. "Trust me, Candy will be *very* put out if she's not included in something that includes extermination."

"Be that as it may," Michael said. "I'm the reason we're in this mess. The only one paying the price of ending the Angel of Mercy is me."

"Well," Missy said, glancing around. "There are certainly a lot of volunteers."

"Clarissa is not a very well-liked individual," my mother said dryly as she leaned in and kissed my cheek. She then touched Gram with reverence and adoration. "I'm so sorry, Mama," she whispered to Gram. "I will make this right for you because I love you, and because you loved my baby and raised her when I couldn't."

"Will it work?" I asked. "Can we truly destroy her?"

My mother paused and glanced over at my father. Their eyes locked and they shared a secret exchange.

"That remains to be seen, Daisy," she said. "And indeed, we shall see."

The End… for now

MORE IN THE GOOD TO THE LAST DEATH SERIES

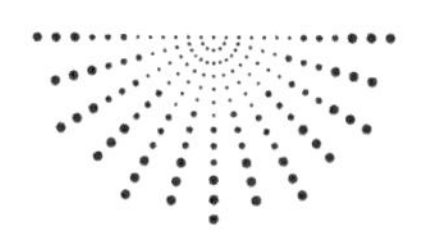

ORDER BOOK FOUR NOW!

My midlife crisis. My rules. And if it doesn't put me six feet under, I plan to live it up in style—possibly for the rest of eternity...

After a Luke Skywalker/Darth Vader moment, I discovered I do indeed have a father. He comes with a hell of a lot of baggage, but I've decided to keep him. Not only do I have a father, I have a kickass new sister, a ghostly family, and super powers to boot. If you add to the mix that I'm dating the Grim Reaper, it's a freakin' party.

The only thing standing in the way of my happiness is the Angel of Mercy, though *Angel of Misery* is more appropriate. She's responsible for almost everyone I have loved, and who has loved me being taken away. With the help of family and friends, I will track her down and show her exactly what a perimenopausal hot flash looks like in action.

Job — Death Counselor — Supergluing ghosts back together and solving their issues is rewarding. For real.

Mission — Bring the seriously evil Angel of Mercy to justice without dying or getting anyone else killed in the process.

Team — A bunch of certifiable Immortals, including one who re-homes vibrators. Yes, you read that correctly.

How to do this? — Wing it. Wine, my Demon boyfriend, a houseful of deceased squatters, and good friends by my side will help.

Midlife's a journey. I will enjoy the ride. The crisis is happening whether I'm ready or not.

ROBYN'S BOOK LIST

(IN CORRECT READING ORDER)

HOT DAMNED SERIES

Fashionably Dead
Fashionably Dead Down Under
Hell on Heels
Fashionably Dead in Diapers
A Fashionably Dead Christmas
Fashionably Hotter Than Hell
Fashionably Dead and Wed
Fashionably Fanged
Fashionably Flawed
A Fashionably Dead Diary
Fashionably Forever After
Fashionably Fabulous
A Fashionable Fiasco
Fashionably Fooled
More coming soon...

SEA SHENANIGANS SERIES

Tallulah's Temptation

Ariel's Antics

Misty's Mayhem

Madison's Mess

Petunia's Pandemonium

Jingle Me Balls

SHIFT HAPPENS SERIES

Ready to Were

Some Were in Time

No Were To Run

Were Me Out

Where We Belong

MAGIC AND MAYHEM SERIES

Switching Hour

Witch Glitch

A Witch in Time

Magically Delicious

A Tale of Two Witches

Three's A Charm

Switching Witches

Your Broom or Mine

The Bad Boys of A$$jacket

HANDCUFFS AND HAPPILY EVER AFTERS SERIES

How Hard Can it Be?

Size Matters

Cop a Feel

If after reading all the above you are still wanting more adventure and zany fun, read *Pirate Dave and His Randy Adventures,* the romance novel budding novelist Rena was helping wicked Evangeline write in *How Hard Can It Be*?

Warning: Pirate Dave Contains Romance Satire, Spoofing, and Pirates with Two Pork Swords.

NOTE FROM THE AUTHOR

If you enjoyed reading *A Most Excellent Midlife Crisis*, please consider leaving a positive review or rating on the site where you purchased it. Reader reviews help my books continue to be valued by resellers and help new readers make decisions about reading them.

You are the reason I write these stories and I sincerely appreciate each of you!

Many thanks for your support,
~ Robyn Peterman

Want to hear about my new releases?
Visit robynpeterman.com and join my mailing list!

ABOUT ROBYN PETERMAN

Robyn Peterman writes because the people inside her head won't leave her alone until she gives them life on paper. Her addictions include laughing really hard with friends, shoes (the expensive kind), Target, Coke (the drink not the drug LOL) with extra ice in a Yeti cup, bejeweled reading glasses, her kids, her super-hot hubby and collecting stray animals.

A former professional actress with Broadway, film and T.V. credits, she now lives in the South with her family and too many animals to count.

Writing gives her peace and makes her whole, plus having a job where she can work in sweatpants works really well for her.

Printed in Great Britain
by Amazon

13395161R00195